Switch

Ingrid Law

Dial Books for Young Readers
an imprint of Penguin Group (USA) LLC

DIAL BOOKS FOR YOUNG READERS
Published by the Penguin Group
Penguin Group (USA) LLC
375 Hudson Street
New York, New York 10014

USA/Canada/UK/Ireland/Australia/New Zealand/India/South Africa/China
penguin.com
A Penguin Random House Company

Library of Congress Cataloging-in-Publication Data
Law, Ingrid, date.
Switch / by Ingrid Law.
pages   cm
"Companion to the Newbery Honor winner Savvy."
Summary: "Gypsy Beaumont's magical savvy switches to its opposite when she learns that her mean and
decidedly non-magical grandma has Alzheimer's and is going to move in with her family"
—Provided by publisher.
ISBN 978-0-8037-3862-1 (hardback)
[1. Magic—Fiction. 2. Families—Fiction. 3. Grandmothers—Fiction. 4. Alzheimer's disease—Fiction.] I. Title.
PZ7.L41836Sw 2015   [Fic]—dc23   2015006965

Printed in the United States of America

1 3 5 7 9 10 8 6 4 2

Designed by Jasmin Rubero
Text set in Stempel Schneidler Std

*To Rick and Shirley, devoted parents
and grandparents*

Chapter 1

"PLEASE, MRS. FOSTER—I'VE SEEN your future, and you really don't want to buy this soap."

"Gypsy Beaumont! Stop making a scene and *let go*."

It was the second Saturday in January, but red and green streamers still hung from the rafters in Flint's Market. A little drummer boy continued to *rum-pum* over the loudspeakers. At the front of the store, a small table held what was left of the holiday clearance: mesh bags of crushed chocolate Hanukkah coins; flattened marshmallow Santas; a torn package of silver confetti; a few scraggly, wilted poinsettias. Meanwhile, halfway down aisle six, I was engaged in a tug-of-war with Mrs. Foster, my former Prairie Scout troop leader and the mother of my *former* best friend, Shelby.

As Mrs. Foster and I battled for possession of a small blue box of Suds o' Heaven bath soap, Shelby pushed her mother's grocery cart down the aisle, away from us. Pretending she didn't know me.

Just like she'd been doing for the past four months.

"What happened to the good citizenship you learned in Prairie Scouts, Gypsy?" Mrs. Foster demanded.

"I'm trying to be a good citizen," I said, wrenching down harder on the box Mrs. Foster and I gripped between us.

Mrs. Foster didn't understand. Couldn't understand. She only tugged back harder. "I never could get you to conform to the conduct of the Prairie Scouts, Gypsy. You were always too flighty."

Yank. Tug.

"Too daydreamy."

Jerk. Pull.

"Too . . . too *odd*. Where are your parents?" Mrs. Foster pried at my clutching fingers, not letting go of the bar of soap that was, unbeknownst to her, as dangerous as an oily banana peel at the top of a staircase.

Hearing Mrs. Foster's voice rise over the post-holiday

rum-pa-pum-pums, I knew I was in trouble. By now, Poppa would have heard the shrieking. He'd be hotfooting it to aisle six, on the double. Mr. Flint would probably be heading our way too. The store owner always kept a close eye on my family when we did our shopping. Things had a way of going wonky when a Beaumont was in the aisles—from exploding cash registers and power surges, to an incident involving all of the ink pens and markers in aisle ten, to an unexplained rainstorm in the bakery that destroyed a dozen birthday cakes and gullywashed fifty loaves of bread into the parking lot.

Mr. Flint had already banned most of my older siblings from the store, for life.

It looked like I'd be next.

I hadn't meant to make a scene. Seeing Shelby and her mother in the store, I'd followed them, slipping away from Poppa in the produce section. When I'd left him, Poppa had been scratching the old scar on his bald head as he sorted through a pile of fresh green beans, trying to pick the perfect ones for Momma. Momma could've grabbed handfuls of the very best beans without even looking, but today Poppa had volunteered to do the shopping. I'd asked to go along. Big mistake.

I'd followed Shelby, spying on her from a distance. I was certain that, if I looked hard enough, I might glimpse a future in which I was a super-mature, card-carrying teenager in Shelby's new gaggle of gawking, squawking gal-pals.

No such luck. I'd seen Mrs. Foster's future instead.

I could feel my glasses slipping down the short slope of my stubby nose. Not wanting to release my two-handed grip on the soap, I used my shoulder to push my glasses back in place. It was either that or close my eyes, and keep them closed. Otherwise things would only get worse.

If Poppa arrived in aisle six now, he'd know I'd been using my *savvy* again. I was supposed to be practicing control. I was supposed to be staying focused on the present. I was supposed to be allowing other people their privacy . . .

But I'd never been too good at remembering my *supposed-to*'s.

"Gypsy!" Poppa appeared at one end of the aisle, just as Mr. Flint materialized at the other. Both of them were frowning. At the same moment, the music inside the market changed. The drummer boy's plodding *pums* faded away, replaced by a lively burst of violins and horns and spritely tambourine: the Russian Dance from *The Nutcracker*. Hearing the familiar melody, my mind filled with a fantasia of dancing thistle-men and orchid women. Lifting my spirits. Compelling my feet to move.

The zeal of the music, and the threat of the three adults closing ranks, bolstered my determination. With one great heave, I snatched the soap from Mrs. Foster's grasp at last. I lingered just long enough to plow every last bar of Suds o' Heaven off the shelf, into my arms. Then I sprang merrily away.

"Gypsy, stop!"

"I can't, Poppa," I called back. "Trust me!" Hop-skipping down aisle six, I hugged my hoard of soap tightly. I couldn't afford to drop any of the slippery boxes; I had to keep them all from Mrs. Foster.

Overtaken by orchestral glee, I only paused when I passed Shelby.

"Come on, Shel. Please?" I begged as I twirled and

hopped around her. "You could help me." All I wanted was to skip away arm-in-arm with Shelby, to giggle and cavort the way we'd done less than a year ago, when we were both still Prairie Scouts, and friends.

Shelby stared at the floor, bug-eyed and red-faced. Completely mortified.

I felt my shoulders droop. But I couldn't dawdle. Mrs. Foster's future was in my hands.

The Nutcracker's Russian Dance only lasts a minute. That was all the time I needed. Before the final tambourine *ting-TANG* buzzed from the speakers, I'd found my way to the seafood section. By the time the others caught up to me, twelve boxes of Suds o' Heaven soap were settling to the bottom of Mr. Flint's empty lobster tank. Sending heavenly suds bubbling through the filters.

Poppa paid for the soap, the cost of cleaning the lobster tank, and our bag of green beans. Then Mr. Flint pointed to the exit. A dozen shoppers looked on, nattering behind their hands.

"Oh, it's that poor man with the peculiar wife and children. It was only a matter of time before something like this happened again."

"I can't understand how someone as nice and as normal as Mr. Beaumont ended up with such wicked children. They're always getting into trouble. It's why they homeschool, you know."

The yakkety-yak of the gossips jackhammered at my insides. We weren't wicked at all! Sure, Rocket had sometimes shocked people on purpose, back when he was young and ornery. And Samson may have turned invisible at church the previous Sunday without meaning to, nearly giving old Mr. Popplewell a heart attack. But those things didn't make my brothers bad.

Tears prickled the corners of my eyes, but I refused to cry. I'd done what I had to do. My savvy vision had been quite clear. If saving Mrs. Foster had cost me future shopping privileges, so be it.

Heading for the exit, Poppa and I brushed past the clearance table. I quickly scooped up a poinsettia flower that had fallen to the floor and tucked it into my hair band, dressing up my knotted mess of curls. Then, without even thinking, I ran my hand through the shimmer of confetti spilled across the table. I was hot in my coat, and my wild dance through the store had made me even warmer; the confetti clung to my sweat-dampened palm.

I couldn't help myself. Soothed by the flower in my hair and the silver bits sprinkling from my fingertips, I momentarily forgot my cares and twirled in the direction of the exit.

"This is exactly why we can't be friends anymore, Gypsy," Shelby said as she and her mother passed me and Poppa, all of us leaving the store at the same time. "You are *waaaay* too embarrassing." As Mrs. Foster pulled her daughter toward the parking lot, Shelby called back over her shoulder, loud enough for everyone in the store to hear:

"We're thirteen years old now, Gypsy. Teenagers! Why do you have to be so weird about some stupid bar of soap? Why do you still act like a silly, dancing, flower-picking baby?"

Shelby's barbs punctured my last bubble of confidence. Her meanness smashed all of the twinkle lights that lit me from inside. I stopped twirling. I hadn't been trying to embarrass anyone. I'd been trying to keep Mrs. Foster from getting a busted elbow and two cracked ribs in a bathtub accident only I could see coming.

But how could Shelby understand? She'd stopped being my friend right before my most important birthday. Right before I turned thirteen. I'd gone away for the summer and lost Shelby to a group of older girls—girls who wore mascara and lip gloss, and skirts too short and tight to twirl.

I sighed as I watched Shelby walk away. It was no use. Even if she had still been my friend, I couldn't have explained. Or told the truth. I'd wanted to share my family's secret with Shelby since the day we met. But I'd always been good. I'd always kept silent. Even when Shelby asked why we Beaumonts were so different.

Different.
Embarrassing.
Baby.

The words knocked around inside my head like bricks. "I'm sorry, Poppa," I said, shivering as we stepped out into the cold with our lonely bag of beans. Fat snowflakes had begun to fall, but I resisted the urge to stick out my tongue and taste them; Shelby might still be watching.

With a shudder, I brushed the last bits of confetti from my palm in a frenzy, as if the clinging bits had abruptly transformed into germs, or prickers, or cockroach eggs. I had to get rid of the sparkles. I had to quit being such a baby.

Poppa took my hand, stopping me. I stifled a sob as he hugged me close. And when he let go again, tilting my chin up with one finger so that I could see his smile, I knew he'd already forgiven me for the soapy scene I'd made inside the store. But there was something sad in his eyes.

"Don't ever let other people's fears or judgments change you, twirly-whirly girl," he said, adjusting the poinsettia in my hair and giving me a wink. "Let's go home now. We've got some beans to eat."

Home. Yes. Home was the best place in the whole wide world—100 percent free from killjoys and party poopers. I was certain there wasn't anything, or anyone, in the entire world that could ever change *that*.

But I would soon learn that sometimes it only takes one person to change everything. To switch things up.

Chapter 2

IN FAMILIES LIKE MINE—SAVVY families—change can hit fast. When I was still teeter-tottering on tiny feet, my family moved away from our home next to the ocean. Momma and Poppa had no choice; my brother Fish had triggered a hurricane along the Gulf Coast on his thirteenth birthday, and we needed to live someplace where he couldn't do as much damage with his storming.

My grandpa moved with us, which was lucky. Originally, my parents were going to relocate the family to Colorado. Closer to Poppa's childhood home.

Closer to Grandma Pat.

Patrice Beaumont was the sourest, least-magical grandmother imaginable. But with the Centennial State still west of sunset, Grandpa Bomba got a twinkle in his eye and we took a detour. Before anyone could say *Jack Robinson*, Grandpa nudged Nebraska farther north and kicked Kansas farther south, using *his* savvy to move and stretch the soil. Just like that, we had our own bit of land, smack-dab in the middle of the country. We called our new home *Kansaska-Nebransas*, and we were happy there.

Grandpa Bomba was gone now, called up to heaven three months ago—right after I turned thirteen. Right after I got *my* savvy. But his room in our house still stood empty. Nobody wanted to disturb it. The air inside those four walls held too much love. Too much magic. I often stuck my nose into Grandpa's room, just to remember what he'd smelled like; I grieved as the scent of sunwarmed sand and freshly turned earth faded slowly into the whiff of dust and memory.

After the fiasco at Flint's Market, I hid in Grandpa Bomba's room, locking the door to keep my little brother out. Still moping over my miserable afternoon, I remembered the last birthday card Grandpa Bomba gave me. He'd jotted oodles of X's and O's inside it. Beneath his hieroglyphic smooches, Grandpa inscribed a quote from Shakespeare, his penmanship wobbly and crooked:

Come what may,
time and the hour run through the roughest day.

Grandpa must have known that I'd have some rough days coming, now that I was growing up. I imagined what Grandpa Bomba would've said if he were still alive and sitting next to me. He might have smiled and kissed the top of my head, proclaiming, "How I love you, Gypsy girl!" or "You look like you need a good yarn to cheer you up." Then he would've reeled off endless stories, his eyes shining bright. He would've told me for the hundredth time how Grandma Dollop had put up radio waves inside of jars the way other ladies put up peaches. Or maybe he would've repeated the story of our first savvy ancestor, Eva Mae El Dorado Two-Birds Ransom, the pioneer girl who fell into the Missouri River on her thirteenth birthday and climbed out covered head to toe in gold dust. Trawling gold, forever after. Generations of savvy folk had been having extraordinary thirteenth birthdays ever since; savvy families dotted the map like sprinkles on a sheet cake.

✳ ✳ ✳ ✳

My savvy birthday had brought its own set of marvels.

On the morning of October eleventh, the sun had slumbered late beneath the deep-blue covers of night, slow to wake on my special day. Swimming up and out of dreamland, I'd wiggled my toes, too woozy and content to move any other part of me. The hum of my parents' voices drifted up from downstairs. Momma was busy cooking a special breakfast. Poppa was setting the table with the unbreakable dishes we always used for savvy birthdays.

My sister, Mibs, would be arriving later in the day with her fiancé, Will Meeks. My oldest brothers, Fish and Rocket, were on their way home too. Fish was bringing his new wife, Mellie. Soon, Samson would come out of hiding, like a moth drawn to the thirteen tiny flames atop my cake, and Tucker would get to sing "Happy Birthday" as big and as loud as he pleased. There would be sparks and hugs and windy bluster as everyone helped me celebrate.

My grown-up siblings had all had their own savvy

adventures. Even Samson had seen his share of excitement. Samson's savvy gave him the power of invisibility, and more. Whenever my reclusive sixteen-year-old brother became as unseen as a ghost, he charged up like a battery, giving him a storehouse of inner strength he could pass to other people with a touch. During a particularly heroic moment the previous summer, Samson had given all his strength away, making it difficult for him to disappear again for months. Making him super-cranky too. By the morning of my birthday, Samson was still working hard to get the full power of his savvy back. But at least he'd gotten to see some spectacular Sardoodledom. Some thrilling drama and excitement.

Now, at last, it was my turn to have some fun.

Despite the slugabed bliss of my early-morning snooziness, I'd shivered in anticipation of what the day might bring. I imagined sprouting a pair of wings as beautiful as those of doves and angels. Or going fishing with Poppa and catching candy necklaces instead of catfish. I pictured myself dancing up to the clouds. Moonwalking to the glowing moon.

I took stock of myself as I lay in bed, trying to decide

if I felt different. But I only felt like same old, same old me. Believing it was safe to start my morning, I sat up and stretched, blinking into the light streaming through my window.

My blurry window . . . inside my completely blurry room.

"Drat and drumsticks," I whispered to myself. "My eyesight is getting worse! If things stay *this* blurry, Momma and Poppa will make me get glasses for sure." No one else in my family wore glasses. No one but Grandma Pat. And I didn't want to share one thing more in common with Patrice Beaumont than I already did. I'd already inherited Grandma Pat's untamable curls— mine the color of sunflower honey, hers now as white as nurses' shoes, or cottage cheese. We both had pointed chins and peachy-cream skin, though Grandma's cheeks were more like wrinkled old fruit in skim milk now. We even shared the same birthday!

I hadn't gotten a birthday card from Grandma since I was ten. That was fine by me. The only things I'd ever found inside Grandma Pat's cards were crumpled dollar bills and sharp words. Words about growing up and toughening up. Words about not standing out, or being different.

Grandma didn't like us. She frowned upon savvy smarts and savvy talents. She hadn't even come to Fish's wedding.

I was still blinking and rubbing my eyelids, trying to bring the world into focus, when little Tuck burst into my room.

"Why are you still in bed, Gypsy?" Tucker demanded. "You should get up. Know why?" My brother crossed the room and leaned against my bed. "Because it's your BIRTHDAY!" he yelled. Then he added, "Momma's making waffles, Gypsy! Waffles!"

At seven—almost eight—Tuck was still years away from getting a savvy of his own, but that didn't stop him from being super-enthusiastic about mine.

"When I'm thirteen"—Tucker jumped onto my bed and started bouncing—"I hope I get a savvy that lets me turn into a cat." My brother's blond hair flew up and down as he made the mattress springs squeak and groan. "Hey! Maybe you'll get volcano power, Gypsy." Tucker leaped to the floor and skip-hopped around my room, pretending his feet were on fire.

"Hot lava! Hot lava, everywhere! Help, everyone—help!"

I giggled. I couldn't help it. Tucker was a clown.

Tuck's cries roused the rest of the house. Samson arrived first, a long, tall shadow in the doorway. Just in time to see Tucker stop, drop, and roll beneath my bed.

"Watch out, Samson!" Tuck called out. "Hot lava is abrupting from the top of Gypsy's head."

"Erupting, not *abrupting*," I laughed, correcting him.

"Lava. Really." Samson had obviously just woken up; his husky voice sounded lower and even more unimpressed than usual. He yawned and leaned against the door frame, fading a little at the edges, like he was thinking about disappearing.

"What's happened? Is anyone hurt?" Poppa's words were taut as he pushed past Samson. He held a cook pot lid in front of him like a shield, and he gripped an industrial-sized fire extinguisher in his other hand. Ready to do battle with any bubbling magma.

Surveying the scene, Poppa relaxed his shoulders. "There is no lava, is there. What a relief!"

I was about to assure Poppa that everything was fine, when something peculiar began to happen to my blurred vision. Every time I tried to focus on Poppa's face, his features began to swirl. The same thing happened when I looked at Samson. My brain felt like a spiral noodle lost inside a cinnamon roll factory—everything was going around and around and around.

By the time I turned to look at Tucker, all I could see was a spinning vortex of moving images. The dizzying swirl spun counterclockwise, then jerked clockwise, before resolving into a single crystal-clear scene. A scene that played out in my mind's eye like a silent movie. Showing me . . .

Tucker.

Older.

Blowing out thirteen candles on a cake, and then—
Gadzooks!

I squeezed my eyes closed and shook my head. I rubbed my eyelids with my knuckles. I'd always had a knack for seeing things other people couldn't, but this was different. This was wackadoo extreme.

I blinked and blinked as Momma stepped into the

room and stood behind Poppa. "I think you can put the fire extinguisher down now, Abram," she said, taking the cook pot lid from him.

Momma turned to me and smiled.

"Good morning, sweetheart. Don't be too anxious. I just know today is going to be a Gypsy-wonderful day!" Momma always knew the right words. She was, after all, capital-*P Perfect*. Her savvy made her that way. My mother never looked rumpled or sloppy. She never stumbled, bumbled, or burned toast. Which was why I was extra, extra confused when my savvy hit full throttle.

I nearly fell off my bed as graceless visions of Momma rioted through my mind's eye. Blinking through a counterclockwise churn, I saw my mother as a little girl. She was sitting on a bench outside a school principal's office, looking as happy as a clam, despite being a wild mess. Her socks slouched and her shoelaces were loose. Her braids were half undone. She had a Band-Aid on one knee and a prize-winning shiner. Momma looked like she'd just gone three rounds with the school bully and won.

I blinked in surprise but didn't take my eyes off

Momma. The swirl of flashes in front of me suddenly jerked and switched directions, spinning clockwise before settling into an all-new scene. An all-new vision.

I saw Momma exactly as she was now—she was even wearing the same shirt. Only, in this premonition, Momma stood on a road lined with tall pine trees, illuminated by the bright lights of a tow truck. It was nighttime. It was snowing. And Momma looked frazzled. She held a half-eaten cupcake in one hand, and she had icing and rainbow sprinkles in her hair, on her shirt, even smeared across her cheek. Our station wagon rested behind her, nose-down in a ditch.

I closed my eyes and refused to open them again for the next half hour; I couldn't look at anyone for more than a few seconds without having another dizzying vision.

There were no candy necklaces on fishhooks for me.

No wings, or moonbeam-dancing either.

My new savvy gave me the power to see willy-nilly into anyone's past or future, but I had no control over which images I got to see. Momma tried to assure me that control would come later, after I learned to *scumble*. After I learned to be the boss of my unique abilities.

"Mastering a new set of skills always takes time, Gypsy," Momma reminded me.

Before my birthday was over, I was the proud owner of a brand-new pair of sparkly purple spectacles, made for me by the one-hour optometrist up in Hebron. My entire family had gone along to help me pick out my glasses. Everyone assured me that the two bottle-thick lenses didn't make my eyes look as huge as I knew they did. But the glasses did the trick, correcting my vision and giving me quick-fix command over my new clairvoyant abilities. As long as my eyesight stayed 20/20 crisp and clear, there was no swirl. No vortex. When I wore my glasses, my savvy visions stayed away.

Of course, that didn't keep me from sliding my new specs down my nose and spying on other people whenever I felt like it. Which was how—three months later, inside Flint's Market—I knew Mrs. Foster was going to take a nasty spill in the bathtub sometime in her future. Slipping on a brand-new bar of Suds o' Heaven soap.

The cordless phone rang in the hallway, bringing me back into the present, back to my mopey-doping inside

Grandpa Bomba's room. From the other side of the door, Tucker shouted, "I'll get it!" There was a moment of silence, then my little brother's voice clanged through the house again.

"Poppa! Hey, Poppa! Some lady named Mrs. Kim wants to talk to—oops! I think I just hung up on her."

There were footsteps in the hall, followed by Poppa's voice. "Hand me the phone, Tuck. Why don't you go ask Gypsy or Samson to play with you until dinner."

"But, Poppa!" Tucker whined as the phone began to ring again. "Gypsy locked me out of Grandpa's room, and I can never find Samson now that he's got his savvy back. He's always invisible. I wish I had *my* savvy already. I hate being the littlest."

At the dinner table that night, I picked at my food. I wasn't hungry, and I didn't feel like talking. All I wanted to do was sit and wait for time to finish running through my awful day.

Poppa was quiet too, and plainly distracted by worried thoughts. Momma, to everyone's surprise and distress, was uncommonly clumsy. Samson and I shared a look of shock when Momma dropped an entire pot roast on the dining room floor but served it to us anyway, seasoned with carpet fuzzies. She had tried to make brownies for dessert, but she'd been talking with Poppa behind closed doors, after the mysterious Mrs. Kim called, and didn't hear the oven timer. The brownies were too burned to eat.

Even with my mind in a fluster over the events and the visions inside Flint's Market, I could tell something was going on. Something was wrong. Really wrong. I knew Tucker and Samson could sense it too. Tucker got cranky, and Samson disappeared the moment he finished helping me wash the dishes. Kansaska-Nebransas brimmed with tension. It felt as if a big, bad wolf lurked just outside our door.

Chapter 3

AT CHURCH THE NEXT morning, Pastor Meeks said a prayer for Mrs. Foster. Despite my efforts, Shelby's mom had slipped and fallen in her bathtub the night before, breaking two ribs and busting her elbow. She must have found a bar of Suds o' Heaven soap someplace else, after leaving Flint's Market.

Mrs. Foster was recuperating at home, but Shelby had come to church with her father. She turned in her pew and glared at me throughout Pastor Meeks's entire prayer, like she blamed me for her mother's accident.

I sighed. In the three months since my birthday, I'd never once managed to change a single bad future I'd envisioned. I'd seen that Tucker was going to swallow a marble; enlisting the entire family to help me, I'd cleared every marble from the house. I told my brother about my vision and instructed him to keep inedible objects out of his mouth. Yet, when Tucker spotted a small green marble in a potted plant at the bank, he put it on his tongue on purpose.

"Thee Gypthy?" he said, trying to talk around the glass ball. "I can thuck on a marble without—" *Gulp!* "Oops."

I barely listened to Pastor Meeks as more and more memories of things I hadn't been able to change came back to me: I'd had a vision of our mailman getting bitten by a dog, and it had happened; I'd glimpsed a bandage on his hand a few days later. I'd seen that Leeba Goldstein, the librarian, was going to drop her wedding band down the sink. When I advised her to never remove the ring before she washed her hands, she thanked me. But she was really thanking me for giving her the idea to wash away her ring. Apparently, Mrs. Goldstein was filing for divorce.

I liked it better when the spinning vortex of my visions shifted counterclockwise, showing me the past. The past was over and done with. There was nothing I could do to change it.

I spent the rest of the church service losing myself in panoramas of other people's lives. I was staring over the tops of my sparkly glasses, watching an amusing, old-timey scene of Mr. Popplewell playing stickball as a boy, when Momma nudged me.

"Please work harder to stay in the present with the rest of us, Gypsy," she whispered as everyone stood to sing "Take Time to Be Holy"—the morning's final hymn.

I pushed my glasses back in place, then hunted for my shoes. I'd kicked them off somewhere beneath our pew. "I swear I was listening," I whispered back.

"Were you?" Momma brushed an unkempt strand of silver-blond hair out of her face and gave me a stern look. Then she accidentally dropped her hymnal. I frowned as I noticed a snag in her cardigan, and a coffee stain on her blouse. Where had my *perfect* momma gone? It was like her savvy had turned upside down.

"I just worry about you, sweetheart," Momma murmured in an undertone as the rest of the congregation warbled: *"Take time to be holy, the world rushes on . . ."*

I winced as Momma bent to retrieve her hymnal and hit her forehead against the top of the next pew.

Rubbing her eyebrow as she straightened up, Momma exhaled tiredly. But she went on talking as if she hadn't blundered.

"It's like you're never really here with us anymore, Gypsy," she said. "You're always too busy looking forward or back."

Clearly grumpy that Momma and I were talking during the hymn, the woman behind us leaned forward and sang extra-extra-loud: *"TAKE TIME TO BE HOLY, BE CALM IN YOUR SOUL . . ."* as if doing so would make us be quiet.

Momma turned and gave the woman a withering look. "*You* be calm in your soul, Myrna Lee," she said. Then she stuck out her tongue. I wasn't sure what had happened to make Momma act so different, but part of me liked this new side of her.

After the service, Tucker made a mad dash for the donut table; Samson vanished into thin air, as usual; and Momma and Poppa joined the rest of the congregation in the fellowship hall. Following on my parents' heels, I paused in the open doorway. I watched Shelby join the older girls gathered by the windows. They were all comparing shoes and nail polish, and taking pictures with their phones.

I looked down at my feet. Drat! I'd forgotten my shoes in the sanctuary again. I curled my toes into the tight gray carpet beneath me, praying Shelby and her friends wouldn't notice I was barefoot. All I could think about was the way Shelby had called me a silly, dancing, flower-picking baby.

When Shelby caught me staring, I waved and gave her my best, most grown-up smile.

Shelby turned her back on me.

Scarcely able to hold back tears, I fled to the bathroom and locked the door.

After taking a few deep breaths, I splashed my cheeks with cold water, adjusted my sparkly spectacles, and considered myself in the mirror. Yesterday, in Flint's Market, I'd taken my glasses off to squint at Shelby, hoping to see a happy future filled with camaraderie. Perhaps I'd been gawking in the wrong direction.

Maybe I should have been looking at *me*.

In the months since my birthday, I hadn't once

worked up the courage to try to see into my own past or future. I'd spent hours peeping into other people's lives. But I'd been careful to never look at myself in a mirror without my glasses on. I'd worried it would be too much like discovering hidden presents before Christmas. I was afraid to see things about myself that weren't meant to be seen. To know things that weren't meant to be known.

"If you can't look yourself in the eye and face your own future," I told my reflection, "when will you ever grow up?"

It was time to take a good look in the mirror. To see how long it would take me to evolve into an honest-to-goodness teenager, and to make some true-blue friends. Friends who would stick by me no matter what. It was time to find out exactly when I'd stop acting like a baby.

Slowly, I took off my glasses, folded them up, and set them gently on the countertop next to the sink. Then . . . I looked.

The swirling images that filled my mind chilled me to the bone.

I saw myself as a feeble old woman with curls as white as thistledown, balancing precariously on an icy ledge—a small thrust of concrete and stone that rimmed a ramshackle clock tower, six stories up.

Snow clouds parted momentarily, and a bright full moon mirrored the round face of the enormous clock. The hands of the clock pointed just shy of midnight. In the vision, I looked out at myself, as if from a vantage point inside the tower. It was like a film camera had been set up in the gap of shattered glass between roman numerals six and nine, capturing a fish-eye view of reaching arms and grasping fingers. Someone in red coat sleeves leaned out through the ruined clock face, trying to rescue me. But I couldn't see any features. Only those red sleeves.

Maybe I would never learn to be less babyish and dippy. Even as an old woman, stuck high up on a tower, I looked ridiculous. I wore a full-length party dress the color of mothballs and old quarters, and a shabby jacket made from white rabbit fur, a single fuzzy pom-pom dangling from the collar. Two oversized Sorrell snow boots stuck out from under the hem of my dress. My knuckles were large and bony, and sparkled strangely in the moonlight. My wrinkled lips were lined in coral lipstick, and a faraway look clouded my eyes behind big, round old-lady glasses. To top it all off, a tarnished rhinestone tiara sat tilted on my head, half of its glass bits gone. Leaving dark spaces, like missing teeth.

In my vision, a mute gust of wind whipped at my dress and made me wobble. I exhaled a fog of breath. Then my lips took the shape of a soundless, startled O.

Staring in stunned horror into my reflection, I watched my future self slip, then start to fall—my skirts flying up over my head, exposing skinny white legs and saggy, floral granny-panties.

With a cry, I shut my eyes. I scrabbled blindly for my glasses, ready to return to the here and now inside the church bathroom.

I hadn't expected to see all the way to the end. My end. I hadn't planned to watch myself plummet. How I wished I could un-see it all: the clock tower . . . the tiara . . . the awful, awful underwear. I wished I could un-know that even the final moments of my life would be a constellation of embarrassments.

I decided then and there that I'd avoid anything and everything that might make my premonition come to pass, even if it was a fate sixty-odd years into my future. I would live a life completely void of sparkles and lace and fur coats of every kind.

I'd keep my feet planted firmly on the ground.

Chapter 4

"YOUR MOTHER AND I have something we need to tell you all." Poppa called a family meeting in the living room as soon as we got home from church. I perched between Samson and Tucker on the sofa. Poppa sat in a chair opposite us, next to the hearth. I wished Poppa had built a fire; I couldn't get my frightening clock tower vision out of my head, and my skin was one big goose bump.

Momma refused to sit. She paced the room instead. Back and forth she went, staring at her feet like she was measuring the length of the opposite wall, the one decorated with photographs of all our relatives. With each new pass, Momma accidentally knocked her elbow into the motley assortment of frames, turning the neat and tidy display of family photos into a crookedy mess.

Poppa scrubbed at the scar on his head. It was a mark he'd carried for almost a decade, after a car crash nearly took his life before my sister's savvy birthday.

"Maybe we won a trip to Disneyland," Tucker whispered loudly in my ear as we waited for Poppa to find his words. I took my little brother's hand and squeezed it, wishing I could be as hopeful.

Samson must have sensed my apprehension, because he wrapped his long, thin fingers around my other hand, making me feel a little stronger. A little calmer too. Whatever was happening, I hoped it had something to do with the phone call Poppa had gotten the day before, and nothing to do with me or Mrs. Foster. Or Flint's Market. Or soap.

"I'm sorry, everyone," Poppa said at last. "Your mother and I have talked it over and, while we know it won't be easy, we've decided we have to bring Grandma Pat here to live with us."

I sucked in a breath and held it.

Samson made a muted choking noise.

Tucker's eyes went wide in horror. He quickly pulled

his fingers out of mine and stuck his hands under his corduroys, protecting his backside. The last time Tucker and Grandma Pat crossed paths, Grandma had given him a swat on the bottom. He'd never forgotten it.

Momma continued to pace, not looking at us. I flinched as she caught the toe of her shoe on the edge of the rug again and again. I knew the odds were against her; if she didn't stop pacing soon, she was bound to trip and fall. But I had bigger worries.

Grandma Pat? Coming to live with us?

"Your grandmother can have Grandpa Bomba's old room, kids," Poppa barreled on, his words gaining sluggish momentum, like an express train bound for dreary destinations. "I suppose that room has been empty long enough. We'll all go to Colorado this week to pack my mother's things and move her here."

"Grandma Pat isn't well," Momma said. "Her neighbors called here yesterday."

Poppa nodded. "Mr. and Mrs. Kim are both doctors, and they feel strongly that my mother can no longer care for herself. Her memory . . . her mind . . . well, she's starting to get very mixed up. But Grandma is family, and we Beaumonts take care of each other, yes?"

No one seconded Poppa's yes. The thought of Grandma Pat moving to Kansaska-Nebransas—*moving into Grandpa's room*—was a bomb detonating inside my chest. I couldn't speak. I could barely breathe. I was certain I was turning inside out.

"We're going to bring Grandma Pat . . . here?" Samson said slowly. His grip on my hand tightened and grew hot—unbearably hot. So hot, I had to let go for fear of being burned. Things were getting worse, and weirder, by the second.

Little Tuck climbed to his feet and stood on the sofa. "But it won't be forever. Right, Poppa?" he said. "Grandma's not coming permanently, is she?"

"Yes, Tuck. Permanently."

"Nooo! Grandma Pat is going to ruin everything." Tucker voiced the potent thought that all of us were thinking. He began to stomp the sofa cushions, shouting: "Grandma hates us! She hates us!"

It was true Grandma Pat didn't like us—Momma and us kids, at least. Poppa was Patrice Beaumont's only child, and her pride and joy. She'd raised him on her own after Grandpa Walter died when Poppa was a boy, and she'd always felt her son should have married someone else. Someone different. Or rather, someone who wasn't so very, *very* different. Savvy different.

At Tucker's cry, Momma stopped pacing and turned toward us, like she'd suddenly remembered she was supposed to comfort us and tell us everything would be okay. Those were the sorts of things a perfect momma would do. But just now, Momma didn't seem too good at remembering her *supposed-to*'s either.

"Kids—" she began. Then her toe caught for the hundredth time on the edge of the rug and she took a tumble, rattling the family portraits on the wall. As the rest of us leaped up to help her, a framed photograph of Grandma Pat landed catawampus on the floor. Upside down and glowering, Grandma looked just as unhappy as the rest of us.

Grandma Pat was no relation to Eva Mae El Dorado Two-Birds Ransom, the first savvy-powered girl from Grandpa Bomba's stories. But maybe she wasn't as un-magical as I thought. Maybe she did have a savvy. Maybe Grandma's savvy was the ability to make a muddle of other people's lives. To turn things topsy-turvy. There was no other explanation for what happened next.

"Um . . . you guys? I feel sorta funny." Tucker stuck out his tongue, lolling it around the way he did whenever he saw cauliflower. Only now his tongue was HUGE. He looked like he was having an allergic reaction to Poppa's news. Already, Tucker's hands and feet were twice their normal size. The rest of him was ballooning fast.

I turned from Momma to little Tuck, then to Samson. "Samson! Look at Tucker's hands and—"

But Samson wasn't looking at Tucker. He wasn't looking at Momma or Poppa. He wasn't looking at me either. He stood staring down at his own hands instead. Rather than vanishing, the way he so often did, Samson had begun to glow. His fingers and palms were turning as orange and as bright as the embers of a campfire, or the burners on a stove.

Like Tucker, Samson looked all wrong.

My brother tugged at his shirt collar, muttering, "Did it just get super-hot in here?"

"Samson!" Poppa gasped, just as Momma shrieked, "Tucker!"

Head and shoulders, knees and toes, nose *and* clothes—Tucker was now three times his normal size. And Samson was on fire.

"Whoa!" Samson barked, glancing down at his hands as each of his fingers lit up in licks of red-and-yellow flame. He looked like he was holding ten candles. A second later, there was a *whoosh* and a *crackle,* and Samson's entire body became a bonfire. His normally dark eyes shone crimson.

Where did Poppa keep that fire extinguisher? I was about to run to look for it, but I stopped short after taking two steps . . . I was beginning to feel a wee bit strange myself.

I forgot about the fire extinguisher as loony-switcheroony sensations twisted through my innards, making me feel sick and weak and peculiar.

Samson's blaze turned the living room oven-hot. The air smelled strongly of struck matches. Yet my brother's sudden combustion didn't appear to be hurting him. Engulfed in flames, his clothes weren't even burning. Samson wasn't *on* fire—he was generating it. But that didn't stop him from dashing out the front door and diving into the snow.

Tucker didn't bother with the door. As soon as he grew large enough for his head to hit the ceiling, my brother boomed: "I TOLD YOU GRANDMA PAT WOULD RUIN EVERYTHING!" He then plowed straight through the wall, like the Kool-Aid Man, leaving a giant, Tucker-shaped hole in the house. While Tucker's tremendous size was shocking—and not at all the talent I'd expected him to get—it was even more shocking because he was so young. Getting a savvy before age thirteen wasn't completely unheard of: My twin cousins, Mesquite and Marisol O'Connell, had been pestering people with their powers of levitation since they were five. Whatever force was jumbling things up, it must have brought on Tucker's savvy early.

Still feeling strange, and hoping *I* wasn't about to grow or catch fire, I followed Momma and Poppa outside as they chased after my brothers. Samson had successfully doused his inferno in the snow; steam rose from his skin as the ice around him melted into puddles. But he continued to lie on the ground, too dumbfounded to move.

Tucker *PUM-PUM-PUMMED* around the yard,

growing as tall as the house itself. Throwing the biggest tantrum ever seen west of the Mississippi—maybe even east of it too—he seemed unaware of his colossal size, or of how powerful his size made him.

"No, Tuck!" I cried as I watched my younger brother uproot trees in our front yard like they were daisies. With the jumbo ears he had now, Tucker should have heard me. But he didn't. Or wouldn't. Or couldn't, over the thunderous sound of his king-sized corduroy pant legs rubbing together. I was thankful Tucker's clothes had grown as big as the rest of him. Otherwise he would have been running around the yard both giant *and* naked.

I watched helplessly as Tucker tossed two leafless maples and a blue spruce into the field across the road. Seeing an old bird's nest and a squirrel's collection of acorns go flying, I whispered a quick prayer for any small creatures hibernating in those far-flung trees.

Poppa hollered, "Tuck! You need to calm down."

Momma cried, "Take a breath, Tucker! Try to—" Then she slipped and fell, landing on top of Samson.

Nothing stopped Tucker's raging. The rest of us

could only stare, openmouthed, as he kicked over the tool shed. As he stepped on the frozen birdbath. As he picked up Momma's knee-high garden gnome like it was a grain of rice and threw it so high, none of us saw where—or if—it came back down.

When Tucker turned around, barreling toward our house head first, like he planned to knock it over, I couldn't watch. I turned away, my heart hammering in my chest. All I wanted to do was forget this terrible moment.

Hunching low, I closed my eyes and pressed my hands over my glasses, shouting: "Stop, stop, stop, stop, STOP!"

And everything did just that. Everything stopped.

Everything but me.

Chapter 5

MY FAMILY MEMBERS WERE statues. A flock of geese paused mid-flight, a frozen V on the horizon. Everything around me had gone dead silent. The only thing I could hear was my breathing. And the pounding of my heart. I counted heartbeats: Ten . . . twenty . . . thirty-three . . . forty-seven . . . fifty. It was like the entire Earth had stopped turning, giving me one and only one moment of time to gaze at: The present moment, motionless and fixed.

The world had become a timeless wintry snapshot instead of a moving picture. Needless to say, I freaked out, right and proper.

"Help!" I cried. "Someone help!" My voice sounded strange in the unmoving air. It bounced back at me, like

I was shouting into a mixing bowl. I didn't know what was happening. Or what to do.

I tugged on Poppa's arm, stopping when his still form began to wobble. I waved my hand in Momma's face; she didn't blink. Delicate beads of melted snow decorated Samson's long hair. More water drops hung suspended around him, untouched by gravity. When I captured one of the drops on the tip of my pinkie, it immediately began to jiggle, and to drip. But when the water slipped from my finger, it fell only an inch. Then it lingered in the air again as if it couldn't move without me. Fascinated, I flicked at the remaining drops, watching each of them sail a short distance, then stop. It was calming to watch the small globules sail and stop, sail and stop. And it gave me hope.

I pressed my fingers against Momma's cheek, thinking she might move if I touched her. She didn't. I poked Samson in the stomach. He didn't twitch a muscle. I placed my hands on Poppa's shoulders.

Nothing.

I didn't try to touch or even look at Tucker as he stood frozen, about to destroy our home. It was Tucker's fault that I'd stopped time, and I was vexed with him.

Stopped time?

Was that what I'd done?

I looked around helplessly. "Wh-what if the world is stuck this way forever?" I stammered aloud. Fear and cold combined to make me tremble; my teeth began to chatter. I took off my glasses and peered at Momma, hoping for a familiar savvy vision, the kind that would show me the precise moment when everything would return to normal.

I bugged out my eyes. I squinted until it hurt. I even tried staring cross-eyed. But I saw no swirl of images inside my mind. No spinning vortex. No dizzying stream of visions, past or future. My rightful thirteenth-birthday savvy was gone. I had a brand-new power to control—a switched-up talent that needed scumbling. And since my everyday eyesight hadn't improved at all with the bewildering switch, I couldn't even throw away my glasses.

Eager to reverse what I had done, I recalled how I'd covered my eyes and yelled *STOP* right before time ground to a halt.

Taking a deep breath, I closed my eyes and hollered the first opposite word that sprang to mind.

"*Go, go, go, go, GO!*"

I peeked one eye open to see if things were moving. No luck. I tried again, using different words.

"Start, start, *START!*"

"Move, *MOVE!*"

I chanted *abracadabra* and *go-back, go-back.* I even offered up a *pretty please.* But I didn't know what cosmic force to push or pull. I couldn't find any magic words.

Frustrated, I scooped up a handful of snow and packed it hard and tight. I aimed my snowball at Tucker's giant head, angry at him for making me say *STOP* in the first place. But my snowball only flew an inch, just as the water drops had, stopping short as soon as it left my troposphere.

I threw snowball after snowball, until I was winded and my hands were numb, and the air was painted in big white polka dots.

I'd always been taught that I was never truly alone. Poppa had said it. Momma had shown it. Pastor Meeks had preached it. And being the fifth of six kids, I'd forever had someone to keep me company. For the first time in my life, I felt like a solitary astronaut on the moon.

Still wearing my Sunday dress, I fell to my knees, clasped my hands, and prayed. I asked God and all the angels to make everything go back to the way it was before Mrs. Kim called . . . before we learned that Grandma Pat was ill and had to live with us . . . before Samson caught fire and Tucker grew big. I apologized to God for not saving Mrs. Foster from her soapy accident. And for talking during the final hymn at church.

Receiving no immediate response to my prayers, I began to cry. I cried until I couldn't cry any longer. Then I went inside, leaving my tears hanging in the air, alongside the water drops and snowballs.

My feet led me automatically to Grandpa Bomba's room before I remembered it didn't belong to him anymore. It was Grandma Pat's room now—or would be, if time ever started moving again.

I fled upstairs to my bedroom instead, where I crawled under my quilt and buried my head beneath my pillows.

At some point, I slept. And when I woke, I sprang up joyfully, believing I'd had a frightful dream. But drawing back my curtains, I found myself staring straight into Tucker's enormous face. I quickly pulled the curtains closed again, still unable to look at him.

Chagrined at having left my family standing in the cold, I put on my coat and boots, and carried blankets and bundles of outerwear outside. I put a hat on Poppa's head, and a scarf around Momma's neck. I jammed wooly mittens over Samson's hands. I couldn't do much for Tucker; he was simply too big. Plus, I was still upset with him for lumberjacking the trees.

As soon as I finished tending to my family, I walked to the highway, wanting to see if my time-stop stretched that far. I only paused once, to glower at a soft country rabbit frozen mid-hop in the middle of the road. "Don't come near me, Mr. Bunny," I said, still remembering my vow from the previous day—my pledge to avoid sparkles and lace, and fur coats of all kinds.

Looking up and down Highway 81, I could see that no one was going anywhere. The cars were like forgotten toys on an empty playground.

I turned around and went home, chewing anxiously on my bottom lip.

Without day turning to night, or any clocks tick-tocking, blinks and heartbeats became my new units of time. Eventually, I decided I'd despaired for long enough. When Momma and Poppa starting moving again, I wanted them to be proud of me. I wanted them to see how responsible and mature I could be without any supervision. Keeping this goal in mind, I straightened the house and did my schoolwork, making pencils float whenever I got bored. I got out a pair of scissors to clip coupons from the Sunday paper, but instead ended up cutting butterflies out of the funny papers, suspending my cutouts in the airspace between my ceiling and my bed.

By the time I slept and woke again, my sense of maturity began to wane. Tummy rumbling, I found a bag of chocolate chips and ate them all. I gobbled cereal straight from the boxes so greedily, I got Cheerios in my hair, and left Corn Chex hovering above the table. Finding it impossible to pour juice from a bottle, or run water from any faucet, I cut into a milk jug with my scissors and scooped the creamy liquid into my mouth with my hand.

I tried on Momma's shoes and dresses. Her jewelry and makeup too.

I even slipped past the DO NOT ENTER sign on Samson's door and plumbed the dark depths of his messy bedroom.

Worried I was going to grow up, grow old, and fall off some clock tower somewhere before another real-time second passed, I began to check the length of my fingernails and measure my hair with a ruler. But I couldn't have aged more than a day or two; I'd only slept twice.

Aside from the question of how to restart time, my biggest problem was Tucker. As soon as I figured out how to make the clocks tick-tock again, Tuck would still be a whisper away from ramming into the house. I had to find a way to distract him the moment his tantrum resumed.

That's when I remembered Poppa's secret stash of gummy bears, the bag he kept hidden in his tackle box. Momma didn't believe in rewarding bad behavior. But it was a well-known fact that Tucker's tantrums ended fast when there was candy handy. The rest of us were not above using bribery to calm him down.

Armed with Poppa's emergency gummy bears, I returned to my bedroom window. Ready to face my brother at last.

As soon as I looked at Tucker—really looked—my anger at him began to melt away. He was, despite his size, just a little boy. The tears that swam in his big blue eyes were so large, I could see myself reflected in them. I suddenly longed to grab a towel and wipe my brother's tears away. I didn't want him to stand there forever, crying. For the first time since I'd stopped time, I felt ready. Ready not to be afraid. Ready to let whatever was supposed to happen next *happen*.

Keeping my eyes focused on Tucker, I raised my hands high, holding the bag of candy out the window.

"It's going to be okay, Tucker," I called out. Then, remembering Grandpa Bomba's words of wisdom in my birthday card, I added, "Come what may!"

I heard the whoosh of wind and the *honk-honk-honk* of geese in the distance. A jumble of surprised cries rose from Momma and Poppa and Samson as they found themselves suddenly and inexplicably dressed up like snowmen. My knees went as jiggly as Jell-O as relief and exhaustion washed through me.

Inside, paper butterflies fluttered to my bed. Outside, my snowballs regained momentum and smacked into Tucker. Making him stop just long enough for me to get his attention.

"Look, Tucker!" I shouted. "I've got gummies! If you settle down—if you *shrink* back down—you can have them all."

"Gummies?" Within seconds, Tucker was back to being the littlest Beaumont, with nothing to show for it except a rip in the seat of his corduroys.

Sighing in satisfaction, I dropped his candy down to him. Then I pulled my head inside the window—just in time to dodge Momma's garden gnome as it fell like a missile from the sky.

Chapter 6

"HOLY GUACAMOLE!" SAID POPPA. "That was like having a bunch of savvy birthdays all at once!" By the time our nerve-mashing day came to an end, Poppa looked shaken, even though he was the only one of us left unchanged. But Poppa's DNA wasn't laced with Muddy River magic; he was immune to whatever mix-up had occurred.

Momma and Poppa were alarmed when they learned about my time-stop. They didn't like knowing I'd been on my own, with no one to turn to for help. Samson could tell right away that I'd explored his room. His eyes blazed at my invasion, but he forgave me. Tucker whined, "You ate all the chocolate chips?" Then, exhausted from his own ordeal, my little brother went to bed and slept for eighteen hours.

Two days later, our ancient station wagon rumbled west, propelling us toward Colorado. The sky hung low over the interstate, as heavy and gray as the mood inside the car. Samson sat behind the wheel, flexing his new driver's license—and his new savvy—the way a fledgling phoenix might flex its fiery new wings. Momma had always been an excellent driver, without a single accident or ticket. But after the nightmarish savvy switch occurred, no one wanted her clumsy feet anywhere near a gas or brake pedal.

It had been kind of fun to see Momma's perfect manners snap in two at church, when she talked back to Myrna Lee. But most of the time, watching Momma blunder was like watching a rare and marvelous butterfly flit-flop on one crumpled wing. It made my heart hurt and my insides feel squishy. It made Samson extra-moody. It made Tucker's bladder overactive.

Tucker had already shouted "I have to pee!" seven times since we'd left home, forcing Samson to stop at every gas station along the highway.

No one complained about Tucker's restless bathroom breaks. None of us wanted to reach Grandma's house quickly. And after Tucker's towering tantrum on Sunday, none of us wanted to watch him grow big inside the station wagon. I imagined Tucker's head popping through the front windshield, his arms and legs each jutting from a different window, making him a giant turtle with a car for a shell.

Thanks to Samson's jumbled savvy, it felt like July, not January. The air-conditioning rattled noisily. Our coats lay in a heap in the back. Samson may have been old enough to drive, but he acted more like a first grader who'd just learned to strike a match. If Samson missed his old savvy, it didn't show; he was utterly enthralled by his bright and fiery switcheroo.

"Will you *please* stop doing that, Samson?" Momma implored as my brother snapped his fingers for the hundredth time, igniting a yellow-orange flicker at the end of his thumb. Once upon a time, Samson was the shadowy moth. Now he was the flame.

"Yeah, Samson, cut it out," I said. "If you lose control, the whole car could catch fire." Samson rolled his eyes at me in the rearview mirror, but the corners of his mouth twitched into a smile, and he temporarily stopped popping flames.

"If *you* lose control, Gypsy"—Tucker raised his voice, looking up from the horde of toys he'd spread across the backseat—"you'll be stuck right here for ages. With nothing to do and no one to keep you company."

"Don't remind me, Tuck," I said. Then I tickled him, making him laugh until Momma told me to stop. Momma knew strong emotions could stir up a person's savvy.

So far, Tucker hadn't been able to make himself grow big on purpose, but he was still super-proud of his new talent.

"Did it scare you to get so big?" I asked Tuck as the miles slipped by. Tucker and I had been playing with his army men and his favorite stuffed cat. We were pretending the cat was a misunderstood monster under attack, only to be rescued by the army men in the end.

"No way!" Tuck said, not looking up from the intricate battle we'd staged between us on the seat. "It was awesome being a giant. I was big enough to do anything! Buuuut—" Tuck hesitated, fiddling with an army figurine that had somehow lost its head. "I didn't mean to wreck so much stuff. That part felt scary *after*. I was just so mad, Gypsy! I couldn't stop." Tucker shrugged.

"Maybe the next time I grow big, instead of wrecking stuff, I'll fight Godzilla, or a dinosaur, and save the whole wide world."

"You're very brave, Tuck," I said. I leaned over and kissed the top of his head. Tucker gacked and sputtered, acting like kisses were toxic poison.

I wished I could say I felt brave. I lived in fear of accidentally stopping time. I knew I'd feel better if I could recall what I'd said or done to make time move again. Momma and Poppa had tried to help me remember, but it had all become a blur too quickly.

"I miss Poppa," Tucker sighed as we passed a sign welcoming us to "Colorful Colorado."

I miss him too, I thought. Poppa had stayed in Kansaska-Nebransas. He needed to board up the hole in the front of our house temporarily, and arrange for contractors to repair the damage in the weeks ahead. But Poppa promised to join us on Saturday, with the moving truck.

We all felt Poppa's absence keenly, perhaps Momma

most of all. The idea of being on her own with Grandma Pat scared the bejeebers out of her, I could tell. Momma tried to hide it, but I could hear her whispering under her breath every now and then, as though she were practicing perfect things to say when we got to Grandma's house.

"How wonderful to see you again, Patrice!"

"It'll be such a blessing to have you in our home."

"No, I'm not a witch who tricked your son into marrying me, and the children aren't a fiendish horde of rabble-rousers."

The night before we left him, Poppa had kissed Momma tenderly on the forehead and said: "Try not to worry, darling. My mother has become so confused, she may have forgotten her narrow-minded opinions. According to Dr. Kim, she may not even remember who we are."

When Tucker heard this, he slapped his palms against his forehead. "That's just crazy! Does Grandma Pat have *Old-timer's disease* or something?"

Poppa didn't smile at Tucker's unintentional eggcorn crack. He merely nodded and said, "Yes, Tuck. Grandma has something very much like that. Things could have gone badly if Dr. Kim and her daughter hadn't found your grandmother the other day."

Poppa had told us how Dr. Kim and her teenage daughter, Nola, spotted Grandma Pat shivering at a local park-and-ride bus stop, wearing her nightgown, her snow boots, and a pair of scorched oven mitts. Befuddled and bad-tempered, Grandma had refused to get into Dr. Kim's car. Fifteen-year-old Nola had walked Grandma all the way home, where she found the smoke alarms shrilling and a burning smell coming from the kitchen. Apparently, Grandma had mistaken the oven for the washing machine; she'd baked a lace tablecloth, three bath towels, and most of her unmentionables at four hundred degrees, until done.

If *done* meant charred and smoldering.

Grandma Pat's mind was becoming just as jumbled as our savvies.

My stomach clenched as the Rocky Mountains appeared on the horizon and we drew closer and closer to Grandma. I considered what I knew about *Old-timer's disease,* as Tucker called it. Loads of old people start to forget things, like where they put their house keys, or what day of the week it is. But Grandma hadn't merely become forgetful. Her illness was much worse than that.

Momma kept encouraging us to share our feelings. She peppered our nine-hour drive with a myriad of medical facts, and a fumbling *what-to-expect* lecture. I knew I should feel bad for Grandma Pat. But traveling seventy-five miles an hour toward Evergreen, Colorado, I couldn't find much kindness. All I could think about was how stern and disapproving Grandma had always been—and how embarrassing it would be to have a grandmother who wandered off in her nightgown.

What would Shelby Foster have to say about that? Now she *really* wouldn't want to be my friend.

The town of Evergreen lay at the ankles of the Rocky Mountains, thirty miles west of the sparkling, mile-high city of Denver. We reached Grandma Pat's house after the sun had set. Tucker snored next to me, not even stirring when Samson turned off the car. Pensive and brooding, Samson stared at the small brick house in front of us, growing hotter by the second.

I shoved my feet into my tight boots, praying

Momma would say there'd been a mistake. That we could return home straightaway, leaving Grandma Pat in Colorado. Instead, Momma took a deep breath and said: "Everybody ready?"

My legs were rubbery after sitting so long. The night sky was studded with stars. The air smelled like pine needles, pine bark, and pine sap. Evergreens stood tall around us. The houses along Grandma's street were built on large lots, with slices of forest between them.

Samson handed me my coat—my fancy one made from red velveteen, with its deep, warm hood and two rows of gold buttons—then he lifted Tucker gently from the car. Tuck nestled his nose into Samson's warm neck, refusing to wake.

"I'm glad he's asleep," Momma murmured.

I was glad too. I knew Momma and I were picturing the same things: Tucker waking up and growing big; Tucker uprooting all of Grandma's trees; Tucker flattening Grandma's brick home like it was made of sticks or straw.

Momma patted Tucker's back, then raised her palm affectionately to Samson's cheek. Making a face, she quickly moved her hand to my brother's forehead.

"Are you sure you feel all right, sweetheart? Your temperature must be a hundred and ten degrees."

"I'm fine, Momma. Really."

Grandma Pat's yard and porch were dark, even though Poppa had told her we were coming. But there were lights on inside. And as we stepped up onto Grandma's front stoop, I could hear a television. Momma was just about to knock, when two bright car beams made our shadows grow and dash across the yard. We all turned to watch a black SUV pull into the well-lit driveway of the bigger, newer house across the road.

A distinguished-looking middle-aged man emerged from the car. When the passenger door opened, a spritely teenage girl hopped out. She wore a puffy white coat, skinny jeans, orange combat boots, and twenty-two layers of black eyeliner and mascara. Wisps of dark hair escaped the girl's slouchy sequined hat. Her lipstick was the color of black plums.

"Dr. Kim and his daughter, I'm guessing," Momma said, waving at the neighbors. "That girl certainly isn't afraid to be herself, is she? I like her already."

"Inside, Nola!" Dr. Kim's voice echoed through the quiet mountain subdivision. "No music until your homework is done." Nola did as she was told. But she hesitated at her front door. Even from a distance, the girl's curiosity was crystal-clear as she stared in our direction. Samson quickly turned away, gazing up at the sky as if he'd just discovered a brand-new love—of astronomy.

"Wait here, kids," Momma said as Dr. Kim crossed the road toward us, looking more like a physician preparing to talk with a patient's family than a friendly neighbor coming to say hello. Adjusting her purse strap higher on her shoulder, Momma stepped down from the porch, only tripping once as she crossed Grandma's scrubby yard to meet him.

"Do you think the Kims know?"

"Know what?" Samson lowered his chin to look at me. He glanced furtively toward the Kims' front door, but Nola was already gone.

"About *us*," I whispered. "About savvies. Do you think Grandma told the Kims our secret?"

Samson snorted. "They wouldn't have believed her if she did."

"What did he say?" I asked Momma as soon as she returned from her brief conversation with Dr. Kim.

"He's glad we've come," she answered. "Your grandmother is getting worse."

"Worse? Worse how?"

Momma didn't have to answer. I found out what *worse* meant a second later when Grandma Pat opened the door wearing large, round old-lady glasses, a tarnished rhinestone tiara with gaps like missing teeth . . . and absolutely nothing else.

Samson immediately swiveled to face the road, his face crimson. Still asleep in Samson's arms, Tucker burbled wordlessly and shifted his head. Momma whipped off her coat and wrapped it around Grandma, pushing her inside.

"I don't need any magazines, if that's what you're selling," Grandma squawked in a voice like a crow's. All I could do was stand in the doorway and gape—not at Grandma's birthday suit, but at the tiara on her head. I'd seen that tarnished crown before, two days ago, in my terrifying vision in the church bathroom mirror.

I'd watched myself fall from the ledge of a ruined

clock tower as two arms reached out to grab me. Two arms in red sleeves.

Still standing motionless on Grandma's front stoop, I slowly looked down at the sleeves of my coat. My fancy *red* coat.

How had I not recognized my own hands and coat sleeves in my vision?

Why hadn't I understood that I was seeing the scene from my point of view? It wasn't *me* who was going to fall sometime in the future. It was Grandma Pat.

Relief warred with guilt inside me. Then I was hit with a brand-new set of fears: Grandma Pat was in terrible danger and I was the one fated to try to rescue her. I had seen no one else in my vision. What if I failed to reach her in time? I wasn't very tall. And my arms were puny! What if I wasn't big enough . . . or strong enough . . . or *brave* enough to catch Grandma and hold on to her?

How would I pull Grandma back to me, when she was already falling?

Chapter 7

OUR FIRST FULL DAY in Evergreen was unseasonably warm, the sky an azure blue so deep, it made me want to swim in it. But not even sunshine and sky-high daydreams could keep me from feeling low, or help me forget the sight of Grandma Pat falling from a snowy tower, dressed like a doddering fairy-tale princess.

I'd slept fitfully the night before, sharing Grandma's lumpy sofa with Tucker—his head on one end, mine on the other. Momma had taken the spare room, while Samson simply stretched out on the living room floor, warming the house like a human furnace.

My clock tower vision puzzled me. Back home, silos, telephone poles, and water towers were the tallest things around; there were no run-down, six-story clock towers anywhere near Kansaska-Nebransas. I hadn't seen one when we'd reached Evergreen, either. And the weather here was beautiful; in my vision, there was ice and snow.

I'd decided to keep my premonition to myself, for now. There was hard work ahead. Momma was already flustered; I didn't want to trouble her more. I didn't want to frighten Tucker, and if I told Samson, his worry might start a wildfire.

As soon as breakfast was over, Momma and Samson began the burdensome business of sorting and packing Grandma's things. I had to babysit. The words *why me?* danced a bossa nova on my tongue, but I kept my mouth shut.

Samson couldn't be in charge of Grandma Pat. Not only was it his job to clear the junk out of the attic, which was elbow-deep in cobwebs, dust, and shadows, Samson wasn't allowed too close to Grandma Pat's white curls, which held enough hair spray to make her dangerously flammable. He'd already scorched holes in the front drapes that morning.

"What're you looking at?" I'd said, startling my

brother into a fit of blazes when I caught him spying on Nola Kim as she left for school.

"There'll be none of that unnatural funny business in my house!" Grandma bellowed as we beat back the flames. "Your ruckus is drowning out my shows."

Mostly, Grandma Pat sat in her recliner and glowered, with her television blaring and Tucker sitting at her feet, playing with his army figures. Aside from the occasional shout or reprimand, Grandma had barely spoken to us since we'd arrived. She refused to acknowledge that we'd come to help her move, even as I worked around her, sifting through drawers, bookshelves, and boxes.

It hadn't occurred to me that Grandma Pat might not want to live with us any more than we wanted to live with her. All morning, Grandma thrummed her fingers on the arm of her chair, waiting for me to turn my back. Whenever I did, she'd pick up a vase, or a basket, or a throw pillow, and shuffle away to hide it. Grandma stuffed an ancient collection of assorted paper napkins down her shirt before I could throw them away. And when I pried open a rusty tin and shrieked, dropping both the tin and the spooky collection of unbroken wishbones inside it, Grandma Pat shouted at me.

"Hey! I was saving those, girly. What do you think you're doing, robbing an old woman of her wishes?"

Grandma never called me Gypsy. Only girly. Or she mistook me for an old school friend named Nettie Arbuckle. It was hard to get used to Grandma's memory slips. They confused me and made me feel unstrung and awkward. Sometimes I felt like yelling back at her when she yelled at me. Other times, I had to try hard not to cry.

A moment later, Grandma Pat's tone of voice changed abruptly. "Has anyone invited you to the winter formal yet, Nettie?" she asked as I gathered up the fragile bones of all her unwished wishes.

"Er . . . are you talking to *me*, Grandma?" I said, sniffling and adjusting my glasses before looking up at her. "What winter formal? I'm homeschooled, remember? I don't go to dances."

"Don't be a goose, Nettie!" Grandma giggled, her eyes lighting with girlish excitement behind her own thick glasses. "The formal is going to be sublime! Especially with Cleavon Dorsey as my dance partner. Daddy doesn't want me to go—he doesn't care for Cleavon. But I don't care what Daddy thinks."

I found myself wishing I could still see forward or backward in time; it was difficult to imagine Grandma Pat as a teenager with a crush, going to an olden-days dance. I would've liked to see it for myself.

By lunchtime, I felt like I was juggling frogs. Grandma had already slipped out of the house and down the road three times, and Tucker had gone to play in the yard twice without asking. To prevent future escapes, I made a makeshift alarm out of some jingle-bells Samson found in a box labeled *X-mas*. I secured the bells around the doorknob. No one would leave the house without me knowing.

Not long after the bells went up, Grandma fell asleep in her chair and Tucker threw a fit. He got mad when I told him he couldn't play with the skinny, scraggly cat sunning herself on the front stoop. Tucker stomped around the living room, growing bigger and bigger, until Samson slid down the ladder from the attic and tossed me a bag of candy. Momma didn't know it, but Samson had secretly stocked up on sweets at every gas station we'd stopped at the day before. He'd hoarded Skittles, gummy worms, and taffy the way Grandma Pat hoarded Cool Whip containers and department store catalogs.

This time, Tucker's tantrum was brief, and he shrank back down without doing any damage. In an effort to keep him calm—and little—I offered to help him feed the stray cat.

Making sure Grandma was still asleep, we opened the last can of tuna in the cupboard. Momma took a break from packing up the kitchen to pour some water into a bowl.

"Hooray!" she exclaimed with a soft chuckle. "I only spilled half of it. Things are looking up."

Happy and satisfied, Tucker grinned as we set the water and tuna out on the stoop. Tucker loved cats. I loved them too—I liked the way they purred and pushed against my leg, demanding my attention and affection. But the stray cat didn't do any of those things. She ran from us and hissed.

"I think kitty needs someone to look after her, the

same way Grandma does," Tucker said as we went back inside. Tuck had become more charitable toward Grandma when she didn't swat him on sight the way he'd expected her to. He'd warmed to her even more when she let him keep a dusty box of chocolates he found under the sofa. Tucker nearly broke a tooth on a fossilized nut cluster before I convinced him the chocolates were too gross and old to eat.

At lunchtime, I made jelly sandwiches for everyone, after Momma somehow managed to burn soup. When I brought Grandma her sandwich, she waved it away.

"I don't want that . . . or *you*. Where is the other girl? The nice girl who brings me sandwiches."

"This *is* a sandwich, Grandma," I said, nodding at the bread I'd sliced into quarters and arranged neatly on a pretty plate. "And *I'm* nice."

Grandma picked up a triangle of sandwich and sniffed it. Then she made a face and let it drop. "Well, it's not tuna. Go get the other girl. The one who knows how to make a tasty, tasty *tuna* sandwich."

"What other girl, Grandma?" I asked, wondering if she meant Momma.

"The *other* girl," Grandma answered. "The girl with the makeup. The one who lives across the road and doesn't rifle through my things."

Grandma Pat wanted the neighbor girl, Nola Kim. I had to work hard to keep my feelings from getting dinged. Was this what every day was going to be like after Grandma moved in?

I tried to be the best granddaughter I could be, even if Grandma Pat couldn't be the best grandmother. I knelt at her side and took her hand in mine, hoping for . . . something. Anything. A gentle squeeze. A kindness. But Grandma immediately wrenched her fingers free, then slathered her hands with a gob of the hand sanitizer she kept next to her chair.

It's not always easy to love someone, even if they're family.

I ate Grandma's jelly sandwich. I didn't tell her that tuna sandwiches were my favorite too. We already had the same curly hair and bad eyesight—the same birthday too. I didn't want to have anything else in common with Grandma Pat.

Chapter 8

SHARING A BIRTHDAY WITH someone isn't too unusual. Samson looked it up for me once when I was younger. He knew how much I worried that our common birthday connected me and Grandma in unpredictable ways.

"Relax, Gypsy," Samson murmured, typing a search into his computer. "You and Grandma Pat are like sugar and steel. You couldn't be more different."

A few clicks of his keyboard, and Samson looked triumphant. "See?" he said. "Nothing to get worked up about."

I leaned over his shoulder, squinting hard as I read aloud: "*Every day, over nineteen million people celebrate their birthday. Three point seven million in China alone. Nine hundred thousand in the United States. Even twenty-seven in Tuvalu."*

I looked at Samson. "Where's Tuvalu?"

My brother shoved his long hair out of his eyes and did another search. "Tuvalu is a tiny island country in the South Pacific," he said a second later.

I sighed in relief. If twenty-seven people in a place called Tuvalu were blowing out candles on the same day as me and Grandma Pat, maybe she and I weren't connected in any unfortunate way after all.

After my episode with Grandma and the jelly sandwich, I wasn't too excited when Nola Kim knocked on the door a few hours later. At the sound of the knock, Samson poked his head down from the attic scuttle in the hallway. Tucker crawled into the cardboard box he'd turned into a spaceship. Grandma jumped in her chair, startled.

"Go away!" Grandma crowed loudly. "I'm not feeding any trick-or-treating beggars, and I don't sign petitions!"

When I opened the door, Nola smiled a cheerful, black-plum smile and blinked eyelids so heavy with dark, uneven eye makeup, it looked as if she'd been in a fight. The girl's short brown hair stuck out in cute wisps and tufts around her face and was highlighted here and there in tints of green and purple. Nola looked like a pugilistic pixie—a colorful punk-rock fairy in orange combat boots. Even with her mess of severe makeup, she was pretty.

Part of me really wanted to like Nola Kim. Another part of me really, really didn't.

Nola stepped inside carrying a bulging plastic bag. She looked as comfortable inside Grandma's house as if she'd been there a thousand times.

"Hi," Nola said, looking at me and then tilting her head sideways to get a better look at Samson. Before Nola could finish saying, *I'm Nola Kim—I live across the street,* Samson had pulled his head back up into the attic.

"Someone's not very sociable." Nola laughed at Samson's sudden disappearance. Then, stepping right past me, she called out, "Hello, Mrs. B.!"

I cringed, waiting for Grandma to say something rude or do something embarrassing.

"Don't worry, Mrs. B." Nola quickly crossed the

room. "It's not Halloween, and you don't have to sign any petitions. It's just me. The girl with the sandwiches. Only, I didn't bring any sandwiches today, just this bag of *bae* for your family."

Nola bent and kissed Grandma's cheek—like she was the granddaughter, and I was the neighbor girl standing awkwardly by the door. Nola didn't appear one bit bothered by Grandma's quirks and quibbles.

Grandma patted Nola's arm and smiled. Smiled! She'd only smiled at me once since we'd arrived, and that was when she thought I was her childhood friend Nettie. Grandma's fondness for Nola was a fast-moving blizzard slamming through my rib cage; I wasn't used to feeling so cold-hearted. So jealous. It did not feel good.

"Hello, Nola," Momma said, trying to wipe her hands clean on a dirty towel as she came into the room. "How nice of you to stop by. I'm Jenny Beaumont, Patrice's daughter-in-law. This is Gypsy." Momma nodded toward me and then looked around for my brothers. "My boys Tucker and Samson are around here somewhere . . ."

"My mom wanted me to bring you these, Mrs. Beaumont," Nola said, holding up her plastic bag. "Mom is at a medical conference in Chicago all week, and Dad is on loan to a hospital down in Pueblo that needed his surgical skills for the next few days. So he's going to be away too. But if you need anything, you're supposed to let me know." She held the bulging bag toward Momma. "I hope you guys like Korean pears. The skins are tough—so you should peel them."

Momma took the bag of fruit, holding it carefully so it wouldn't break. "You're all alone in that big house, Nola? Would you like to stay for dinner?"

Say no, say no, say no, I thought.

To my relief, Nola smiled and shook her head. Just as she said, "I'm okay, thanks," Tucker jumped out of his cardboard box, and shouted, *"BOO!"*

"Ah! That boy is loud and sticky," Grandma said. Taking Nola's hand, she whispered up at her: "Please take him with you when you go."

Little Tuck looked wounded.

"That's Tucker," I told Nola, giving her an uncertain smile. Nola smiled back, but her eyes darted to my sweatshirt. Maybe she was just noticing that I was wearing it inside out. I sometimes wore my clothes that way on purpose, to stop scritchy seams from making my life extra-scratchy. I felt myself blush. Poppa had told us Nola was fifteen—fifteen and already staying by herself! I didn't want the neighbor girl to think I was some baby who couldn't even dress herself properly. Had I brushed my hair that morning?

"Is that your fort, sprout?" Nola turned back to Tucker, saying nothing about my shirt.

Tucker furrowed his brow. "What's a sprout?"

"It's a little plant that still has a lot of growing to do."

"I'm not little," said Tucker. "I can grow really, really big. Really, really fast. I got my savvy early and now I become a giant whenever I get mad. And this isn't a fort. It's a spaceship."

Momma and I both tensed at the same time. Tucker had been told time and again to keep our family's secret *secret*. But Nola didn't know about savvies. She only knew about the oversized imaginations of little boys.

"Well, I think you may have scraped your really,

really big chin on one of your sensor arrays or photon torpedoes," Nola said. Tuck raised his chin and we all saw a long red scrape.

"Oh, Tuck!" said Momma, stepping toward him with her dirty towel. Nola reached into the pocket of her jeans and pulled out a colorful assortment of Band-Aids.

"I've got this, Mrs. Beaumont. Don't worry."

Momma laughed. "Do you always carry first aid supplies with you, Nola?"

The girl shrugged. "I guess that's what happens when both of your parents are doctors." Nola dressed Tucker's boo-boo with no fewer than five Band-Aids— one of each color—while Tucker beamed up at her like she was made of gumdrops and rock candy.

Tucker asked, "Are you gonna be a doctor, when you grow up?"

Nola grimaced. "No way. I have much more exciting plans." After stuffing the empty Band-Aid wrappers back into her pocket, Nola spread her fingers wide and traced an arc above her head. Her eyes reflected imaginary flashbulbs as she said, "Someday I want to see my name in lights and hear crowds of people cheer for me. It's my dream to stand on a stage and sing for an audience. To get a standing ovation!"

I wished I had half of Nola's confidence. She obviously knew what she was good at and wasn't afraid to share her talents with the world.

"Do you sing for other people often, Nola?" Momma asked.

"No." Nola sighed. "I signed up to sing in the school talent show last fall. It was going to be my big debut. But then Bo Peters tried to play his piccolo blindfolded and riding a unicycle, and he pedaled off the stage. Bo's accident ended the show. I never got my chance to shine."

That evening, after dining on delivery pizza and Korean pears, Samson and I hauled bags and boxes of garbage down the driveway. Music thumped loudly from the house across the road. In the darkness of the mountain subdivision, it was easy to see into Nola's second-story bedroom. Her curtains were drawn back and she was dancing around her room like a pop star, wearing a sparkly tank top and zebra-striped pajama pants. Nola held a hairbrush to her lips, pretending it was a microphone. The only thing missing was the cheering crowd.

And Nola's name, in lights.

Chapter 9

OUR SECOND DAY IN Colorado wasn't any better than the first. After breakfast, Tucker let the stray cat zip inside. The growly old grimalkin scaled the holes in the scorched drapes, then leaped to the top of a bookcase, where she hissed and clawed at everyone.

After lunch, Samson accidentally set fire to the dead leaves and pine needles in the yard. He quickly soaked the flames using a garden hose, but someone in the neighborhood saw smoke and called 911. Samson endured a long lecture on forest fires and the dangers of cigarettes, lighters, and matches, before the fire trucks drove away.

As soon as Nola got home from school, she knocked

on the door again, carrying a plate of sandwiches. "Just habit, I guess," she said.

Grandma was happy to see her. "You must have known these people are starving me!"

"Grandma—!" I began to object, wanting to assure Nola we were doing no such thing. Nola gave me a sympathetic eye roll. I liked her better for it. I liked her even more when she nudged my arm and said, "Looking after Mrs. B. is hard work, Gypsy. Don't take anything she says too personally." After she left, I sampled one of Nola's tuna sandwiches. Grandma was right. They were tasty.

That evening, Grandma Pat wandered down the hallway wearing swim goggles and a polka-dot bikini. She gripped a stocking filled with loose change. There was a hole in the toe of the stocking and with every step Grandma took, a nickel, a penny, or a dime spilled to the floor. Momma and I led Grandma back to her bedroom. While Momma wrangled Grandma into a nightgown, I took her sock of coins and laid it gently on the dresser.

"I want my son to meet you," Grandma told Momma

as Momma helped her into her slippers. "I like you better than that so-called *perfect* woman he married." Momma stiffened. Then she relaxed her shoulders and laughed.

"I'm not sure if that was a compliment or an insult."

When Grandma was asleep, Momma went for a walk to clear her head. She returned lickety split, reeking head-to-toe of skunk.

At midnight, I got up to get a drink of water and found Momma sitting at the kitchen table in front of an entire store-bought sheet cake. She cradled her head in one hand as she stabbed at frosting flowers with a fork. I slumped into the chair next to her, resisting the urge to hold my nose. Even though she'd washed and scrubbed, Momma still smelled awful.

"Cake?" Momma offered me her fork. I shook my head. Cake was for parties; I couldn't think of anything to celebrate.

"Things will be all right in the end. Won't they, Momma?" I tugged on a loose thread that dangled from the cuff of my sweatshirt, watching the stitching unravel. Momma stopped me, weaving her fingers through mine.

"Let not your heart be troubled, Gypsy," she recited. *"Neither let it be afraid."* Momma squeezed my hand, then added: "Of course, sweetheart. I'm sure everything will be A-okay. Eventually." I tried to take comfort in Momma's words, but she didn't know about my vision of Grandma and the clock tower. I was about to tell her everything, when Momma reached up and removed my glasses, wiping the lenses on her shirttail. It was a bad sign. A week ago, Momma never would've grabbed my glasses without asking—without giving me time to close my eyes, to avoid seeing any savvy visions.

"Do you think our savvies will ever switch back?" I asked, taking my glasses from her.

"Honestly, Gypsy?" Momma looked at me with tired eyes. She paused for a long while, sitting so still, I began to wonder if I'd stopped time without knowing it. But eventually she laughed her beautiful laugh and said, "I have no idea what's going to happen. I kinda wish *you* did."

I kinda wished I didn't.

The sound of the television woke me with a start. It was Friday morning. On Saturday, Poppa would arrive with the moving truck and we would all be together again. At least, that had been the plan.

"Brace yourselves, folks," the Channel 3 weather lady trilled. "We have a winter storm warning in effect starting at six p.m. Temperatures will drop this afternoon, with snow showers beginning around . . ."

I hunted for my glasses, wishing my eyesight had gotten better with the switch. Samson and Tucker were awake now too. We all listened as the meteorologist continued her crummy forecast with enthusiasm.

". . . tonight's fast-moving blizzard is expected to dump up to twenty-six inches of snow on the Denver metro area by midnight. Officials are asking people to stay indoors this evening, and to—"

"Snow?" I cried, thinking, *No-no-no-no-no!* First there was the tiara. Now there was a blizzard on the way. Drat and drizzle! More and more pieces of my snowy clock tower vision were falling into place. The last two days of sunshine and warm weather had tricked me. I'd thought there was no danger of my vision coming to pass any time soon.

"I hope the weather doesn't delay your poppa,"

Momma said, brushing cake crumbs from her shirt as she joined us in the living room. I wondered if she'd slept.

"Don't worry, Momma." Tucker yawned. "Not even a snowstorm could stop Poppa. He never gives up. That's his ordinary, everyday savvy."

"That was before the switch." Samson's words were soft, but bleak.

"Tucker's right, kids," Momma assured us. "Your poppa would never give up on us—switch or no switch. Besides, no one but us has had a problem with things changing."

I'd heard Momma talking on the phone to Fish and Mibs, and to Aunt Dinah and Uncle Autry too, trying to figure out what happened to our savvies. But nobody else's abilities had turned upside down. No one knew what we should do to fix ours, either. I gave Grandma Pat the side-eye, still half convinced the switch was *her* fault . . . even though I was beginning to see that Grandma's life was getting switched up too—and not in a way that could be fixed or scumbled.

As predicted, a bitter wind began to rattle the windows by mid-afternoon, and the temperature outside dropped like God had just opened the door of His refrigerator. I was glad I was wearing my favorite cozy sweatshirt—the oversized sea-green one that hung nearly to the knees of my soft gray leggings.

I'd spent most of the afternoon sorting through boxes of old photos and mementos. Shuffling through a stack of faded images of Grandma as a smiling, curly-haired girl, I pretended not to notice that young Patrice and I could've practically been twins. There were plenty of photographs of Poppa as a boy as well, making me wonder for the thousandth time how Poppa had turned out so sweet and so loving with such a hard-hearted mother. But Poppa always said that Grandma hadn't been a terrible parent—just a strict one, one who'd had to work very hard to raise him on her own, after his dad died.

I was studying Grandpa Walter's funeral program when something caught my eye. Something that made my heart stop and my breath catch in my throat.

Hands shaking, I pulled a stiff rectangle of ice-blue paper from the box. It was an invitation: an invitation to the Larimer High School Winter Formal, in Denver,

Colorado, dated nineteen hundred and forever ago. I wondered if it was the same dance Grandma Pat had asked me about on Wednesday, when she thought I was Nettie Arbuckle.

But it wasn't the invitation itself that spooked me, it was the image of the building engraved in silver at the top of it—a high school building with a frighteningly familiar-looking clock tower. I knew that tower. Its architecture was burned into my mind's eye.

Grandma snatched the invitation from my hands, startling me.

"How I wish Daddy would let me go to the dance, Nettie!" she said. Just like that, I was Nettie Arbuckle again. "Did I tell you Cleavon Dorsey asked me to be his date? I *have* to find a way to go. I just have to! I hate Daddy for saying no." Hugging the invitation to her chest, Grandma began to spin and shuffle. Dreaming about Cleavon, she twirled around the room the way I'd always loved to twirl, before I'd been made to feel dumb for twirling inside Flint's Market.

Rising to my feet, I watched Grandma teeter, pirouette, and totter. I hovered closely, arms at the ready, following her the way a parent follows a tiny child just learning how to walk. Sometimes it felt like Grandma was getting younger and younger, while I had to work harder and harder to grow up.

Chapter 10

AN HOUR LATER, THE odds of keeping my clock tower vision from coming to pass went from bad to worse. In the short time it took me to go to the bathroom and wash my hands, Grandma Pat changed her clothes.

"She says she's going to some dance," Samson muttered, thrusting his chin in Grandma's direction as I stepped out of the bathroom. My brother leaned against the living room wall, arms crossed, watching Grandma struggle to get her feet into a huge pair of Sorrell snow boots. The lace and netting of her voluminous silvery party dress kept getting in the way, and her tarnished tiara slipped sideways in her downy curls every time she bent down to tie her bootlaces. Tucker sat on the sofa, stroking a white rabbit fur coat with two dangling pom-poms.

A snowstorm was on its way, and now Grandma Pat's clock tower costume was nearly complete—her lips were even painted coral pink. But if Father Time thought he had Grandma Pat's destiny firmly in his grip, he had another think coming. I had no intention of letting anything bad happen to my grandmother. Not that night, or any other. I would get Grandma to change out of her party clothes. Then I'd make Samson torch them.

But no matter how I begged and pleaded, Grandma Pat refused to take off the awful dress. Pushing me away, she grabbed her coat from Tucker. Then she stomped down the hallway and locked herself in her bedroom.

Momma peeked into the living room. "Everything okay in here?"

I nodded, grimacing. Then I shook my head. I opened my mouth to share my dreadful vision. "Momma, I—"

"We're out of cake—I mean, *tape*. We're out of packing tape," Momma interrupted me, yanking on her coat and grabbing the car keys.

"You're going out?" Samson uncrossed his arms and started toward her, his eyes glowing with concern.

"Momma! You're not going to drive, are you? Let me take you."

"I'm only going to the store, Samson. I'll be fine. I'll even bring back dinner. I promise I'll be careful." Momma stood straighter, putting her fists on her hips like Wonder Woman. "I won't let my new talent for blunders keep me from living my life. I laugh in the face of flubs and goof-ups. Ha-ha-ha!"

"Wait, Momma!" I tried again as Momma headed for the door, chuckling at her own bravado. "I really need to tell you someth—"

"Bring back jelly beans, Momma!" Tucker shouted over me. "Jelly beans! Jelly beans!"

Momma was gone before I could get her to listen. When I turned to tell Samson about Grandma's dress and Grandma's fall, he'd already disappeared into the attic.

For the next hour, I sat with my back against Grandma's bedroom door. Tucker watched cartoons in the living room. Samson hid upstairs, probably reading a book by the light of his own thumb. Grandma's ill temper seemed to gust through the cracks in the door frame, swirling around me like a cold wind. But after a few noisy thumps and bumps, no sounds came from her room.

Maybe she went to bed early, I thought, sighing with relief as I imagined Grandma snug and warm beneath her blankets. The sun set and the house grew dim. I refused to leave my post, even if it meant sitting in the dark. If Grandma tried to leave her bedroom wearing her party getup, I'd be there to stop her.

After a while, Tucker turned off the television and wandered down the hallway, hugging his stuffed cat and dragging a blanket behind him.

"What are you doing, Gypsy?"

"Making sure Grandma Pat stays safe."

"Because she's got the Old-timer's?" My brother settled down next to me, leaning his back against the locked door too.

"Yes, Tuck. Because of that. And because of . . . other things." I didn't want to tell Tucker about my vision. He was too little to help, and I didn't want to frighten him. Besides, with both of us sitting in front of her bedroom door, Grandma wasn't going anywhere.

I rubbed my eyes behind my glasses, replaying my clock tower vision over and over in my head, until a barrage of urgent knocking at the front door made me look up.

I leaped to my feet, thinking Momma had returned at last and needed help carrying the groceries. Tucker followed me to the door.

Knock-knock-knock!

Bang-bang-bang!

Jing-a-jing-jingle!

My makeshift jingle-bell alarm made it sound like Santa Claus was frantically clamoring to be let in. But it wasn't Santa banging on the door. It wasn't Momma, either. It was Nola Kim.

"Where is Mrs. B., you guys?" she demanded, barging past us in green skinny jeans and purple combat boots. Nola dropped a hard-sided silver cosmetics case and half a dozen Mall of Denver shopping bags onto the floor. Finding Grandma's recliner empty, she grabbed me by the shoulders.

"Tell me she's still here! Tell me your grandmother didn't do what I think she did."

"Grandma hasn't left her room for the last hour," I said, bewildered. But a sickening feeling was already squiggling through my stomach.

"What's happening?" Tucker looked from me to Nola.

Nola didn't answer. Instead, she raced down the hallway, dodging stacks of boxes and shimmying around the ladder to the attic. Tucker and I were right behind her.

Nola jiggled Grandma's doorknob. It was still locked.

"She's sleeping," I said, hoping I was right. Already knowing I was wrong.

"I'm pretty sure she *isn't* sleeping." Nola pulled a bobby pin out from under her sequined hat, then dropped to one knee. Straightening the pin, she jammed one end of it into the hole in the middle of the doorknob, trying to open the lock.

My heart thump-bumped in my chest. I hadn't been able to stop Tucker from swallowing a marble. I hadn't kept Mrs. Foster from slipping on a bar of soap. Why had I thought I could stop *any* future vision from happening?

"What's going on?" Samson's voice made me jump as he appeared beside me. His black T-shirt was smeared with dust, and he had a thin paperback book tucked into the pocket of his torn blue jeans. The edges of the pages were all singed black. Samson *had* been reading in the attic, just as I'd suspected.

Seeing Nola crouched in front of Grandma's door, Samson gave a start. This time, he didn't bolt. But he did quickly pull the armpits of his T-shirt to his nose to see if he smelled okay. I'd never seen Samson act so loopy around a girl before. It was weird. If the situation hadn't been so dire, I would have teased him.

"What's going on?" Samson repeated.

"I was shopping with some friends in Denver—they just dropped me off . . ." Nola began to explain, not looking up as she continued to fiddle with the lock. After a few more unsuccessful tries, Nola threw her bobby pin on the floor in frustration and stood up. "I was waving to my friends as they drove away, when I saw . . . well . . ." She paused and shook her head. "You're just going to have to see it for yourself. It's bad. It's really, really bad!"

Nola turned and slapped her palm against the unyielding doorknob. Tucker made a determined face and pushed his pint-sized shoulder against the door, trying to help. I pictured Grandma lying on the floor of her bedroom, unable to get up. I imagined her hurt, or dead. Samson must have been picturing something similar, because he raised the heel of his boot and kicked in Grandma's door.

Grandma wasn't in her bed or on the floor—she wasn't in her room at all. Now we could see why Nola was freaked out. A thin blast of wintry air billowed Grandma's curtains, giving the rest of us our first glimpse of the knotted bedsheets hanging out the window. It was only a three-foot drop from the windowsill to the ground; Grandma must have thought the window was higher up when she was making her escape plan. She'd done her best to close the window behind her, but the twisted linens kept the pane from lowering all the way.

It was clear to us all . . . Grandma Pat was gone.

Chapter 11

"DID GRANDMA REALLY LEAVE this way?" Tucker leaned out over the sill, holding the window open above him, inspecting Grandma's escape route with admiration. "Hey, Gypsy! Samson! Can I climb out the window too? Just once—just to try it?"

"No, Tuck," Samson and I answered in unison.

"Aw! The ground isn't even that far down."

"We have to call 911," Nola said, taking charge. She paced from the window to the bed, then back again, fumbling in her pockets for her phone.

"Maybe we should wait to call the police until we've looked for Grandma," I said. "She could still be close by. She probably just wandered down the road a little way." I crossed my fingers, hoping, hoping, hoping.

"Gypsy's right." Samson nodded his agreement. I knew my brother and I shared the same fears about calling in the cavalry. What if Tucker threw a gigantic fit just as the police arrived, picking up patrol cars and throwing them like toys? What if Samson belched a plume of flames, setting an officer's hat on fire?

"I'm *not* waiting." Nola dialed 911 and raised her phone to her ear, giving Samson and me a reproachful look. "Maybe you don't realize yet how sick your grandmother is," she said as she waited for an operator to pick up. "We can't mess around, not when it's dark outside and there's a blizzard coming. I'll talk to the sheriff's office and have them issue an alert. You three go start knocking on doors. We'll get the whole neighborhood to help us search. Where's your mom?"

"She went to the store," I said. *A long time ago,* I thought.

Grabbing Samson's wrist, I wrenched his arm toward me, trying to check the time on his battered wristwatch. "It's nearly six o'clock," I said, shaking Samson's arm. "Momma should've been back by now. She said she was going to bring back dinner."

"I should never have let her drive," Samson berated himself under his breath. Then, louder, he snapped, "Ow! Let go, Gypsy! You're gonna break my arm." I did let go. Fast. Samson's skin was growing hotter. I was afraid he was about to lose control.

"Samson, you need to—" I began, but before I could say more, Samson's eyes glowed and a pillar of flames shot straight up from the top of his head, scorching the ceiling.

Nola screamed and stumbled backward as a swirling storm of glowing embers popped and sizzled around Samson. Her phone flew out of her hand; I watched it sail straight toward the windowpane directly above Tucker. Tuck was still holding up the window and leaning out into the night, scanning the front yard for Grandma Pat. He turned just as Nola's phone smashed through the glass above his head.

My heart thumped wildly. I couldn't think. I threw my arms across my face and closed my eyes as tight as they would go, not wanting to see my little brother get cut to ribbons. Someone had started yelling—someone who sounded exactly like me. One long, drawn-out word was erupting from my mouth, reverberating through the house . . . circling the planet.

"STOOOOOOOOOOOOOOOOOOP!"

I'd done it again. Stopped time in its tracks. Once more, I was alone in an unmoving world. I could have paused to take a breath. I could have sat down on Grandma's bed to pull my wits together. But I had too much adrenaline pumping through my veins. I didn't know how long this time-stop would last.

Heart pounding, I moved quickly. I shot across the room and dragged Tucker out from under the shards of glass hanging in the air above him. Like a tiny UFO trying to fly back to the stars, Nola's cell phone hovered just beyond the busted window.

Nola's gaze was fixed on Samson: on his glowing eyes and flaming hair, and on the fantastical swirls of red-orange embers that circled him like fiery hula hoops. Distorted by shock, the girl's features had frozen in an awkward, mouth-twisted, half-blinking expression. She looked like a screwball snapshot of herself. An unflattering picture any teenage girl would quickly tear to pieces if she could.

Not knowing how else to stop the neighbor girl from seeing more of Samson's fire show, I grabbed Grandma's sleep mask from her bedside table and secured it over Nola's eyes. Then I raced to the kitchen and brought back a footstool and plastic pitcher of iced tea. Avoiding Samson's flames and embers as best I could, I stepped onto the footstool and turned the pitcher upside down on top of my brother's head. I left it there, like a hat with a water balloon in it, ready to pop. I hoped a gallon of iced tea would be enough to douse Samson's blazes as soon as time resumed.

Stepping down from the footstool, I saw the faded invitation to the Larimer High winter formal taped to the mirror above Grandma's dresser. Alongside it, Grandma had hung a note she'd scrawled on one of the paper napkins from her collection—one with a scalloped edge and a border of blue snowflakes. The message she'd left behind was obviously meant for her long-dead, disapproving father. My hands shook as I read the note.

I don't care what you think.
I'm going to the dance at Larimer High tonight.
Don't come after me!

I wasn't surprised to see where Grandma was headed, but I did feel defeated. No matter how hard I tried, I wasn't changing anything. I wasn't keeping any terrifying futures from coming to pass. It was like the Suds o' Heaven soap fiasco all over again. Only this time, the stakes were higher. Six stories higher.

Grandma Pat didn't know it, but her future depended on me and me alone.

"Don't be ridiculous," I told myself in the mirror. "Denver is miles away from Evergreen. There's no way Grandma could get that far on foot. She doesn't drive, or own a car. Now that time has stopped, she won't get a step farther." I leaned closer to the mirror, nearly touching noses with my reflection.

"You *can* stop your clock tower vision from happening," I whispered. "You *will* stop it!"

I snatched the invitation and the note. Then I grabbed my coat, crammed my feet into my snow boots, and bolted out the front door after Grandma.

The TV had been issuing dire warnings about the approaching storm all day. Now the blizzard crouched in the distance, heavy and ominous, an enormous white wolf poised to swallow the moon and stars. I imagined Grandma's illness gobbling up her memories the very same way, and I got a glimpse into how frightening that might be for her.

I was looking up and down the curving road, wondering which way to go, when a small flash of silver caught my eye. Moving to investigate, I discovered the glint came from a shiny dime lying on the asphalt. I picked up the coin and put it in my pocket. A few feet ahead, I spotted a penny. Then two nickels and another dime.

Passing house after house, pine tree after pine tree, I followed the white line on the edge of the winding road, pursuing Grandma's trail of pocket change, hoping there'd be enough coins in her stocking to lead me straight to her. Every step I took down the hill made me feel more lonesome and forlorn.

When I couldn't find another penny or nickel anywhere on the road ahead of me, I was about to turn back, sure I'd lost Grandma's trail in the darkness.

That's when I saw it. Not another coin, but a white

ball of fur: one of the pompoms from Grandma's coat. The pompom lay on the ground across the road, at the foot of the bus stop at the Hiwan Park-n-Ride. The Park-and-Ride was a large lot tucked between a woodsy park and a small church, where people could leave their cars and board buses into the city. I crossed the street and snatched up the fuzzy pom-pom. Grandma was nowhere to be seen.

The last time Grandma was here, Nola and her mother had found her before she could make it any farther. Nola had walked her back home. Had Grandma Pat really managed to board a bus to Denver this time, dressed the way she was? I sucked in my breath. Buses and Beaumonts didn't always mix.

I pulled Grandma's winter formal invitation from my pocket and looked at it again. My hands trembled as I ran my fingers over the engraved image of the Larimer High School clock tower. Denver was huge. It had suburbs and skyscrapers and roller coasters. Having lived most of my life between two tallgrass prairie states, surrounded by summer corn, winter wheat, and big, long stretches of nothing, I'd spent the little end of *never* in big cities. I was overcome by the thought of Grandma all alone in Denver, and overwhelmed by the idea of going there myself to search for her. A country mouse in the metropolis.

With time caught in a gridlock, the only way for me to get to Denver would be to hike thirty miles of highway.

I needed to restart time.

I dashed back up the winding road. As I listened to the dull thud of my boots clomping through the stillness, I tried to remember what I'd said or done to restart time the previous Sunday. But my memory of that day was still a blur.

Keeping my eyes glued to the asphalt, I jogged forward, repeating streams of words. Hoping to eventually stumble across the right ones.

"Start, start, start . . ."

"Go, go, go . . ."

"Tick, tick, tock . . ."

"Please, please, please . . ."

I had tried the same sets of syllables last time. None of them had worked on Sunday; they didn't work now, either. What were the magic words?

I was having a rough day. Grandpa Bomba's savvy had given him the power to move mountains, not see into the future, but he must have guessed that I'd have a bad day or two ahead of me. Why else would he have put that quote in my birthday card—the one from Shakespeare—about time and the hour running through the roughest day? Right now, time wasn't running at all. I was. And I was getting tired.

Halfway up the hill, I slowed my pace, then stopped. Both my legs and my lungs needed a break. Sucking in crisp mountain air, I tried to assure myself that this night *would* end, one way or another.

Looking up from the asphalt and the gravel, I took in all the sights around me—the hills, the stars, the trees, even the rising storm front, heavy with snow. Maybe there was a purpose to it all. A grand master plan. I didn't know. I *did* know that I couldn't hold an entire blizzard at bay forever. I had to face the fact that a storm was coming.

"You're as ready as you'll ever be, Gypsy," I told myself. I took a long, slow breath, and held it. When

I breathed out again, I whispered, "Come what may." Then I did the same thing three more times. Breathe in. Breathe out. *Come what may.*

Feeling a little better, a little calmer, I began to jog up the road again, softly chanting the words Grandpa Bomba had given me inside my birthday card.

A sharp blast of arctic air plastered my curls across my face, making me shiver. A snowflake landed on my nose. I jogged on, listening to the wind shaking the evergreens, and to the sound of traffic, far away in the distance. A car horn honked, startling me. I turned, hoping it was Momma returning from the store at last with bags full of cake and packing tape. When a stranger in a pickup truck drove past me, I realized with a jolt that time had started moving again without me noticing.

Had I found the right set of magic words at last? Perhaps Grandpa had given me one final gift before he died, when he wrote *come what may* inside my birthday card.

"Thank you, Grandpa!" I shouted to the frosty sky.

As more snowflakes began to fall, my jog turned

into a celebratory skip-hop-jump. The thought that I'd found a way to scumble my switched-up savvy made me want to spin and twirl and sing a chorus of *hallelujah*s. But I couldn't slow down. Now that the world was whirling again, the real race to find Grandma was on.

Chapter 12

WHEN I RETURNED, SAMSON and Tucker were in the middle of the road, calling out for me and Grandma. The front door of Grandma's house stood open, spilling light into the yard. Nola clung to the door frame, like she'd just lived through an earthquake—a major shake-up of everything she thought she knew about the world. Witnessing my family's abilities for the first time sometimes had that effect on people.

I tried to imagine what it must have been like for Nola when time started again. One moment, she was watching Samson light up like a house on fire; the next moment, she was blindfolded . . . Tucker had moved away from the window in a flash . . . Samson's flames were out and he was dripping iced tea . . . and I'd completely vanished.

"Gypsy!" Tucker shouted when he saw me running up the road.

"There you are!" Samson met me in three long strides. He gathered me up in a warm, damp hug. "As soon as that pitcher hit me, I knew you'd stopped time again. Plus, I had that same queasy feeling in my stomach we all got the last time you stopped and started time.

"Yeah, me too," Tucker whined, holding his tummy. "I don't like it when you do that, Gypsy."

Samson hugged me fiercely. "When we couldn't find you—"

"Erf," I mumbled into the front of my brother's shirt. "I love you too, Samson, but you're squishing me. And roasting me."

"How long were you on your own this time?" Samson asked, taking a step back but not letting go of my shoulders. His worry brought a smile to my face. My older brothers all shared a steadfast overprotective streak.

"Not long," I said. "But we have to get moving." I

pointed up at the sky. "The storm is here, and I'm pretty sure Grandma is on a bus headed into Denver."

"A bus? Into Denver?" Samson's jaw dropped.

"Where's Denver?" Tuck wanted to know.

I pulled out Grandma Pat's winter formal invitation, the note scrawled on the napkin, and the fur pom-pom, displaying them all for Tucker and Samson.

"I was trying to tell everyone earlier," I said, "but nobody would listen. Right before the switch happened, I had a vision—a vision of the future. A vision of *this* night . . ."

Still standing in the yard, I rattled off a shortened version of my clock tower premonition. I explained how, at first, I'd thought the old woman in the vision was me, a long time from now. I didn't share the part about the hands reaching out from the red sleeves, and how it was going to be up to me to save Grandma. I knew it would only double Samson's distress, and I couldn't risk the possibility of more blazes.

Tucker looked more confused than anything else. Nola crept closer as I spoke, staring at the rest of us like we were a family of purple unicorns.

By the time I finished telling Samson about my vision, I was trembling. "Why isn't Momma back yet?" I cried. "We need her!"

"Don't worry, Gypsy," said Samson. My brother led me back toward the house, brushing past Nola, who still stood gaping. "We'll use Grandma's phone to call Momma—to call the police too, just like Nola wanted us to do. I don't know where Momma is; she should have been back by now. As soon as she gets here, we'll all go after Grandma. But without a car—"

"I-I have a car." Nola's voice stopped us in our tracks. "I-I mean, my mom's new SUV is in the garage. She's still in Chicago, at her medical conference, and Dad is two hours away, in Pueblo—probably in the middle of removing someone's gallbladder, or something. But my mom's car is here." Nola pointed over her shoulder, toward her house. She looked both wired and uncertain, like she was offering a getaway car for a diamond heist.

"Only . . ." Nola paused, looking back at the rest of us through her bandit mask of black eye makeup. "I don't turn sixteen until next month. I don't have a driver's license yet."

"Samson's got one," Tucker piped up, jabbing Samson in the arm repeatedly with one finger.

"Would you really let us use your mother's car, Nola?" I asked.

"Only if you guys tell me everything—and I mean *everything*. And only if you take me with you."

Things moved quickly after that. We all rushed back into Grandma's house, where Samson ran to use the telephone in the kitchen, and Tucker and I stood in front of Nola, spilling the entire can of beans about all things savvy-secret. We talked over each other in our haste, explaining *everything* as fast as we could. Starting with the tale of our first savvy ancestor and ending with the switch, we condensed an entire pot of spicy chili into quick spoonfuls and small bites. Worried that Nola might be scared of Samson now, after nearly getting flambéed by his fire show, I told her how heroic my brother could be; I divulged how he'd once pushed his old invisibility-and-strength-giving savvy to its limits to help save the day. How he'd lost his powers completely for three miserable months afterward.

Nola kept her eyes narrowed, her arms crossed, and her lips pressed tight, like she didn't trust a single word Tucker and I were saying. But she couldn't deny what she'd already seen.

By the time Samson rejoined us, glancing nervously at the neighbor girl, Nola was a little calmer. But she still kept her distance, uncertain if it was safe to get too close to any of us.

"I'm not sure I believe half of what you guys just told me," she said. Then she added, "But I'm still going with you. I'm worried about Mrs. B." None of us argued with her. We needed her. Nola knew the city; we didn't. And we needed her mother's car.

"Did you talk to Momma, Samson?" I asked as my older brother clasped my shoulder with one broiling hand, like he was trying to make me feel stronger, the way he could before the switch. I was grateful for the gesture, even if it did make my skin feel like it was going to blister.

"Did you call the police? Are they going to put out an alert for Grandma? Are they going to look for her?"

"Momma's phone went straight to voicemail,"

Samson said, glowering. "Either her battery is dead, or she turned off her phone by mistake. And the police?" Samson scoffed softly. "They thought I was a prank caller—said if I didn't stop playing on the phone, I could face penalties. I suppose I shouldn't have told them Grandma is trying to get to the top of a clock tower dressed like one of the Twelve Dancing Princesses."

"It's up to us, then," I said, even though I knew that, in the end, it was going to be up to me, and me alone.

I helped Tucker find his coat and mittens while Nola retrieved her cosmetics case and shopping bags from the entryway. Samson didn't need a coat. He was warmed naturally from the inside out.

The snow fell in droves as we all trooped across the road to the Kims' garage. Nola punched a code into a small keypad, opening the garage door. She then moved quickly to her mom's spotless, pearl-white SUV, where she opened the rear hatch and tossed her shopping bags inside.

"You do have a driver's license, right?" Nola asked Samson as she grabbed a set of keys from a peg on the wall and dangled them in front of him. When Samson nodded, blushing, Nola sighed and said, "Lucky." Then she slapped the keys into my brother's palm and climbed into the passenger seat of the car.

Tucker and I were in the backseat in a flash.

"This is crazy," Nola said as Samson backed the mammoth car down the driveway. "I bet I'm dreaming all of this." She clutched her slouchy sequined hat, fingering a few of the silver sequins that had warped and melted during Samson's fire show. "I'm in the car with a bunch of kids with kooky powers, my elderly neighbor is missing, and my phone is trashed. I should probably try to call my dad, down in Pueblo—but what would I say? If I told him the truth, he'd want to X-ray my brain."

Nola ranted on and on as Samson got us on the road. "Three weeks! I was going to get my driver's license in three weeks. If my mom finds out we took her car, she won't let me take my driving test until I'm older than Mrs. B. And I won't be allowed to stay home alone again, ever."

"But you and your parents have been caring for Grandma Pat," I said from the backseat, fastening Tucker's seat belt, then mine. "Wouldn't your mom want us to go look for her?"

"Not in *this* car." Nola took a long, exaggerated sniff. "Smell that? That's New Car Scent. When it comes to this SUV, the president of the United States could be sinking in quicksand, and Mom would be too worried about getting the floor mats dirty to rescue him. So nobody make a mess or . . ." She pointed at Samson. "Or set any part of this car on fire."

"What about *our* momma?" Tuck asked, twisting in his seat to watch Grandma's house disappear into the distance. "Momma's savvy is all messed up, and she's been gone forever. What if she's in trouble?"

"Momma will be okay, Tuck," Samson said, even though he didn't sound entirely convinced. "Who knows why her phone is off? With her savvy all switched up, I suppose anything could've happened to it."

Tucker nodded gravely. "Maybe she dropped it in the potty. And then an alligator ate it."

Samson smiled. "I suppose it's possible."

"Drat! I know exactly why Momma is so late," I said. I felt like kicking myself as the memory of one of my very first savvy visions came rushing back to me. How had I not remembered earlier? On the morning of my thirteenth birthday, I'd looked into Momma's face and seen a tow truck, pine trees, snow, and a cupcake.

And our station wagon nose-down in a ditch.

When I shared the things I'd foreseen three months ago, Samson pounded his fist against the steering wheel. A ball of fire scorched the windshield in front of him and quickly dissipated.

"I knew I shouldn't have let her drive!" he said, ignoring Nola's shrieking as he rubbed a black scorch mark from the glass. "Now we have to search for Momma too."

"No we don't, Samson," I assured him. "You were right when you said Momma's fine. She isn't hurt. And a tow truck *will* come for her—it might already be on its way. I saw it, Samson. Momma will be safe, I promise. Grandma won't be." I shuddered. My premonition of Momma and the tow truck was just one more thing I hadn't been able to keep from happening. How would I ever save Grandma?

Chapter 13

SNOW GUSTS BUFFETED THE SUV, but thanks to Samson's brooding, we were plenty warm. We'd barely left Evergreen before Nola took off her jacket, revealing a flowing leopard-print scarf and a tight purple T-shirt with the words *Pop Star* bejeweled across the front. She opened the hard-sided cosmetics case she'd stowed at her feet and rummaged through it.

"I feel like my eyelashes got toasted," she said. Using the mirror on the back of her sun visor, Nola applied six new layers of mascara.

Samson drove top speed, following Nola's directions into Denver. The storm gnashed its big teeth at us, trying to swallow us whole. Making the roads and highways spit-slippery.

For the first ten miles, we sat in silence, filling the inside of the SUV with unspoken thoughts and worries. Samson snapped his fingers nervously, igniting the tip of his thumb over and over again. I tried not to picture Grandma Pat wandering down some dark alley in the wind and weather. Nola knew where Grandma's bus from Evergreen would stop once it got to Denver; she didn't know where the old high school was. So we were headed for the bus terminal, hoping to catch up to Grandma there.

The clock on the dashboard was too small for me to see. I asked Samson for the time so often, he took off his watch and gave it to me. I secured the canvas band around my own wrist, even though the watch itself was hot, hot, hot. If anyone needed a timepiece, it was me. It was 6:25. We had to find Grandma Pat before midnight. I tried to relax. We had plenty of time.

But as the skyline of the Mile-High City grew bigger and bigger in the windshield, I realized that we could search for a week and not find Grandma.

Nola continued to fiddle with the melted sequins on her hat, like she was still trying to process everything she'd witnessed, and everything we'd told her.

"So let me see if I've got this right," she said, after instructing Samson to take the next exit. "Before everything got 'switched up,' as you say it did"—Nola made air quotes with her fingers, then pointed to my older brother—"you could turn invisible *and* make other people feel calmer or stronger, or whatever, when you reappeared. But now you're Fire Guy, making people like me collapse in fear?"

"Fire Guy?" Samson jerked his head back at the nickname. But when I caught his reflection in the rearview mirror, I could see him smiling. He liked his new savvy!

"And before this so-called *switch*"—Nola turned to look at me—"*you* used to be able to see into the past or future, right?"

"She totally could!" Tucker said, kicking Nola's seat. "Gypsy even had a vision of me burying Poppa's fifty states quarter collection in the backyard when I was five. That was when I liked to pretend I was a pyrite."

"*Pirate*, Tuck. Not *pyrite*," I corrected him.

"Yeah, a pirate." Tucker dismissed my interruption with a wave, still kicking Nola's seat. "After Gypsy had her vision, we all went out with shovels and dug up the quarters. It was fun! Gypsy is always taking off her glasses and spacing out. Momma says it's not good manners to stare, but Gypsy stares at people all the time. She gets this really dopey look on her face and—*whammo!* She gets a vision." Tucker bulged out his eyes and made a silly face. "At least, she used to."

"I don't get a dopey look on my face!" I squeaked, completely mortified. "I don't, do I, Samson?" Samson winced apologetically in the rearview mirror.

"Sorry, Gypsy . . . you sort of do. Or, did. But it was always kinda cute."

"Your vision-face even makes Momma and Poppa laugh sometimes." Tuck chortled. "But they said we have to be polite."

I slipped lower in my seat and covered my face with my hands. It was no wonder Shelby Foster didn't want to have anything to do with me: I twirled down grocery aisles, I stuck flowers in my hair, I tossed glitter around like a giddy fairy princess . . . *and* I stared at people. Making stupid, dopey faces.

"Only now you *stop* time instead . . . right, Gypsy?"

Nola spoke slowly as she sussed out the details of our switched-up savvies. I could hear the disbelief beginning to fade from her voice, gradually being replaced by awe and wonder.

"Now, instead of seeing someone else's past or future, you get trapped in the present. Wow!" Nola paused as she pondered the idea. "It's like you get a single lasting moment that's yours, and yours alone. That's pretty cool." Nola sounded like she was trying to be kind. Like she could tell I felt self-conscious about what Tucker and Samson had said about my face, and was applying a gentle Band-Aid over my embarrassment. I wondered if anyone had ever made fun of Nola and the way she wore her makeup.

"I bet you don't look dopey at all when you stop time, Gypsy," Nola said reassuringly. "How *do* you do that, exactly?"

I straightened up a little in my seat, listening to the steady *thwap-wap* rhythm of the windshield wipers.

"Um, I think I just say *stop*. Really loudly. Or over and over again, like: *Stop-stop-stop-stop-STOP!*"

I clapped my hand over my mouth, realizing what

I'd just done. But this time, nothing happened. Everyone and everything kept moving.

Nola raised one eyebrow. "Okay . . . so, you just said stop, loudly and a bunch of times. Did time stop?"

"No." I shifted uncomfortably. *Why hadn't it?* I thought I'd finally gotten my new savvy scumbled. I thought it was all about finding the right words: *stop* to make everything freeze; Grandpa's *come what may* to make things go again. Now I didn't know what to believe.

"I guess I'm still working out the kinks," I said. Then I chewed my bottom lip.

When Tucker booted the back of Nola's seat again, she twisted around and scowled at him. "Hey, sprout! Stop with the kicking already!"

Tucker scowled back. "I'm not a sprout. I told you when you came over the first time, I can grow into a giant. Wanna see me try?"

"No, Tuck. She doesn't," Samson said. He reached into his pocket. "Want some Skittles?"

"Or a piece of taffy?" I said, pulling out my own supply of just-in-case candy. Both Samson and I had stocked our pockets before leaving Grandma's house.

"Wait . . ." Nola narrowed her eyes again, looking suspiciously at little Tuck, then back at me and Samson. "You guys told me a person has to be thirteen to get a . . . a—"

"A savvy," I reminded her.

"Now you're telling me that the sprou—that Tucker has got powers too? Why would that happen if he's only seven?"

Samson shrugged. "Unexpected things happen in our family."

"And the switch made things even more unexpected—and unexplainable," I added. "It made Tucker grow big."

"How big are we talking?" Nola sized up my little brother.

"Really big!" said Tuck. "But only when I'm mad. I've been trying to make myself grow big other times too. I try . . . and I try . . . and I try"—he slapped his hands to his forehead, then spread his arms wide—"but all I do is fart." Tucker chose that moment to demonstrate. He scrunched up his face and concentrated with all his might. The noise that ripped from his caboose could've put the World's Largest Tuba out of work. And the smell?

"Whoa! Tuck, no." Samson quickly rolled down all the windows, not caring about the snow. "Give us some warning next time, buddy."

Nola waved one hand in front of her face and held her nose. "There goes the new-car smell."

Tucker sighed in disappointment. "Someday I'll learn to scumble," he said. He looked so deflated, Samson and I each gave him a handful of candy.

When Nola heard the crackling sound of taffy wrappers, she said, "Remember! No messes, Tucker. My mom can't know we took her car. Though, after that stink bomb you just dropped, there may be no way to hide it."

"I won't make a mess, Nola," Tuck assured her through a mouthful of taffy and Skittles, spitting colorful bits of sweets everywhere. Already, there were sticky fingerprints on the inside of Tucker's window and on the soft black leather seats, five Skittles and three taffy wrappers lay on the floor, and the back of Nola's seat was covered in size-four boot prints. It was going to be hard to keep Mrs. Kim's SUV looking—and smelling—shiny-new.

By the time we reached downtown Denver, it was

6:40. The SUV's wiper blades worked overtime to clear the snow from the windshield as Nola gave Samson turn-by-turn directions. Directions that were mostly right.

"Turn left up ahead, Fire Guy. No, wait!" Nola grabbed Samson's wrist and pulled down on it. "Go right instead! We're nearly there. The bus station is just a few blocks ahead, but all these streets are one-way." Clearly flustered by Nola's back-and-forth commands, and by Nola's fingers touching his wrist, Samson didn't turn left or right. Instead, he held the steering wheel steady and kept driving forward. Running a red light.

Someone honked and Samson swerved. The SUV went sliding. Nola's shopping bags tipped over in the cargo space behind me, spilling half their contents. A can of pop rolled out of one of the bags and crashed into the rear hatch. With a *bang-pop-FIZZ* the can burst open and began to spin like a lawn sprinkler, showering the back of the car—and the back of my head—with sweet-smelling orange soda.

Nola's eyes were two dark wells of horror as she turned to look at the mess. Her dismay multiplied when a police siren chirped behind us.

Chapter 14

THE PATROL CAR DREW up on our tail, lights flashing. Samson cursed under his breath and started scanning the street for a place to pull over.

"No, no, no," I said, wiping orange soda from my cheek. "We can't stop. We're almost to the bus station!"

"It's right there." Nola pointed to an open plaza ahead of us. "The bus terminal is underground."

Samson maneuvered into a loading zone. The police car parked behind us, blinding us with its lights. A couple of small, electric shuttle buses waited by the plaza. A trio of bearded men with cardboard signs and overburdened grocery carts sat beneath a shelter. The snow was already inches deep on the streets and sidewalks. People of all sorts rushed to and fro, moving up and down a nearby pedestrian mall, and going in and out of a small glass building at the center of the plaza: The entrance to the underground bus station.

My heart leaped. We were so close. I prayed we'd find Grandma Pat in the bus station, twirling in her boots and ball gown.

"Be cool, got it?" Nola looked at Samson, then glanced back at the cop car. "Don't do anything too— too flamey. Just explain to this guy about Mrs. B. Maybe he'll help us look for her, and not give you a ticket . . . or ask whose car this is."

I couldn't wait for the police officer, or sit patiently through explanations. I felt bad about abandoning Samson, but my brother was going to have to deal with the police on his own.

I raised the hood of my coat and opened my door. "I'm going to look for Grandma."

"Wait for me!" Tucker snatched his coat and mittens. "I'm coming too." Tucker and I jumped from the SUV and fled hand in hand through the snow. The entrance to the bus station stood fifty feet away. The patrol car's lights dazzled the snowflakes.

"Gypsy, no! We need to stick together." Samson climbed halfway out of the car to call after me. A glance over my shoulder showed me that my brother's eyes were glowing ember-red. The falling snow melted and evaporated around him, leaving him bone dry.

"Gypsy!" Samson called again, his voice miserable and exasperated. But Samson wasn't the only one who was unhappy with Tuck and me for running off.

"Hey! You kids!"

I looked over my other shoulder and saw a square-jawed police officer. The officer circled two fingers in the air, then pointed them at Mrs. Kim's SUV, like he was trying to round us all up with a single lassoing gesture. "Return to your vehicle!"

Tuck and I both hesitated, stopping midway to the bus station.

"We could really use some help, officer." Samson raised both hands in the air, the way people do in police shows. "We're looking for our grandmother. She's—"

"Get back in your car, son. Then we'll talk." The officer cut Samson off before he could explain that our grandmother was sick and lost, and that we were desperate to find her.

Samson did as he was told. But before he got back in the car, he caught my eye and thrust his chin toward the station, mouthing the word *GO*. Apparently, Samson had changed his mind about us sticking together. He knew how important it was that we find Grandma Pat.

Gripping Tucker's hand tighter, I broke into a run.

"You two! Come back here," the officer called after us.

"Just give us a minute," I turned to shout, trip-skipping backward toward the entrance. "My brother has to go to the bathroom."

"No I don't!" Tucker tried to pry his fingers out of mine as I tugged him in the direction of the sliding doors. "I don't have to go, Gypsy."

"Shh! I'm only pretending so the policeman will let us go."

"Ohhhh," Tucker exclaimed. "I get it. It's a trick." Mustering his most monumental voice, Tuck shouted: "Boy, oh boy! I have so much pee in me, I could fill a swimming pool."

"Go for it, kid. Write your name in the snow," one of the drifters under the shelter called out, rolling his cart of belongings out of the way to get a better view. "If you let loose right here, we might have ourselves a sunny-yellow skating rink by morning."

Surely Tucker couldn't grow big enough to make that kind of splash! But the thought left me wondering: Just how large could Tucker grow? I hoped I'd never have to find out.

Despite the cold and snow, people on the street were beginning to stop and stare. I knew my face had to be as red as my hood and coat. I didn't like being on the other side of the peeking and the prying.

"Ha! That man was funny, Gypsy," Tucker said, hopping at my side. I pulled my brother through the sliding doors, then onto the escalator that would carry us down into the underground terminal.

The bus station was filled with benches and clocks and shops, and every sort of person imaginable. I could hear the muffled rumble of engines beyond the loading gates, while a pungent potpourri of coffee, popcorn, sweat, and exhaust fumes made my nose twitch. The clocks all read

7:05. Passing a small convenience store, then a coffee stand, I turned around and around, scanning the crowd. I saw no tiaras. No poufy party dresses. No Grandma Pat.

Tucker tugged my sleeve. "Look, Gypsy! Kittens!"

"Wait, Tucker—no!" Tucker ignored me. He made a beeline toward a young woman with blond dreadlocks who was sitting on the floor behind a large cardboard box, directly across from the row of shops. Inside the box were four mewing kitties. The word *FREE* was inked on the outside in orange marker—the same color as the striped kittens.

Part of me wanted to run to the box of purrs and whiskers too. But I was on a mission.

Keeping one eye on Tucker, I zoomed inside the convenience store, hoping to ask the boy working behind the counter if he'd seen Grandma Pat. In my haste, I cut in front of two older kids—one skinny and white, one huge and black—who were also making their way into the store.

"Sorry!" I said. "Pardon me!"

The skinny boy just glared. His skin, spotted with pimples, reminded me of slippery cave-dwelling salamanders. The pale kid gave me the shivers. His chest was so sunken, it made me wonder if he was missing his front ribs, his sternum, or his entire heart.

"Yo, Del!" the spotty kid greeted the boy at the cash register, but the greeting sounded more like a threat than a hello.

Looking me up and down, Mr. Salamander snorted. Then he and his large friend ambled to the back of the store, picking up magazines and key chains and batteries—even perfume bottles from a dusty cosmetics counter—then quickly putting each item down again, as if everything bored them. The two older boys eyed me, then Del, like they were waiting for me to leave. Like they had some bad business to conduct with the boy behind the counter and didn't want a witness.

Del didn't look much older than me. He wore a gray hoodie over a blue button-up shirt, and sported a spiffy yellow bow tie. His thick puff of black twists made him appear taller than he was, but he was still short compared to the other boys. Del's friends—if they were his friends— were in high school, I guessed. Like Nola and Samson.

"Can I help you?" Del said, barely glancing at me.

He kept his eyes fixed on the older boys. Beads of sweat dotted his smooth brown forehead, like dew dappling a summer cattail.

"I hope you can," I said. Then, checking to make sure Tucker was still squatting safely by the kittens, I explained why I was there.

"I'm looking for my grandmother. Maybe you've seen her? She would've been hard to miss. She's wearing a party dress and a tiara. She's not well." My voice wobbled. "She . . . she thinks she's going to a dance at Larimer High School tonight."

As soon as I said the word *tiara,* I had Del's full attention. His eyes widened, and he began to nod. He'd seen Grandma Pat, I could tell. But before he could say anything—

"Did I hear something about a dance at the old high school?" The spotty kid and his friend moved closer. Too close for comfort.

"A rave?" salamander-boy asked in a slippery voice. "Tonight? I like it! A party during a blizzard—I'm down for that." The boy tugged one of my curls and let it spring back. Then he jumped up to sit on the counter.

He grabbed a candy bar, tore off the wrapper, and took a bite. I wrinkled my nose; the older boy chewed with his trap open and talked with his mouth full.

"Who's this, Del? Your girlfriend?" *Chew, chew, chew.* "Do you guys hang out? Gossip? Paint each other's nails? Or do you two smoochy-smoochy whenever your uncle Ray isn't around?"

On the other side of the counter, Del flinched. Then his expression grew stony mad. He squared his shoulders and stood tall. His hands curled into tight, tense fists. Whatever was happening, or about to happen, I didn't want to get involved; I had a grandmother to rescue.

I backed up a step and ran into the larger boy, who was standing right behind me. "Oops!" I said. "Um . . . sorry."

"No worries," said the big kid, his voice so soft and quiet, I almost didn't hear him.

He didn't let me pass.

"You're gonna pay for that candy bar. Right, Tripp?" Del said through clenched teeth. "Ray will be right back—he's next door, getting coffee. Or should I call

George over?" Del nodded in the direction of the bus station's lone security guard. The man looked twice as old as Grandma Pat. He sat at a desk fifty feet from the shop, chin drooped against his chest. Snoring.

Tripp chortled, and took another bite of the candy bar. "Oh, Del," he said, spitting pieces of chocolate and peanuts as he spoke, the way my seven-year-old brother was still learning not to do. "You make me laugh, dude." *Chew-chew-chew*. "You're not going to call George over. Or your uncle. Is he, B-Bug?"

I looked over my shoulder at the boy towering there. B-Bug shook his head slowly. With the exception of Tucker, B-Bug had to be the biggest kid I'd ever seen; his coat was six sizes too big for a grizzly bear. Yet somehow I was more afraid of Tripp. Tripp had meanness in his eyes, pure and simple.

"And *why* won't Del call for help, B-Bug?" Tripp snickered. B-Bug didn't answer. He just sighed. But he sighed softly, like he didn't want Tripp to hear.

"That's right!" Tripp went on, not needing B-Bug or anyone else to have a conversation. "Del won't call for help, because I've got *this*." He pulled a phone from his pocket and waggled it in Del's face. "You, my young friend, are going to give me a permanent five-finger discount at your uncle's store. If you don't, I'm gonna make this picture I snapped last Sunday go viral. You're just a few clicks away from everyone at school seeing *this*." Tripp pressed a button on his phone, illuminating the screen. Shining its light directly into Del's eyes.

Del's nostrils flared. His jaw muscles tightened as he stared at Tripp's phone. But he said nothing.

"Once this image gets around"—Tripp waved his phone in a tight circle—"you'll never be able to show your pretty, pretty face at Park Hill Academy again. Either that, or I could just have B-Bug rearrange your teeth. Go ahead, B-Bug! Give Del a pop on the nose. Prove I'm not joking."

After another almost-silent sigh, B-Bug stepped around me and advanced on Del.

Del looked anxiously at Tripp's phone, then even more anxiously at B-Bug's raised fist, which was roughly the size of a brick. "You aren't really gonna hit me, are you, B-Bug?" Del said, his voice shaking with anger or dread, or both. "Your mom was friends with my gran, remember? Gran used to do her makeup here in the shop sometimes, when she'd get off the bus to go to work."

"I remember." B-Bug hesitated, but he didn't lower his knuckles. Looking at his pasty pal, he rumbled, "Del's an old friend of mine, Tripp. Are you sure you want me to hit him?"

Tripp exhaled sharply. "No, B-Bug, ya big doofus. I want you to give him a kiss on the mouth, just like that old lady in the ball gown did after she jumped into your arms and called you *Cleavon*. Ha! You should'a seen your face!

"Of course I want you to hit him!"

Old lady in a ball gown? Cleavon? These bullies had seen Grandma Pat.

"Wait!" I said, a million questions springing to the tip of my tongue. But none of the boys even looked my way. B-Bug was already reaching over the counter. With an apologetic look, he grabbed the front of Del's hoodie. Then he pulled back his arm, aiming his knuckles at the smaller boy's face.

"Do it, B-Bug!" Tripp leaped off the counter and started jumping up and down, throwing punches in the air, like a spectator at a boxing match. I saw Del brace himself for the coming blow and felt my own face scrunch up too. Like I was the one about to get hit, not Del.

I didn't want anything to do with this awful moment. I turned away, closing my eyes and plugging my ears.

I heard Del cry, "Time freeze! Freeze now!" even as I opened my mouth and shouted: *"Stop, stop, STOP!"*

When the familiar curtain of silence fell, I opened one eye and turned, peeking warily at the stalled-out smack-down in front of me.

B-Bug's right fist was less than an inch away from the tip of Del's nose.

Tripp had frozen while jumping up and down. He now had both feet off the ground.

I looked at my watch. It was a quarter past seven and I was alone again, just me against the frozen world. Or . . . maybe not.

"Ha! That'll teach you losers."

I nearly shot out of my skin at the sound of the words. Apparently, I wasn't by myself after all. Time *had* stopped. Just not for everyone.

Chapter 15

DEL AND I STARED at each other. The boy waved his hand. I waved back. Del slowly shook his head. I shook my head too. I silently counted heartbeats: ten . . . twenty . . . thirty-three . . . forty-seven . . . fifty. I wondered if Del was counting heartbeats too.

"Whoa," he said at last. "Why are you still moving, Specs? You should be a statue, like everyone else. How are you messing with my atomic time-freeze?" Del's voice sounded muffled and distant, but I got used to the effect quickly. With time stopped, it was a wonder we could hear each other at all.

I watched Del try to squirm out of his hoodie, which was locked inside B-Bug's grip. My heart pounded ten more times before the full meaning of Del's words hit me . . . *Why are you messing with* my *atomic time-freeze?*

The boy from the convenience store thought *he'd* stopped the clocks. He didn't know I'd done it.

Del disappeared momentarily inside his hoodie as he slipped B-Bug's snare. It was funny to see the sweatshirt hanging empty from the other boy's big paw. It made B-Bug look like a human coatrack.

"In case you haven't noticed, Specs"—Del flashed me a grin as he smoothed his shirt and tidied his twists—"you are in the presence of an honest-to-goodness superhero. I just stopped time and saved the day!" Del took a strut-step backward, spreading his arms wide.

A snort of laughter erupted from my nose as Del tripped over a bundle of newspapers. His arms became two propellers as he tried to catch himself. Then he fell, landing squarely on his brash behind.

I stepped forward and stuck out my hand, offering to help Del off the floor.

The boy clasped my fingers and scrambled to his feet. He cleared his throat, straightening his bow tie—and his dignity—like he was the coolest kid on the planet and I was a total nincompoop for not knowing it.

"Maybe you oughtta be my sidekick, Specs—you know, since you're the only one still moving around and all. Why *are* you moving? What makes you different?"

I wondered the same thing about him. So far, I hadn't run into one other person who was immune to the power of my switched-up savvy.

"I-I must be special, I guess," I said with a shrug. Then I asked, "Why were those boys picking on you?"

"Aw, that?" Del tried to maintain his easygoing bluster, but he tensed as he glanced at Tripp and B-Bug. "That was a whole lot of nothing, Specs. We were just goofing around."

"It didn't look very goofy," I said. "Here, I think you bit your lip when you fell. You're bleeding." Del licked his lip and winced. I handed him the paper napkin from my pocket, the one with Grandma's note on it.

As soon as Del took the napkin, I wished I hadn't given it to him. His eyebrows rose as he read Grandma Pat's note aloud:

"*I don't care what you think . . . I'm going to the dance at Larimer High tonight . . . Don't come after me.* That's right!" he said, snapping his fingers once before dabbing his bloody lip with the napkin. "You were looking for the old lady who came through here a while back—the one in the thrift store party outfit. She's your grandmother?" Del studied me for a moment, then nodded.

"Yeaaah, I totally see the resemblance. I could tell your gran wasn't well, Specs. But if I'd known she was trying to get to the old high school . . ."

I shifted uncomfortably, not sure if Del would understand what a tall order it was to have a grandmother like mine—one who did and said and wore weird things. One who couldn't remember what decade it was, or recognize her own granddaughter. Even if we did look alike.

"Your gran told Uncle Ray she needed to get to Aardman's Flowers," Del went on. "Said she had to pick up a boutonniere she'd ordered for tonight. Ray gave her directions. I told him not to—I told him she was off her nut. But Ray just said, 'Del, we offer customer service here.'" Del lowered his voice as he mimicked his uncle. "'I don't judge my customers, or make mental health determinations. If I did, I'd lose half my business.' Then Ray packed her off to Aardman's so that she could get her boutonniere."

"Her *boot* and *ear*?" I repeated, thinking Grandma had lost more of her marbles than I'd realized. Del blinked at me a couple times, then laughed.

"*Boutonniere,* Specs. You know, a flower that goes on a guy's lapel?" Del gestured to his chest, as if to demonstrate. "People get them for fancy parties. Like weddings, or—"

"Or high school formals?" I asked.

"Yeah, sure. They can be for dances too. But it's kinda old-fashioned. Your gran isn't really trying to get to Larimer High tonight, is she? That place has been boarded up for years. It's dangerous. Only miscreants and troublemakers go there now. People like *them.*" Del pointed over his shoulder at Tripp and B-Bug.

The words *miscreants* and *troublemakers* worried me. What if Grandma reached her old high school and found herself dancing with some wrong-doing lowlife? I imagined Patrice Beaumont fending off muggers, gangs, and hooligans, unsure who would win.

Wanting to think about anything else, I looked out of the shop's open doors, into the bus terminal. The bus station could have been a warehouse of shop-window dummies; Del and I were the only people moving.

"So . . . is this the first time you ever, you know, stopped time?" I asked Del, trying to sound casual, like I was asking him about a movie or the weather, instead of a case of mistaken abilities.

"What? Nah. I do it all the time."

"Really?" I turned back to him and raised an eyebrow.

"Okay, if you gotta know, this is only the third time I've done it. It's the second time today, though. That must mean I'm getting better at it, right? When it happened the first time, last Sunday, I thought the clocks were never going to move again. When they did—" Del glanced at Tripp and B-Bug, then stopped talking as if he were remembering something bad.

Del swabbed his lip with the napkin one last time, then he crumpled Grandma's note and threw it in Tripp's direction. The napkin flew an inch from his fingertips, then stopped, hanging suspended in the air the same way my snowballs and pencils and paper butterflies had. It was strange to think that Del had been wandering around on his own during my last two time-stops.

Maybe Momma and Poppa and everyone else were right—maybe we never are completely alone.

Del looked at me apologetically. "My uncle really should have called someone to come get your grandmother—but he just thought she was a batty old ding-a-ling."

"Don't call her that," I snapped, surprised by my defensiveness.

"I *didn't* call her that, Specs. I'm just telling you what Uncle Ray said."

"My grandmother isn't crazy. She's sick. She gets mixed up a lot."

Del's face softened. "I wasn't making fun of her, I swear. In fact, I'll help you look for her. You and I appear to have an unmoving minute on our hands. Your gran can't have gotten too far. I know where Aardman's Flowers is. It's down the mall, less than a mile. That shop has been around for decades."

With a grunt, Del pried the phone out of Tripp's rigid fingers and slipped the device into the pocket of his jeans. Del laughed when he noticed the way Tripp hovered three inches off the ground. He pulled the other kid toward him, then pushed him back again, toying with Tripp like he was a balloon made from pale, pocked marble.

Flashing me a wicked grin and waggling his eyebrows, Del pushed and pulled Tripp's still form until he was on the other side of the counter. He positioned his tormenter directly in front of B-Bug's clenched fist. As soon as time regained momentum, B-Bug would punch Tripp instead of him. The two bullies were in for a big surprise.

"Don't just stand there, Specs. Help me! It's seven fifteen, and it might be seven fifteen for a good long while. I'm still new to this superpower stuff—I don't actually know yet how I've been making time *start* again. So we may as well have a little fun, then go find your gran. It's not like she's going anywhere at the moment, am I right?"

I chewed my lip, torn between my need to find Grandma Pat and the lure of having a bit of fun for the first time during one of my time-stops. I stood in place and watched as Del darted into a storeroom and returned with two rolls of toilet paper. He handed a roll to me, but I didn't know what he wanted me to do with it. I wavered between disbelief and delight when Del started wrapping Tripp and B-Bug in swathes of white, turning them into mummies.

"Sorry about this, B-Bug," he said as he reached up to wrap bath tissue around the boy's thick neck, talking to B-Bug like the larger boy could hear him. "I used to like you, dude. But now that you let this idiot Tripp order you around all the time, I've got no sympathy. It's not like you don't deserve this. You *were* about to hit me." When he ran out of toilet paper, Del turned back to me.

"Come on, Specs, live a little! Why are you just standing there?"

I felt a smile tug at the corners of my mouth. My heart thumped a bit faster. Setting down my roll of toilet paper, I looked around. TP-ing someone wasn't my style, but there was a bucket near the door filled with five-dollar bouquets of mixed flowers. While Del tied B-Bug's shoelaces together—and then moved on to Tripp's—I fashioned two quick circlets out of flowers.

"Ha! I like the way you think, Specs." Del grinned when he saw what I was doing. He gave me a leg up, helping me crown both bullies. After which, I stuck a long-stemmed rose between Tripp's front teeth.

"How did you make those daisy chains so fast?" Del asked, stepping back to admire our handiwork. "You braided those stems like lightning."

I felt myself flush.

Silly, dancing, flower-picking baby.

"I've had a lot of practice," I said, waiting for Del to make fun of me.

But Del just nodded and said, "Cool."

When we were done giving the bullies their May Day mummy makeover, Del wiped his hands on his jeans, like he was wiping them clean of the older boys.

"That was some serious entertainment! If only I had some special-effects makeup—I could scare the pants off these two numbskulls by making them look like gruesome, gnawed-on zombies." Del turned to me, still grinning.

"What's your name, Specs?"

"Gypsy," I answered. "Gypsy Beaumont."

"I'm Antwon Delacroix," Del said, pressing a thumb

to his chest. "But only my parents and teachers call me Antwon. You can call me Mr. Kool-A Iced-Tea Time. That's what I'm thinking of calling myself now that I can stop the clocks. I've always wanted to be a super-hero."

I didn't have the heart to tell Del the truth. I didn't want to be the one to take away his swagger. I needed this boy. He knew things about Denver I didn't. And it was nice to have company. If I crushed Del's superhero fantasy by telling him my secret, would he still want to help me?

I couldn't take that risk.

I couldn't risk trying to restart time yet, either; it would be easier to find Grandma Pat if she was standing still. Maybe Del and I could shortstop her at Aardman's Flowers and keep her from getting anywhere near Larimer High.

I was halfway up the unmoving escalator, ready to execute Plan A—Intercept Grandma at Aardman's Flowers—when I remembered Tucker.

"Drat and drabble! I almost forgot my little brother!"

Chapter 16

"YOU'VE GOT A BROTHER?" Del asked, pulling on his coat as we sped back down into the terminal.

"I've got four," I called over my shoulder. "A sister too."

"Are they all here?"

"No, most of them are grown up. Only Tucker is here—and Samson. Samson's outside, in the car."

Del and I threaded our way through the frozen crowd inside the bus station. We found Tucker squatting in front of the three orange kittens in the box. He held his coat tightly closed around him, like he was trying to keep himself small and contained despite his enormous love of cats.

"Help me pick him up." I hooked my fingers under

one of Tucker's elbows, motioning for Del to grab the other.

"Are you serious? We're just going to lift the little guy and carry him? He's not a cooler full of Gatorade."

"We can't leave him," I said. "And he's not going anywhere on his own now that I—er, now that time has stopped."

"That's true," Del said, and he helped me hoist Tuck off the floor. "You know, Specs . . . you're taking this whole time-freeze business pretty well. Most people would be flipping out right now."

"I guess I'm still in shock." I wasn't lying. I was still shocked—shocked to meet someone who was completely unaffected by my savvy.

"How can a kid this small weigh so much?" Del complained as we half lifted, half dragged Tuck up the escalator—*bump, thump, whump.* "I always thought it would be nice to have a little brother, but this gives me a newfound appreciation for being an only child."

When we reached the top of the escalator, the automatic doors wouldn't open. "We're going to have to pry them," I said. Del glanced back down into the terminal, imagining, perhaps, that two toilet-paper mummies were about to rise up and grab him. Working together, we wrested the doors open wide enough to squeeze through them. Then we stepped out into a field of snow, and a wall of cold.

The city's glow illuminated the wintry night, turning the sky into an otherworldly yellow-gray dome. Snow-flakes hung like magnified dust motes in the time-stilled air. I smiled as the most delightful idea popped into my head: I wondered if I could make upright snow angels, just by doing jumping jacks.

How I longed to try!

"Wow," Del whispered next to me, sounding as awe-struck as I felt. I almost suggested that we try out my jumping-jack snow-angel idea together. Then I remembered the way Shelby had looked at me inside Flint's Market, and I made myself as still and as motionless as Tucker.

I would *not* embarrass myself in front of city boy Antwon Delacroix.

"Tell me that's not your other brother over there in the SUV," Del said. "The one with the five-oh sitting on his six?" Poppa was ex-military, so I knew the word *six* could also mean *behind*. But—

"Five-oh?" I gave Del a quizzical look.

"*Five-oh.* The *police,* Specs. The police."

"Oh. Yeah. That's him." I frowned, feeling every inch a country bumpkin.

"Ouch!" Del winced. "Who's the girl having the serious makeup malfunction next to him?"

I narrowed my eyes at Del, trying to see if he was making fun of Nola. But his concern seemed more humanitarian than mocking, like he was a first aid worker witnessing a natural disaster.

"That's Nola Kim. She's Grandma's neighbor. We sort of borrowed her mother's car after Grandma Pat climbed out the window."

Del raised his eyebrows. "Your gran went out the window?"

I nodded. "I've got to find her, Del."

"Come on," he said. "Let's put this little dude in the back of your ride. Then he'll be safe and sound, and you and I can make a break for Aardman's Flowers. Your gran can't have gotten too far, right? Especially now that

I stopped time. Don't worry, Specs! Mr. Kool-A Iced-Tea Time is on the jo—"

"No!" I stopped him. "I can't leave Tucker behind."

"What?" He blinked at me. "Why not? I'm all for helping find your gran—it's exactly the sort of thing we superheroes do. But you can bet your badink-a-dink that I'm not gonna lug a little kid all the way down the 16th Street Mall in the snow."

"I promised I'd look after him," I said, wishing I'd done a better job of looking after Grandma. "And Tucker might get . . . *upset* when he realizes we took him away from the kittens. And when my brother gets upset . . . well, let's just say Tucker knows how to throw a really big fit. The kind I wouldn't want the police—I mean, the *five-oh* to see."

Del glanced down at Tucker with new respect. "That must be one heck of a tantrum."

"You don't know the half of it."

"I'm still not carrying him all the way to Aardman's."

I pushed my glasses higher on my nose and looked around the snowy plaza, searching for a solution. The three bearded men were still huddled under the shelter with their cluster of shopping carts.

Eyeing the buggies, I turned to Del and smiled. "I have the best idea."

"This was *not* the best idea," Del said after we'd gone two blocks.

"That's because you keep steering us crooked, Del." I gave the grocery cart a shove, trying my best not to look at Tucker; it was unsettling to see him lying on his back inside the basket, with his limbs cramped up like a dead bug, and a silly, kitten-loving grin glued to his face. Our cargo wasn't heavy. We'd removed everything from the cart before dumping Tucker into it, but it was still difficult to push. I felt guilty for taking it. Guilty for skipping out on Samson too.

Before leaving the plaza, I'd left Samson a note. Using the brightest shade of lipstick in Nola's cosmetics case—a tube of Twisted Tangerine—I scrawled a message across the dashboard inside the SUV.

MEET US AT AARDMAN'S FLOWERS
—G

I knew Nola was going to be mad, but I had to risk

it. Grandma or no Grandma, I was going to restart time as soon as I got to the flower shop. I only hoped Samson and Nola would be able to find the place. With Poppa still in Kansaska-Nebransas, and Momma waiting for a tow truck somewhere in Evergreen, my family had already become too fractured. I didn't want to be separated from Samson for too long. We Beaumonts were supposed to stick together.

But I'd never been too good at remembering my *supposed-to*'s.

"I'm not steering us crooked, Specs," Del said, giving the cart a shove. "We boosted a buggy with a bum wheel. This thing won't roll straight." Shoulder to shoulder and hip to hip, Del and I bumped our way down Denver's outdoor pedestrian mall, forcing the cart ahead of us through the snow. The 16th Street Mall was lined on either side with towering skyscrapers and old, historic buildings. Lacy snowflakes caught in our hair and on our coats as we pressed forward.

"We've got to go faster," I said, scanning everywhere for Grandma's tiara and poufy dress. I threw my weight against the cart, trying to maneuver around an unmoving squirrel out in the storm past its bedtime.

"I think we've already reached top speed with these wheels, Specs. It feels like we're trying to push through a river of my gran's hamburger gravy. That stuff was *thick*." Del chuckled, and the smile on his face was the sort people get when they're remembering something they love, or someone they miss.

"Whoa! Do you see that? Or am I losing it?" Del swiveled his head, pointing up at a building we'd just passed. I followed his gaze to a second-story window, where two identical girls with ebony hair buns and pink leotards stared down at us. Bouncing on their toes, and waving frantically, they looked just as astonished to see us as we were to see them. The girls were twin ballerinas-in-training. A sign below the window read: *Michelle Robin School of Dance*.

I glanced up and down the mall, listening and looking. "Has time started moving again, Del?"

"Uh-uh." Del slowly shook his head. "Should we stop?" he asked. "Go up there and introduce ourselves?"

He waved halfheartedly at the dancers and sighed. "Maybe we should form a club, or team, or something. We could call ourselves The Timeless Crusaders. I wonder how many more people can resist the power of my time-stops."

I still didn't have the heart to tell Del that I was the one stopping time. I had no clue why Del and the girls in the window weren't frozen in place. Just then, I knew only one thing:

"We can't dilly-dally. Time or no time, my grandma needs me."

I kept my eyes peeled for more moving strangers. First Del . . . now a pair of girls who looked like twins? I couldn't ignore the likelihood that there were even more people in the world who were unaffected by my savvy. Was there a Dutch boy awake in the night in Holland, wondering why the windmills had stopped turning? A tour guide on the Great Wall of China, baffled by a sea of unmoving tourists? Would those people want to be Timeless Crusaders too?

"Aardman's Flowers." Del read the sign above the win-

dow when we arrived at the flower shop at last.

I stared gloomily at the notice taped to the door. *"Closed for the blizzard."*

A man wearing an orange-and-blue parka and a matching ski hat stood like a statue at the door, key poised in the lock.

There was no sign of Grandma Pat.

Del studied the frozen florist for a moment, then he snapped his fingers twice and opened his palm. "Hand over that lipstick you brought with you, Specs."

I fished in my pocket for Nola's tube of Twisted Tangerine. "What do you need it for?" I asked, entrusting the lipstick to Del.

"I want to paint this guy's face orange. He won't mind; he's a Broncos fan." Del pointed to the team colors on the man's coat.

I shook my head. "I think we've had enough fun for one time-stop, Del. Besides, Nola's already going to be mad at me for raiding her cosmetics case. Let's not make a bigger mess of her lipstick than I already have."

"Aw, come on, Specs! My gran was a makeup *artist*. I learned more than a thing or two watching her do makeovers behind the cosmetics counter in my uncle's store." As he spoke, Del reached up and drew the profile of a charging bronco onto the shopkeeper's left cheek. When he finished his sports-fan makeover, Del prodded the frozen florist with three fingers, making the man tilt to the left, then to the right.

"Stop it," I said, trying not to laugh. "If you leave him like that, he'll tip over as soon as I make time go again. Besides, we need to figure out what to do next." But I already knew what I needed to do next. It was time to go to plan B. It was time to reunite with Samson and Nola, and then go directly to the old high school building. We'd wait for Grandma there and keep her from climbing to the top of the treacherous clock tower. Only, every time I thought about the tower, I wanted to run and hide. I didn't think I could face it. Not in person. Not for real. Just watching the scene play out in the bathroom mirror had been terrifying enough. I wasn't ready to discover if I had the strength to catch Grandma and hold on to her.

What if I failed?

I was nothing but a baby. Silly and afraid.

"Gypsy? Hello? Are you in there, Specs?" When I looked up, Del was waving one hand in front of my glasses.

"What?"

"I *said,* you mean *I* have to make time go again. Right?" Del frowned. "You said you have to do it, but—"

"Del—"

"Shh! Just stand back and let me work. I'm going to start the clocks again, just for you, Gypsy Beaumont. Then we can ask this flower guy if he's seen your grandmother."

My shoulders drooped as I watched Del try to restart time. He jumped up and down. He punched the floating snow. He closed his eyes, clapped his hands, and cried, "Bibbity . . . bobbity . . . bacon double cheeseburgers!"

"Abba-dabba-doo-cadabra!"

"Shazbot!"

Del quickly ran out of fancy moves and funny incantations, but he didn't stop trying. He wanted to help and he wasn't afraid to face the situation head-on.

"Maybe you should try *come what may,*" I mumbled, lamenting the loss of what I'd believed to be my own magic words.

"Come what may?"

"It's part of a Shakespeare quote my grandpa shared with me before he died," I explained. *"Come what may, time and the hour run through the roughest day."*

"I like it." Del nodded his approval. "It's kinda like saying: Whatever happens, time will keep on moving and bad days will always end. Yeah?"

"Yeah."

"But 'come what may' could also mean: *Bring it on!* Don't you think?"

"Er . . . yes, I suppose so," I agreed again, this time with more than a thimble-full of hesitation.

While Del spread his arms wide and turned up the volume on his swagger, shouting: "Hey, time! Come what may! Bring it on!" I wrestled with the knowledge that words alone couldn't stop or start time. I had learned that lesson in the SUV with Nola when I said *stop* and nothing stopped. I was still missing something. There was an essential puzzle piece I was overlooking—one that would let me scumble my mixed-up savvy. One that would allow me to switch time off and on at will.

I glanced at little Tuck, who was still all bent up

inside the shopping cart, and I remembered the first time I stopped the clocks, five days ago. I'd blamed Tucker. He'd made me so mad. He had also made me afraid—a hundred times more afraid than the crazy switch had made me. Fearing Tucker was about to wreck the house, I'd closed my eyes and turned away. I'd done the same thing at Grandma's, when the bedroom window was about to shatter; and at the bus station, when B-Bug was going to knock Del's block off. Each time, I'd turned away, not wanting to face what was happening, or what was coming next. Unwilling to bring *anything* on.

My chest began to burn, and I realized I was holding my breath. I emptied my lungs, then filled them again, turning my attention back to everything there was to see in the frozen moment in front of me—the snow, the city, the lampposts, the shopkeeper, Del and Tucker. It had been a long and interesting interval since I stopped time back in the bus station. But I was growing keen to move on to the next moment . . . and the moment after that.

"Are you really ready for time to start again, Del?"

"Are you kidding? I'm half past ready. Aren't you?"

"Yes, I am," I said. "Come what may, I'm ready." This time, when I said the words, they felt deep and true. I also knew now that I didn't have to say them at all. Keeping my eyes open, I spread my arms wide, the way Del had, like I was welcoming back time with a waiting hug. Ready to embrace, or experience, or overcome whatever was going to happen next . . . and next . . . and next.

I tried not to think about the things I couldn't change. About the things I was afraid might happen. I could feel Del watching me, like he could sense the powerful pull that radiated out from where I stood—a pull that made the whole world turn again.

Chapter 17

THE HUBBUB OF THE stormy night returned in a rush. A glacial gust slammed the floating snowflakes sideways, gluing them to newspaper boxes, street signs, and us. I bubbled with pride at the return of the blizzard.

I'd started time again—on purpose!

Ignoring the wind and weather, I twirled a triumphant twirl. Then I slipped on a patch of ice and fell. I felt like Jack Frost was mocking me, reminding me that I was supposed to be growing up and acting my age, not spinning and dancing around in the snow like a ninny.

Lying flat on my back on the sidewalk, I heard Tucker cry, "Hey! What's going on? How'd I get in this cart?" and the shopkeeper say, "Where'd you three come from? Are you okay, kid? Did you hit your head?"

Rushing to help me off the ground, Del and the shop-keeper both dusted snow from my coat and leggings.

"I'm okay," I said, feeling foolish. "Nothing hurts."

Nothing but my pride.

I didn't know how long it would take Samson and Nola to catch up to us. But once I explained our situation to the shopkeeper, he kindly allowed us to wait inside. He was worried I might have injured myself in front of his store. Like it was his fault I fell on the ice, not mine.

"No self-respecting Aardman would leave three kids standing alone on a city curb in a blizzard, after dark," the man said, introducing himself to us as: "Thomas G. Aardman, fourth-generation florist to the governor of Colorado." Then he hoisted Tucker out of the shopping cart and escorted us into his store—completely unaware of the decorative orange markings on his face.

Mr. Aardman turned on all the lights. Colorful ribbons snapped and fluttered from the rafters, rippling in the warm currents issuing from the heating vents. The shop was filled with the aroma of hundreds of cut flowers blooming by the bucketful inside glass coolers. I closed my eyes and sucked in the scent of roses, freesias, and carnations. For half a heartbeat, I was able to forget where I was, and why. I imagined I was standing in a meadow of wildflowers, surrounded by towering glass jars—jars like the ones my savvy grandma, Dollop O'Connell, once used to can storehouses of radio waves.

How I wished Grandma Pat could have been born into a savvy family too! Why couldn't Patrice Beaumont have a touch of shimmer-glimmer in her DNA, the way both of my mother's parents had?

I was disheartened to learn that Mr. Aardman hadn't seen my grandmother. The snow was coming down so hard now, I wasn't sure what I was beginning to fear more: Grandma Pat making it to the clock tower, or Grandma Pat *not* making it to the clock tower. What if she was already a grandma-shaped Popsicle?

Tucker started acting strangely the moment he was out of the cold. He barely glanced at Del, even after I explained, in a rapid whisper in his ear, how Del had helped me, and how, for some reason, Del didn't freeze with the rest of the world when I stopped time. I thought Tuck would be brimming with questions. Instead, he wiggled and squirmed, hugging his arms across the front of his coat, like he was working hard to keep his heart from popping out of his chest. I hadn't seen Tucker so jumpy since he tried to smuggle a dozen freshly baked cookies out of Momma's kitchen, in his underwear— not realizing the cookies were still hot.

"Do you have to go to the bathroom or something?" I asked him, looking around the shop for a washroom.

"Nope, nope!" Tucker shook his head. Then he ducked away from me and Del, whispering soothing things into his coat, as if trying to reassure his own belly button that everything was going to be all right.

"He could be feeling queasy," I told Del, remembering my brother's tummy troubles after previous time-stops. Mr. Aardman was holding a hand over his stomach too as he disappeared into the back room.

Del also looked like he felt sick. No . . . not sick. Bereaved. Deflated. Disappointed. Robbed. Del had watched me restart time; his belief that he had super-powers had just been totally obliterated.

I pressed my eyelids together tightly. I was begin-ning to understand a thing or two about scumbling my savvy now. Closing my eyes was an important part of stopping the clocks. Drawing in on myself was another. More out of habit than anything else, I silently mouthed the words *stop-stop-stop,* sticking a pin in time so that Del could have a semi-private moment to recover. I could feel myself do it this time. I could feel the way the world slowed to a standstill, like I was pulling on the reins of a runaway horse.

When I opened my eyes again, I was enormously pleased with myself. The floral coolers had fallen silent. The ribbons overhead had stopped waving. Del's lips were pressed into a tight line.

"Seriously?" Del rolled his eyes, then mumbled, "Show-off." But the corners of his mouth tugged into a grudging smile when he said it, so I knew he wasn't entirely angry.

"I just thought—"

"Gah! Will you just start time again, Specs?"

"Yes, of course! I . . . I could use the practice." I grimaced and whispered, "Sorry." Then, standing tall and strong and ready—and with my eyes wide open—I released the reins again and let time gallop on.

Mr. Aardman returned a moment later, carrying a

snow shovel, a bag of ice melt, and a first aid cold pack.

"Really, I'm fine," I told him, when he thrust the cold pack at me. "I swear, I didn't hurt myself on the ice." Mr. Aardman looked so addlepated with distress, I took the cold pack and held it to the back of my head, just to make him feel better. Nodding to me and Del, the shopkeeper carried his shovel out the door, determined to make the sidewalk in front of his store safe for twirly-whirly girls like me.

Del and I slumped into two of the cushy chairs in the bridal consultation corner, waiting for Samson and Nola to arrive with the car. I continued to hold the cold pack to my head, even though I didn't need it. Del fidgeted with the zipper pull on his coat.

"Soooo, did you trip over a radioactive sundial or something?" he asked. "Or were you bathed in magical clock oil on the day you were born?"

I sighed, knowing I owed Del a proper explanation. I had wanted to let him believe he had the power to stop time, hoping to spare him the disappointment he felt now. I knew I was going to have to tell Del the whole impossible-to-believe truth.

For the second time that night, my family's secrets came spilling out—thirteenth birthdays, savvies, the switch, my clock tower vision. I told him everything. Del listened without interrupting, but the truth only seemed to make things worse. Del looked more depressed than he had before I'd told him anything.

Mr. Aardman was still shoveling the sidewalk, barely getting a section cleared before the snow covered it up again, when the front door opened and Samson rushed inside, with Nola at his heels.

"Gypsy! Tucker! We got here as fast as we could!"

Chapter 18

"**DON'T EVER DO THAT** again, Gypsy!" Samson said as he and Nola joined us inside Aardman's Flowers. "We can't split up like that. What if we hadn't been able to find you? That police officer thought I was crazy when I pointed to your message on the dashboard and asked him for directions to Aardman's Flowers."

"Did you have to use my lipstick, Gypsy?" Nola gave me an exasperated look. "Couldn't you think of a cleaner way to leave us a note? Erm, hey there . . . who're you?" Nola noticed Del for the first time.

"Me? I'm nobody," Del said glumly. "Nobody special, that is." Del frowned as he studied Nola's heavy, inexpertly applied makeup.

"This is Del, you guys," I said, waving my cold pack

in his direction. "Don't worry, he knows everything. I've already told him about savvies, and he's been helping me look for Grandma. You're not gonna believe it— Del's not affected by my time-stops! He helped me—"

"Gypsy!" Samson's eyes blazed ember bright as he ignored Del and crouched down in front of me. At first I thought he was going to get angry at me for telling another person our family secret. But then he said, "Why were you holding an ice pack to your head, Gypsy? Did you hurt yourself?"

"Let me look at her!" Nola pushed my brother aside. Before I could object, Nola began a two-handed examination of my scalp, searching for a bump that wasn't there. Peering intently at me, she held up one finger and moved it back and forth in front of my eyes.

"What are you even doing?" Del asked, stifling a snort of laughter. I was relieved to hear him laugh. Maybe Del wouldn't stay unhappy with me forever.

"I'm checking to see if she has a concussion," Nola answered curtly.

"I don't have a concussion, Nola. I didn't even—" I stopped talking when a small orange-striped kitten zipped past us, followed closely by Tucker.

"Tucker? Tucker!" I called after him. "Did you take that kitten from the bus station?"

"I was gonna put him back, Gypsy!" Tucker called over his shoulder. He reached down to snatch up the kitten, then he carried it back to where the rest of us were sitting. "I was only cuddling him for a minute. Then I blinked and I was in that shopping cart. It's not my fault Cap'n Stormy hitched a ride. *You're* the one who stopped time and took us both away."

"Cap'n Stormy?" I repeated as Tucker plopped the kitten into my lap. I couldn't help but smile when the tiny cat began to mew.

"Captain Stormalong Fuzzypants," Tuck announced the name proudly. "I think it suits him. He's got pretty fuzzy pants."

"What if he's a *her*?" Nola asked, stroking Cap'n Stormy's silky tail.

"Don't be dumb," Tucker said. "Girls can be captains too. Right, Gypsy?"

"Right, Tuck," I agreed.

From that moment on, Captain Stormalong Fuzzypants was a girl, and we had one more companion in our search for Grandma Pat.

The appearance of the kitten calmed everyone. It is impossible to stay unhappy or distressed when a super-soft ball of adorability curls up in your hands, closes its eyes, and purrs.

We all sat together in the bridal area. Samson took a turn petting the kitten. Then Del. When Del handed Cap'n Stormy to Nola, he said, "So, you live next door to the grandmother? Do these people's supernatural powers rub off, if you hang around them long enough? I suppose you have some reality-crushing talent too."

Nola automatically touched the melted sequins on her hat. "Trust me, I'm not a part of this crazy family. But I've got big plans of my own." She passed Cap'n Stormy back to Tucker and hopped to her feet, striking a playful, pop-star pose. "Someday I'm going to sing in front of crowds of people and listen to them cheer."

"She wants to see her name in lights," said Samson.

Nola glued her fists to her hips. "Do you doubt me, Fire Guy?"

"Not at all," said Samson. "In fact, I can put your name in lights right now." My brother stood too, then he held up one hand and set it blazing. Using his fiery fingers, he made a quick series of motions in the air, leaving a lingering trail of orange embers that spelled out Nola's name. Samson's pyrotechnics only lasted for a second. When he was done, he blew out his hand like it was a giant match. Nola and I clapped. Samson blushed and took a bow.

I giggled. My moody-broody brother was showing off. Trying to impress a girl. It appeared to have worked too. Nola looked smitten. Her eyes still glowed from the light Samson had practically burned into her optic nerve.

Del shook his head, taking it all in. After a minute he turned to Tucker and said, "I wish I was a part of your family, little guy. I bet you can't wait to turn thirteen and get powers of your own."

"I don't have to wait," Tuck said, grinning. "I got my savvy early. Watch this!" Before any of us could stop him, Tuck scrunched up his face and farted.

Then he doubled in size.

"Yippee! I did it! I didn't even have to get mad this time."

Startled, itty-bitty Cap'n Stormy scrambled up and over Tucker's enormous shoulder. Then she clawed her way down the back of his coat and jumped to the floor.

"Aw, man!" Del stared up at Tucker, slack-jawed and jealous.

It didn't take much to get Tucker to shrink back down to normal size. We didn't even have to give him any candy. A few plaintive mews from Captain Storm-along Fuzzypants did the trick. Soon Tucker was his regular small self again, cradling his new pet in his arms.

I looked at my watch. It seemed impossible, but less than two hours had passed since we'd left Grandma's house—two hours by the clock. For me, it had been a whole lot longer.

"We've got to go get Grandma," I told the others. "I don't want her anywhere near the Larimer High School clock tower at midnight. I don't even want her to be in the city."

"Don't worry, Gypsy," Samson said. "We have loads

of time. It's only eight o'clock. We're going to find her, I promise. Are you ready to go?"

I nodded, then paused. "We should try to call Momma. If she made it back to Grandma's house, she'll be worried. If she goes back out in the snow to look for us, she might trigger an avalanche."

Samson agreed. "We can use the shop phone, before we go."

"Del has a phone," I said, remembering how Del pried Tripp's cell phone out of the bully's stony grip and slipped it into the pocket of his jeans.

Samson reached toward Del. "Can I borrow it?" When Del didn't hand over Tripp's phone, pronto, Samson's eyes lit in a fierce red-orange glow.

"Whoa, dude, cool your jets!" Del quickly dug inside his pocket. "No need to get combustible." As soon as Del slapped Tripp's phone into Samson's hand, I felt bad for bringing it up, remembering how Tripp had tried to blackmail Del into letting him steal from his uncle's store. Threatening him with an image stored in his phone. It wasn't too long ago that I could've stared at Del over the tops of my glasses, trying to see into his past, sifting through his history without him even knowing I was looking. Suddenly, I was glad I couldn't do that anymore. I liked Del. He deserved his privacy.

The glow from the phone lit Samson's face as he slid his thumb across the screen, trying to access it. My brother paused, squinting at the image that came up automatically behind the lockscreen. He looked at Del, then back at the phone again.

"Is this your sister, Del?" he said, waving the phone once in the air. "She looks just like you. Only prettier."

"Let me see!" Nola chirped, reaching for the phone. "I want to see his sister." Del leaped out of his chair and grabbed the device before Nola could get a hold of it. A memory tickled the back of my brain . . . something Del had said when we were leaving the bus station. But I couldn't pry the memory loose.

"Everyone back off," Del said, raising his arm in front of him protectively. "I'm gonna use this phone to make a couple calls of my own. You guys can use the phone behind the counter."

Samson raised his eyebrows in surprise, but he didn't force the issue. He simply nodded at Del, then sauntered over to the phone next to the cash register. Del jabbed at Tripp's phone, cursing under his breath when he discovered it was password-protected.

As Del got up to join Samson at the shop counter, Tucker found a peacock feather in one of the store's silk flower arrangements and began using it as a cat toy. He and Cap'n Stormy jumped and dashed around the store while Samson and Del made their calls.

"Do you want to call anyone, Nola?" I asked as we watched Tucker and Cap'n Stormy play.

"Nah," she said. "Like I said before, my mom and dad don't even know I'm gone. That's one silver lining, right? It means we'll be able to clean up Mom's car before my parents get home."

"Momma's phone is still going straight to voicemail," Samson said when he rejoined us. "I left another message. Hopefully the tow truck from that vision of yours didn't break down, Gypsy, just because Momma got a ride in it."

"Well, that's taken care of," Del said, clapping his hands together once as he too rejoined us. "I told my uncle I went home, and I told my parents that I'm staying with my uncle. Hopefully, my butt is covered for a few hours. Maybe you guys could give me a ride home, after we find your gran?" Del's face grew thoughtful, then troubled.

"Specs . . ." he said, looking at me. "You said your gran is going to be at the top of the clock tower at eleven fifty-eight?"

I nodded, glad that it was only eight o'clock.

Del's frown deepened. "Yeah . . . well, remember how I told you the old high school building has been boarded up for decades? I hate to tell you this, but that clock hasn't worked in years. Its hands are *stuck* at eleven fifty-eight. That's the only time it ever tells."

I dropped Mr. Aardman's cold pack on the floor. I could feel the color drain from my cheeks. "I think I'm going to throw up."

"You definitely have a concussion," Nola said, retrieving the cold pack and handing it back to me. "You should really take it easy, Gypsy."

"I didn't hit my head, Nola!" I said in frustration. "Don't you see what Del is saying? If the clock from my vision always reads eleven fifty-eight—"

"Then for all we know," Samson cut in, "Grandma could be up there right now."

"We've got to go!" I said.

Del held out his hand, offering to help me out of my chair. I let him. I was surprised—and goofishly, girlishly pleased—when he didn't let go of my hand, once we were both standing.

Gathering hats and coats and mittens and kittens, we all raced for the door. But Del stopped me, dragging me back toward him as the others exited the shop ahead of us.

"You know, Gypsy. I feel sort of . . . dumb, I guess." Del's shoulders wilted. Even his spiffy yellow bow tie seemed to sag. "Here I was, going on and on about stopping the clocks," he said, "when it was you the whole time."

"Now that you know," I said, feeling the warmth of his fingers around mine, "do you still want to be my . . . I mean, do you still want to help me find my grandmother?" I really wanted to ask Del if he still wanted to be my friend. But I wasn't sure I could take it if he said no and pulled his hand away.

"Of course, Specs. Just—" Del paused, like he was

searching for a chuckle of the laughter he always kept so close. "Just do me a favor, okay?" He held open the door with his free hand, looking glum. "Please don't stop time again for a while. I don't want to be reminded of just how much I'm *not* a superhero."

"I'll try not to," I said, sorry I'd dashed the dreams of Mr. Kool-A Iced-Tea Time. I wanted to assure Del that he *was* extraordinary, even if he couldn't stop time. I already knew Del was funny and caring and brave, and that he had a massive talent for mummifying people in toilet paper. I was certain he must have other abilities too. His very own sort of savvy. I was determined to think up a new superhero name for Del, before the night was over.

Chapter 19

SAMSON MADE SHORT WORK of clearing away the flurries that had already fleeced the car. Del sat between Tuck and me in the backseat. Tucker kept a firm grip on Captain Stormalong Fuzzypants, even though she was squirmy and wanting to play.

The engine revved and roared as Samson powered Mrs. Kim's white SUV through the snowbound city. The night sky was an alabaster vault, withholding the moon and the stars and the darkness. Except for the occasional passing snowplow, the streets of Denver were emptier than they'd been an hour earlier. The lady on Channel 3 had been right about the storm, and people were heeding her warnings.

According to my watch, it was 8:07. But time hardly

mattered now. I tried not to replay my vision of Grandma Pat's fall over and over inside my head. But I couldn't help it. I kept picturing her coral-pink lips making that silent O. I kept seeing her white curls fly up around her face, her poufy skirts puffing out all around her. I tried not to be afraid. But it was impossible not to be. I longed to stop time. But if I did, Del and I would be forced to walk all the way to Larimer High. Samson and the SUV would get us to the high school faster. Del assured us it wasn't far.

Using an entire package of makeup-removing wipes, Nola scrubbed at my note on the dashboard. It was no use. The Twisted Tangerine letters smeared across the vinyl, but didn't come off.

"My life is over," Nola said, giving in to defeat. "I'm never going to be allowed to take my driver's test now. My mom is going to kill me. Then, because she's a car-diologist, she'll pull out her defibrillator paddles and restart my heart—just so she can kill me again."

"Drama, drama, drama," Samson muttered, but he was smiling. Nola ignored him, stuffing handfuls of used cleaning wipes back into her cosmetics case. Del eyed the case with interest.

"You know," he said, "if we had more time, I could give you a slammin' makeover. My gran was a pro. I learned a lot watching her work. I could fix your makeup for you. Easy."

"There's something wrong with my makeup?" Nola pulled down her sun visor and slid open the mirror. Puckering her lips, she scrutinized her appearance.

"Did your gran teach your sister about makeup too, Del?" I asked, thinking of the girl Samson saw on Tripp's phone.

"Sister?" Del wrinkled his brow. Then he remembered and rolled his eyes. He scrunched lower in his seat. "Yeah, no. About that, Specs—"

"What are you talking about, Del?" Nola interrupted him. She turned on Del, her eyes narrowing to thin slits behind her thick veneer of eyeliner. "There isn't one thing wrong with my makeup!"

"Seriously?" Del raised his eyebrows. "Dang, girl. I hate to tell you this, but you look like the Lone Ranger. That mask is hiding all the good things you got going for you. You're not letting yourself shine."

"I'm not?" Nola looked in the mirror again, studying

her face more thoughtfully. "But I think I'm pretty."

"You are!" Del agreed with enthusiasm. "You're just covering all the pretty up. If you'd just—"

But Del didn't have time to give Nola any makeup tips before Samson slammed down hard on the brakes and the SUV slid sideways.

There was a man standing in the middle of the road, waving his arms for us to stop.

Samson carefully edged the SUV closer to the man in the street. Dressed for the weather in a hooded gray parka, the fellow jogged toward us, jabbing a thumb over his shoulder toward a green sedan stalled out in the opposite lane. The car's hazard lights blinked feebly, smothered by the storm.

Samson lowered his window as the man approached.

"Thanks for stopping, kid." The man gasped for breath, his face framed by the open window. "My car broke down, and I'm about to have a wife!" The stranger paused and shook his head, leaning one hand against the door of the SUV to steady himself. Then he pointed once more toward his car.

"I mean, my wife's about to have a Stephanie!" Barking a deep, hysterical laugh, the man panted for breath, then tried again. "Let me start over. My wife—my wife, Stephanie—she's going to have a baby. Our first baby!" The father-to-be thumped the edge of Samson's open window with his palms. Then he started hopping up and down in the snow in excitement. Or to stay warm. Or both. I couldn't actually tell.

"Fingers and toes, man!" the man shouted over the whistling wind, announcing his joy to the snowy night. "Fin-gers-and-*toes*! Any minute now, I'm going to be counting fingers and toes. I'm going to be a father!"

"Your wife is in that car?" Nola asked, leaning toward Samson's window. "How close are her contractions?"

"Every two minutes," the man answered, eyes wide.

Nola shot Samson an *uh-oh* sort of look.

"How can we help?" Samson asked, his low voice becoming a nervous, high-pitched jangle.

"Can you squeeze us in?" The man peered deeper into the SUV; his expression was hopeful as he waved to Del and me, then to Tucker. "Can we get a ride? I'm Jimmy, by the way. James Walker." Mr. Walker stuck a hand inside the car for Samson to shake. Then he resumed hopping up and down, and pointing.

"I was driving Stephanie to Mercy Medical when our car ran out of gas. I tried calling 911, but I couldn't get through."

"Mercy Medical Center is back that way," Nola told Samson, pointing behind us. She turned to look at me, her face drawn in worry and uncertainty. I felt sick to my stomach again, not because of a time-stop or a non-existent concussion, but because I knew exactly what Nola was going to say.

"If we drive these people to Mercy, Gypsy, it'll mean turning around and heading in the opposite direction of the old high school. It'll mean putting off our search for Mrs. B. a little longer. But . . . these people really can't wait."

I knew everyone in the car felt torn in two. But there seemed to be an unspoken agreement between the others that I should be the one to make the decision: Help the Walkers get to the medical center so that their baby could be born, safe and warm and dry . . . or leave the parents-to-be stranded on the street, and continue toward Grandma and the high school.

"Gypsy?" Samson met my eyes in the rearview mirror, waiting. Del and Tucker both watched me intently. Everyone was calling on *me* to captain the futures of both a new life and an old one.

"We have to help them," I said, trying hard to keep myself from bursting into tears. I felt like I was betraying Grandma Pat. Del took hold of my hand again, giving it a reassuring squeeze.

"I'm scared for your grandmother too, Gypsy," Nola murmured, turning so that she could rest her fingers on my shaking knee. Lips pressed tight, Samson nodded to me in the rearview mirror, as if he were trying to give me a boost of fortitude the only way he knew how. Then, without another word, he maneuvered the SUV closer to the Walkers' car.

"We'll drop Mr. and Mrs. Walker off at the medical center and get right back on the road," I said, doing my best to sound confident and commanding.

Three minutes later, Tucker, Del, Captain Stormalong Fuzzypants, and I were all crammed into the rear of the SUV, nestled among the spilled contents of Nola's Mall of Denver shopping bags. There were no seat belts in the cargo space, but we were going to have to make do; James Walker and his very pregnant wife, Stephanie, needed the backseat.

Mrs. Walker did her best to smile at us as her husband pushed her into the car. She began to say hello. But her greeting turned into a loud "Hel-OW!" instead, as a new contraction began.

Gunning the engine, Samson aimed us in the direction of the medical center. Mrs. Walker punched Mr. Walker in the chest.

"I told you to gas up the car before the storm, Jimmy! So help me, if I deliver our first child in some stranger's SUV, I'm going to—"

"I know I asked you not to, Specs," Del whispered. "But maybe this would be a good time to stop the clocks."

"I can't, Del," I whispered back, wishing that I could. "Not this time."

"Why not? Did you lose your mojo?"

"No. It's just that it wouldn't do any good now. You and I can't get Mrs. Walker to the medical center by ourselves. It's too far. And it's not like we could stick a pregnant lady in a grocery cart, even if we had one. If I stop time now, Del, I'll only be stalling the life that's trying to happen."

Mrs. Walker gave another groan. She gripped the corners of the seats in front of her. "I really, really appreciate the ride, young man," Mrs. Walker told Samson through clenched teeth. "But do you think you could possibly drive faster?"

"The kid is going as fast as he can, Steph." Mr. Walker rubbed his wife's back, trying to soothe her. "The only way he could get us there quicker would be if he could melt all the blang-dang snow that's in our way."

Samson hit the brakes and smacked a red-hot fist against his forehead. His eyes were already glowing when he swiveled in his seat and said, "Why didn't I think of that?"

"Nola," Samson said, low and quick. "Since you have all the medical genes, you sit in the backseat with Mrs. Walker and try to keep her calm. Mr. Walker . . ." Samson turned to the soon-to-be father. "Right now, I need you to do three things for me." Samson raised a rosy-glowing finger with each of his demands:

"One, I need you to trust me. Two, I need you to drive. Three, I need you to *not . . . freak . . out.*"

Two minutes later, all I could see of Samson were his boots and his lower legs, where they dangled down into the SUV through the open sun roof. The view out the front windshield was something from an epic movie. Two spectacular jets of orange-and-yellow flame arched down from the top of the car, melting the deep snowdrifts in front of us. Leaving scorch marks and puddles on the road. I could picture Samson sitting above me, braced against the wind, his long hair whipping in tongues of fire as he stretched out his arms in front of him, like he was driving a pair of blazing steeds. From the waist up, Samson had to be as fiery as the sun itself. To any passersby, Mrs. Kim's SUV probably looked like the chariot that carried Elijah up to heaven.

If Momma and Poppa ever found out what he was doing, they'd probably homeschool Samson all the way through college. Then he'd have to find a way to work from his bedroom, because our parents would never let him leave the house again.

"Am I the only one who's worried about this plan?" Del asked as he and Tucker and I bumped and jostled into one another in the back of the SUV. "Cars run on gasoline. Gasoline is highly flammable."

"I'm worried!" squeaked Tucker, holding tight to Cap'n Stormy.

James Walker was plainly worried too. He careened around corners, driving like a maniac. When he glanced over his shoulder at his wife, he was as bug-eyed and sweaty as if he were sitting on a stick of dynamite. I wondered if he regretted having waved us down.

Maybe I should *stop time,* I thought as Mrs. Walker cried out in pain—or in panic. I couldn't blame the poor woman; witnessing Samson's switched-up savvy in action was akin to having hot sauce poured directly on your brain. Fortunately, all of Samson's heat was going up and out and forward, not down on us. Otherwise, we would've all been roasted. Or blown to smithereens.

"My parents made me watch a medical video about childbirth before I started high school." Nola raised her voice over the sound of my brother's barely controlled inferno. "I'm no doctor, but I do know that you shouldn't push yet, Mrs. Walker." Then, a little softer, she added, "I hope you've learned some lullabies. You're going to be singing to this baby soon."

Cap'n Stormy cowered inside Tucker's coat. Tucker looked like he couldn't decide if he should be cheering for Samson, or coming unglued from all the chaos.

"Here, Tuck," I said, pulling the last piece of taffy from my pocket.

"Yo, I've got a better idea for helping the little dude get through this," Del said. "Scoot over, Specs, and let me work." Del searched inside Nola's shopping bags, fishing out what he needed to help Tucker stay calm and small.

When I understood Del's plan, I smiled and left him to it.

By the time Mercy Medical Center came into sight, on the other side of the city's skyscrapers, Tucker's face was artfully painted to look like a rainbow-whiskered cat; Nola looked panicked, like she was contemplating the untidiness there'd be if Mrs. Walker gave birth in the backseat of her mother's car; and Samson was exhausted.

My brother was running out of blazes.

Workmen in coveralls pushed snow blowers along the sidewalks of the medical center. They all looked up in surprise as Samson's final jets of flame fizzled and went out.

By the time Jimmy Walker barreled into the parking lot, Samson didn't have enough fire left in him to light the first candle on Baby Walker's birthday cake.

Mr. Walker drove as close to the emergency room doors as he could before he hit the brakes. The SUV jerked, skidded, then stopped with a *crunch* at the base of a concrete pylon.

"Samson!" I cried, watching my brother's feet disappear through the sun roof as he was thrown over the side of the SUV.

"Get me out of here," Stephanie Walker shouted. "I think I've been hallucinating from the pain, and this baby isn't going to wait another second."

Everyone emptied from the car. The Walkers ran into the hospital without even turning to say good-bye, or thank you. The rest of us understood. Even if Samson *had* just given his all to help the couple, he may also have traumatized them for life.

I found my brother a moment later. Samson lay on his back in the grainy ice melt sprinkled on the sidewalk, staring up into the falling snow. His knees were bent toward the sky and he hugged his right arm across his chest. Snowflakes caught in Samson's hair and gathered on his jeans and T-shirt. When I reached him, he was awake. But he felt cold for the first time in days. From the way he cradled his right arm, I knew he was hurt.

"I think I may have done it again, Gypsy," he said weakly, trying to blink snowflakes from his eyelashes.

"Done what, Samson?"

"I think I may have pushed an all-new savvy to its limits." Samson shot me a satisfied half grin. "Also? I think I may have dislocated my shoulder."

Chapter 20

IT *HAD NEVER BEEN* the plan to go inside Mercy Medical Center. Not with Grandma Pat still unaccounted for, and Larimer High now several miles back the way we'd come. But Tucker had to go to the bathroom, for real this time, and Nola thought she could fix Samson's shoulder if we could get him out of the snow and cold.

"I promise we'll be fast, Gypsy," Nola said as she helped Samson through the sliding doors of the med center.

The waiting room inside Mercy Medical was chaos. Part of it had been sectioned off, converted into an emergency storm shelter with cots and blankets, making room for those who had gotten stranded, and for the homeless who needed to get off the streets. There was also a small mob seeking medical help, clutching stomachs or wearing bandages. A line of people waited to be checked in at the front desk, where a frazzled clerk sat shuffling papers and entering information into a computer. The latest weather report burbled from a television on the wall.

". . . Snow showers should begin to lighten earlier than expected in this fast-moving storm. Plows are out in force, but please continue to use caution as . . ."

Somewhere close by, a toddler shrieked and an old man coughed. A boy tossed a paper airplane across the room, hitting the beleaguered desk clerk in the eye. It was easy to slip past the pandemonium. Nobody looked our way.

Nola half supported, half shoved Samson ahead of her, looking for an empty exam room or an unlocked storage closet where she could try to fix his shoulder without anyone asking questions, taking names, or calling for a real doctor to help. If the staff of the medical center got involved, we'd get waylaid. Then we'd never reach Grandma Pat in time.

"*Ow.* Stop pushing me," Samson complained in a

whisper as Nola jostled him down a yellow hallway. "I'm in pain here, remember? Just saved the day?" I barely heard Nola's reply as they disappeared around a corner.

"Stop being such a baby."

After what Samson had just done—with the fire jets, and the snow-melting, and the falling off the top of the SUV—I doubted *he* was worried about being called a baby.

While Samson and Nola followed the yellow hallway, Del and I steered Tucker down a blue one, searching for a bathroom away from the brouhaha inside the waiting area.

"I really, really gotta go, Gypsy!" Tucker tugged on my sleeve as he shuffle-hopped between me and Del. Cap'n Stormy peeked her head out of the top of his coat and mewed. Tuck held his kitten tight, twitching his own rainbow-colored whiskers. Del had done the best job of face painting I'd ever seen, with the kinds of details only a professional makeup artist would think to add. I'd forgotten how easy it was for little kids to feel transformed, just by getting their faces painted. I'd taken my own turn as a cat . . . and as a flower, a dragon, and a tiger. But I'd never had my face painted as beautifully as Del had painted Tucker's.

"Gypseeeeeee," Tucker whined, still yanking my sleeve. I knew Tuck was getting tired. It was 8:40, and it had already been a long, action-packed evening. If we'd been home, in Kansaska-Nebransas with Poppa and Momma, Tucker would've already finished brushing his teeth and changing into his jammies. He'd be getting ready for a story and a snuggle and a good-night kiss.

"Guess what, Tuck?" I said as I led my little brother to the door of a men's room in the middle of a purple corridor. "You didn't need a savvy to turn you into a cat. Del worked that magic for you."

"Mrowww," Tucker meowed as he handed Captain Stormalong Fuzzypants to me. I hoped Momma and Poppa would let Tucker keep the kitten.

While Tucker took care of business in the men's room, Del and I slid down the wall across from the restrooms, sitting on the floor to play with the tiny kitten. Exhaustion threatened to overtake me. But the night wasn't over yet. I couldn't give in to my tiredness. If my vision came to pass, I'd need every ounce of strength I could muster. If only I were a superhero, like Del dreamed of being; then even my muscles would have muscles, and I'd rescue Grandma with ease.

Be-deep! A tone sounded from inside Del's coat pocket, startling us both. Perplexed, Del fished out Tripp's phone and stared at it, scowling.

"What is it?" I asked.

"Text message," Del answered. "From Tripp." He showed me the message, which appeared on the screen without requiring a password.

> I know u got my phone
> dunno how u did what u
> did but we r coming 4 u

I looked worriedly at Del. "Tripp wouldn't really try to come after you tonight, would he? Not in a blizzard." I remembered how Del had wrapped Tripp up in toilet paper and aimed B-Bug's fist at him, actions akin to stomping on a wasps' nest. I had probably made matters worse by adding my own flowery touches to the scene.

Del stuck the phone back in his pocket. "He's only trying to scare me," he said. "It's not like Tripp and B-Bug know where I am." Del's tone was cavalier, but his jaw muscles tightened. The message had rattled him.

"I miss the old B-Bug," Del said after a pause as we listened to Tucker play with the automatic hand dryers in the bathroom, turning them off and on, and off and on. "His real name is *Byron*. Byron Berger. He used to be a decent guy."

"Well, he seems pretty rotten now," I said. "If I hadn't stopped time when I did, your friend Byron would have punched you in the nose."

"Yeah, probably." Del shrugged. "But only because Tripp told him to. When my gran was still alive, Byron would come into my uncle's shop. He'd hang out by the cosmetics counter, like she was his gran too. My grandmother always liked B-Bug, and if Gran liked him, he can't be all bad. She was a good judge of character." Del made his voice high and wobbly, imitating his beloved grandmother:

"That Byron Berger is as sweet as a spoonful of sugar. But that's only half as sweet as you, Antwon—you're my double spoonful."

Del smiled, remembering.

"B-Bug always treated my gran with respect," he went on. "Then Gran died and Travis Kaminski the Third transferred to Park Hill Academy. Tripp changed things big-time when he arrived. He had the entire school under his thumb by the end of his first week, switching everything up." Del shook his head and laughed. "Switching it up—ha! That's what you guys say too, right? It's nutso-redonkulous how fast life can change. Isn't it, Specs?"

"Nutso-redonkulous indeed," I sighed, stroking Cap'n Stormy's tiny ears.

"You're lucky you still have a grandma," Del said. "I miss mine something awful."

I didn't say anything. Having a grandmother like Patrice Beaumont wasn't exactly like riding a gravy train with biscuit wheels.

When the hand dryers continued to go on and off inside the men's room, I ran out of patience. "Tucker! Your hands are dry already. It's time to go."

Our brief rest was over. It was time to find Samson and Nola, and get back on the road.

As soon as Tuck emerged from the men's room,

Del picked up Cap'n Stormy and I took Tucker's hand. Together, we wound through a labyrinth of color-coded corridors, searching for the others.

Turning down a green hallway, I got the shock of my life.

The very best sort of shock ever.

"Look, Gypsy!" Tucker shouted, pulling his hand out of mine and racing down the hall. "It's Grandma Pat!"

Chapter 21

MY SPIRITS SOARED. TUCKER was right. Grandma Pat sat at the end of the hallway, asleep in a wheelchair, seemingly forgotten next to a vacant nurses' station. She had a blanket over her lap, and her chin nodded against the soft white fur of her moth-eaten coat. Her tiara was askew and her glasses had slipped down her nose. Some kind soul must have found my grandmother wandering disoriented through the snow, and brought her to the medical center.

I was surprised when I felt a sharp prickle behind my eyes. Even more surprised when I found my cheeks wet with tears. It may have only been relief, but I felt an unexpected surge of love for Grandma Pat.

"Come on, you guys!" Tucker shouted over his

shoulder. "I want Grandma to meet Cap'n Stormy."

"Shh, Tucker! Don't wake her!"

"Why not?" Tucker whispered loudly as Del and I caught up to him at the foot of Grandma's wheelchair. Del kept ahold of Cap'n Stormy, while I bent down next to Tuck. I smiled at the single wilted daisy Grandma gripped tightly in one hand; a makeshift boutonniere, perhaps, for her phantom beau, Cleavon Dorsey.

Grandma looked so bent and frail in her wheelchair, and so oddball with her big Sorrel snow boots sticking out from beneath her blanket and her fancy dress, I wanted to hug her.

A water bottle sat untouched in Grandma's lap, and a hospital bracelet hung loosely from her wrist. There were numbers printed on the plastic band that were meaningless to me. There was also a barcode, and the words *DOE, JANE*. Grandma Pat hadn't even told the hospital staff her name. I wondered where, when, and who she'd thought she was when she first got here. I wondered if she'd been scared, or if she'd thought they would want her to buy a magazine subscription or sign a petition.

"It's going to be easier to get Grandma out of here if

she stays asleep," I explained quietly to Tucker.

"But . . . why do we want to get her out? Won't Grandma be safe here if we stay to protect her?" Gently, Tuck traced the veins on the back of Grandma's hand with one finger. His touch was soft, softer than when he petted Cap'n Stormy, but three petals still fell from Grandma's daisy.

"Your brother makes a good point, Specs," Del said. "Mercy Medical is probably the safest place your gran could be tonight."

I took off my glasses and wiped my eyes with the back of my wrist. As I looked into Grandma Pat's blurry face, I recalled it all: The old high school. The clock tower. The parting clouds revealing a big, round moon. Grandma falling.

My hands shook as I put my glasses back on. I knew full well that my savvy hadn't switched back—that it might never switch back. I was only remembering the things I'd seen before, and even though Grandma looked like she was out of danger, those remembered things still spooked me. I wouldn't breathe easy until Grandma was out of the city and as far from the Larimer

High School clock tower as I could get her. Fate might twist and turn in unexpected ways, but if I could just get Grandma Pat home to Evergreen, I knew I could keep her safe. I'd make it impossible for her to find her way back to Denver. I'd handcuff myself to her, if I had to.

"We're leaving," I said stubbornly, my single-minded determination turning my voice into steel. "I'm taking Grandma home. Let's find Samson and Nola, and get out of here."

I found a pair of scissors behind the counter of the nurses' station and used them to cut off Grandma's plastic bracelet. I let Tucker push Grandma's wheelchair as we went to retrieve Nola and Samson. Grandma stayed asleep, which was for the best. If she woke up and raised a fuss, she might draw unwanted attention. No nurse or doctor would let five kids wheel an old woman out of the medical center during a snowstorm.

"Are you sure about this?" Del asked as we found our way back to the yellow hallway.

"I'm sure," I said, knowing I probably wouldn't even sleep again until Poppa arrived with the moving truck and we were all on our way home. Home to Kansaska-

Nebransas, where Grandma Pat could have Grandpa Bomba's bed, and Grandpa Bomba's rocker. Where she could fill Grandpa Bomba's room with *her* smells and live out the rest of her days in safety, surrounded by her family.

"What's happening? Where am I?" Grandma jolted awake, grasping the handles of her wheelchair with a start. Dropping both her daisy and her water bottle, she twisted to look back at Tucker, Del, and me. "Who are you people? Are you kidnapping me?"

"No, Grandma," Tucker said, patting her arm reassuringly. "We're here to rescue you, and to introduce you to my new kitten." Tucker seized Captain Stormalong Fuzzypants from Del and held her high, her tiny paws flailing. The only thing Grandma said when she saw the cat was, "Humph." But to Tucker, she said, "I know you. You're the loud, sticky one. The one who's a whole lot bigger than you look."

Tucker beamed, standing tall. "You remember!"

Grandma gave another "Humph." But something about her face made me think she looked relieved, as though she might actually be glad to see us.

"Don't worry, Grandma," I said. "We've come to bring you home."

"Well, it's about time." Grandma pursed her lips.

Del laughed and swooped up Grandma's fallen flower. "Hey there, Mrs. Beaumont. I'm your granddaughter's friend Antwon Delacroix." He tucked the daisy behind Grandma's ear and straightened her tiara. Then he made a show of jumping backward, saying, "Whoa, step back! I didn't know Gypsy's gran was a bona fide beauty queen!"

Grandma snorted once and waved dismissively at Del. But pink bloomed in her cheeks, and her eyes lit with a bashful, girlish sparkle. Del's grandmother had been right; when it came to sugar, Antwon Delacroix *was* a double spoonful.

"Flattery will get you nowhere, young man," Grandma said, but Del's charm had enlivened her. She gripped the blanket on her lap and scooted forward in her wheelchair, trying to make the wheels turn with the power of her skinny rump alone. "Can't you kids drive this thing any faster? You and this young sweet-talker are going to have to be speedier, Gypsy, if you're going to get me home in time to watch my shows."

I stood dumbstruck. Had Grandma really just called me Gypsy? A laugh welled up from someplace deep inside me and bubbled over. For the first time in three days, Grandma Pat had called me by my real name—like she remembered me.

"Don't worry, Grandma, we can go faster. Hang on!" Unable to keep from grinning, I grabbed the handles of Grandma's wheelchair and ran up the hallway, heading for the place we'd last seen Samson and Nola. When Grandma let out an enthusiastic *yeeeeeehaw!* I smiled wider yet.

"That's more like it, Nettie," she said. "Now we're cooking with gas. Faster, faster! We'll be at the winter dance in no time." And just like that, the moment passed and I was Nettie Arbuckle again.

I didn't try to correct Grandma this time. She had remembered me once. That meant that somewhere in the maze of her mind, a girl named Gypsy Beaumont still existed. Maybe that was all I needed to know.

Chapter 22

IF NOLA AND SAMSON hadn't been arguing, we might not have found them. They were in an empty X-ray room, and they were in the middle of a standoff.

As soon as they both got over their initial shock and relief at seeing Grandma Pat, their argument began again.

"I can't fix your shoulder if you won't let me touch you."

"I thought you wanted to be a singer, not a doctor. Why don't you sing me a song instead? I have a feeling it'll hurt less."

"Gypsy? Will you please tell your brother that he needs to stop being such a—?"

"Samson is not a baby," I butted in, defending my

* 219 *

older brother. Then I turned on Samson, raising one finger. "You! Stop being such a . . . such a *clodpate* and let Nola try to help you. She seems to know a thing or two about patching people up."

"Have you ever done this before?" Samson asked Nola, reluctantly giving in.

"Um." Nola hesitated before answering. "No . . . not exactly." When Samson's eyes widened in dismay, Nola quickly reassured him. "But my dad had me watch him do it during the talent show last fall, after Bo Peters pedaled off the stage on his unicycle. I may not have gotten to sing that night, but I did learn how to fix a dislocated shoulder."

"Just get it over with." Samson closed his eyes.

When we emerged from the X-ray room five minutes later, Samson's right arm was secured in a sling made from Nola's leopard-print scarf. His face was as pale and gray as ashes, making the dark, plum-colored lipstick mark on his cheek stand out like a bruise.

Nola had counted *one . . . two . . . three* and jammed his shoulder back in place. Then, while Samson was still busy howling and cursing, she had kissed him on the cheek.

I was nervous about trying to wheel Grandma Pat past the desk attendant in the crowded waiting room, but our escape went off without a hitch. There had been a pileup on the highway, and some of the accident victims were being brought in from an ambulance, boosting the bedlam inside Mercy Medical another notch. A St. Patrick's Day parade could have marched through every hallway, and the overburdened doctors and nurses would've remained fixated on the patients who needed their attention most.

With Del at my side, I pushed Grandma Pat's wheelchair through the waiting area and out into the parking lot. The cars in the lot looked like giant marshmallows. It was still snowing, but the winds that had deviled us throughout the night were beginning to die down.

"Oh, no! No, no, no!" Nola cried as we approached her mother's car, which was still parked where we'd abandoned it upon arrival. We had all been distracted when we'd first arrived; but now, as we neared the SUV, an entire inventory of automotive injuries came into focus. A small snowdrift had built up inside the car, because nobody had thought to close the sun roof. One headlamp was broken, where it had collided with the concrete pylon, and the front bumper had a crumple. But the damage to the bumper and the headlight was small compared to the blackened circle of cracked and peeling paint that marred the roof. We could clearly see where Samson had sat, firing his savvy-powered flame throwers. His butt-print was scorched into the steel.

"How am I ever going to explain *this* to my parents?" Nola looked devastated.

"We'll think of something," Samson said, trying to sound positive. "But we need to go now, Nola. Gypsy thinks Grandma will be in danger as long as we're in Denver. This night's not over yet."

Nola raised an eyebrow. "Are you going to clear the roads for us again? All the way to Evergreen?" Samson canted his head back in the direction of the medical center, wincing from the pain in his shoulder.

"I won't need to," he said. "The TV reports say the city's got plows out and the snow is supposed to stop earlier than predicted. That's good. Because, right now, I don't think I could melt enough snow to give Grandma a drink of water. But if I drive carefully enough, I think I can get us back to Evergreen in one piece."

"Oh, no you won't!" Nola wagged her finger at Samson as they both grabbed for the driver's-side door handle at the same time. "There's no way you can drive safely through this snow with your arm in a sling. We need someone who can keep both hands on the wheel."

Samson frowned, but he let go of the door handle. "Who's going to drive then? You?"

"Yes," said Nola. "I may not have my license yet, but I do have a learner's permit. I've been practicing for months. My driver's test is only three weeks away. We'll bring Del home—carefully—and then the rest of us will make our way back to Evergreen—extra-carefully. Like you said, with snowplows on the roads, how bad can it be?"

Del and I brushed the drift of snow out of the car as best we could, then we helped Grandma Pat out of her wheelchair and into the backseat, buckling her in tight. Tucker and Cap'n Stormy got comfy in the cargo area. As soon as Grandma was situated, Del and I both looked at the empty wheelchair, then at each other, thinking the same thing:

We needed to take it.

We both remembered how useful the grocery cart had been to us earlier. Without saying anything to Nola and Samson, we quietly folded up the wheelchair and loaded it in the back of the car, alongside Tucker and Nola's shopping bags.

Tuck was happy to be in the back of the SUV again, where he could curl up like a momma cat around his kitten. For the first time since Grandma went out the window, I felt like everything was going to be all right. I knew we were going to have plenty of explaining to do to my parents, and to Nola's parents too. But the important thing was that Grandma Pat would soon be safe.

As Nola put the car in reverse and backed away from the concrete pylon, I racked my brain for ways to help pay for the damage to Mrs. Kim's car. Maybe I could go to work for the government—I could get a job as a spy. My ability to stop time could be quite handy in that line of work. If ever there were a time bomb that needed defusing, the president could call me up and tell me to say *stop*. I'd halt the ticking countdown in its tracks. Then maybe there would be someone else, someone just as impervious to my savvy time-stops as Del was, who could defuse the bomb, while the rest of the world remained safely frozen. Or maybe I could learn to do that too.

I glanced at Del where he sat on the other side of Grandma, and wondered again why time never stopped for him—or for those twins we'd seen earlier. What could we all have in common? What could possibly connect us?

Now that Samson wasn't a hundred and ten degrees, it was frigid inside the car, even with the heater set to high. Beyond the windshield, everything was blanketed in white. Even the traffic signals wore white top hats, and their flashing red and yellow lights were coated in icy frosting. Except for the occasional *crash-a-rattle-whoosh* of a passing snowplow, the streets of Denver were deserted. Nola could drive as slowly and as carefully as she needed to.

Even so, Nola's knuckles were white as she gripped the steering wheel. She piloted her mother's SUV around slippery corners at a pace that would have made snails yawn.

"I could've walked to my uncle's house and gotten

there faster," Del murmured, too low for Nola to hear. But I suspected Del didn't really mind the pace. Maybe he didn't feel ready to say good-bye any more than I did.

"Toughen up, Patrice," Grandma mumbled next to me, caught in the monstrous brain cloud that was gobbling up her memories.

"What did you say, Grandma?"

"That's what Daddy is always telling me to do, Nettie," she went on, sounding blue. "'Toughen up,' Daddy says. 'Follow the rules, Patrice. Know your place in this world, and don't embarrass the family by trying to stand out or be different. Don't ever let me catch you dallying with a boy like Cleavon Dorsey again, either! Nothing good can come from hobnobbing with those who aren't like us.'

"You know what, Nettie?" Grandma hooked her arm through mine and leaned her white curls against my golden brown ones. "I think Daddy might be right. Maybe I have been acting like a dumb-cluck fool. Maybe it's time for me to grow up and get my head on straight."

"He isn't right," I said softly. "You didn't need to worry so much about standing out, or about liking people who were different from you. Your daddy was wrong."

It made me sad to realize that Grandma may have once been open-minded and full of pluck. At some point she must have decided to start believing the hidebound things her father preached. When had his fears begun to change her?

Tucker pulled himself to his knees and leaned against the back of Grandma's seat, as if he too wanted to assure her that she'd never needed to toughen up. He stroked the shoulder of Grandma's fur coat, and said:

"Wanna hear a story, Grandma?" Then, without waiting for a yes or no, he began telling Grandma Pat the tale of our first savvy ancestor—the pioneer girl who had attracted gold the way some people attract mosquitos. To my surprise, Grandma Pat sat up a little straighter, listening with interest.

I looked at my watch. It was 9:15.

Tucker was already up to the part of the story where young Eva Mae climbed out of the Missouri River covered in gold dust, when Nola made a sharp turn and the SUV spun out into the middle of an intersection.

"Watch out!" cried Samson. "There's a car coming, Nola."

"I see it. I'm trying!"

The other car, a rusty Jeep, honked its horn as it sped around us.

"How rude," Nola spat. Then she started forward again, the windshield wipers clunk-thunking to the same rhythm as our pounding hearts.

"I think you need to turn around," said Samson. "Or get off this road as fast as you can." Wincing in pain, he craned his neck, trying to get a look at the snow-covered street signs. "I'm pretty sure we're on a one-way street—going the wrong way."

"Everything's fine," said Nola, brushing off Samson's concern. "We're on Welton, and Welton is a one-way street going west."

"East," Del quickly corrected her. "Welton Street is one-way going *east*."

"Well, that can't be right, because I'm driving west." Nola tapped the compass reading on the SUV's dashboard, then she shifted her gaze away from the road and looked over her shoulder at Del. "Are you sure Welton runs east, Del?"

"Pretty sure!" Del's voice jumped three octaves. He braced one hand against the back of Samson's seat, pointing toward the enormous snowplow headed straight for us.

Just when I thought I'd been wrong about every future vision I'd ever had—when I thought I might have no future at all—Nola careened around the snowplow and turned off Welton.

The new boulevard we slid onto was bisected by a small ravine. A creek and a snow-covered bike path ran along the bottom of the gorge, fifteen feet down. We all lurched and bounced in our seats, holding on tight as the SUV bumped up and over the buried curb, onto the buried sidewalk at the top of the ravine. Nola's cosmetics case ricocheted around like a piece of popcorn in a popper. Sitting unsecured in the cargo area, Tucker bounced into the air. So did Cap'n Stormy.

"Find something to hang on to, Tucker!" I cried, wishing I'd been more diligent about making sure my little brother was safely buckled in. I glanced at Grandma; she was fully awake now, but her eyes were wide and unfocused.

"Try to get the car back on the road, Nola," Samson said, working hard to keep his voice low and calm.

"I am trying," Nola said as she plowed through a series of low-hanging tree branches. The branches slapped *thwap-thwap-thwap* against the windshield, and scraped along the side of the car like fingernails on a chalkboard.

"Hit the brakes," Samson, Del, and I all shouted at the same time as we caught sight of a safety railing looming large in front of us.

"Okay, okay!" Nola shouted back. She slammed her foot down hard, missing the brake. Flooring the gas pedal instead.

Chapter 23

THE SAFETY RAIL SHOULD have stopped us, but it
didn't. Nola was driving too fast. I didn't need my old
savvy to see what was going to happen next—to see
that the SUV was going to take a flying leap into the
gulch that divided the two sides of the boulevard. We
were going to plunge straight down into the creek.

"Everyone hold on!" Nola cried as all four of our tires
left the ground. Like a ride at the county fair, the car
began to rotate wrong side up, and its front end lurched
down into the ravine below.

My heart bump-thumped, as if preparing to explode.
Had I created an unhappy ending for us all, by trying to
change Grandma's fate?

I squeezed my eyes closed and screamed *stop-stop-*

STOP—if only for good measure. I may not have needed the words to trigger my savvy, but saying them couldn't hurt. Nor was I the only one screaming.

My head spun and my stomach writhed as though we were still falling. But the car had stopped. The shrieking had stopped. Everything had stopped, just like I'd willed it to.

The SUV hung suspended sideways in midair. The nose of the car pointed down at a crazy angle, two feet from the creek, where ice-fringed waters sloshed and churned.

I heard Del whistle one low note, then say, "That was close, Specs. Maybe next time, you could pause things a little sooner?"

All I managed to answer was, "Uh-huh . . . yeah . . . okay."

Del and I leaned hard against our seat belts, gasping for breath. The others were all frozen in place. Most of them, anyway. I nearly had a heart attack when Grandma Pat elbowed me in the ribs and said:

"I don't like the way the sandwich-girl drives. I'm getting out!"

✳ ✳ ✳ ✳

"Grandma!" I cried. "You're still moving!"

"Of course I'm still moving, girly. I'm not dead yet." Before Del or I could stop her, Grandma Pat unfastened her seat belt and fell sideways. She tumbled tuchus over teacup against Del's door and window, smothering Del in a silvery cloud of lace and netting. I'd stopped time to save us, but Grandma Pat was still finding her way into trouble.

"It looks like we can add your gran to the ranks of The Timeless Crusaders," Del said through the muffle of fabric around him.

Patrice Beaumont may have been a senior citizen, she may have looked thin and brittle, but she still had plenty of moxie left in her old bones, even if her mind was growing slushy. Grandma had braved her bedroom window . . . the bus . . . the night . . . the snow . . . the cold . . . and the big city, in hopes of reaching her old high school. Just so that she could go to a dance—the ghost of a dance—that her father had forbidden her to attend sixty years ago.

I was only three years old when my sister, Mibs,

decided that our poppa's ordinary, everyday savvy was the ability to never, ever give up. I understood better now who Poppa had inherited his determination from: Grandma Pat didn't own any white flags. She may have let her dreams get squashed when she was younger, but she refused to surrender those same dreams now. Even if they were only illusions.

Maybe Grandma had a savvy after all, in the same way Poppa did. Maybe Grandma Pat's savvy made her a stubborn daredevil—a strong-willed dynamo of an old lady who was unaffected by my time-stops. Thinking back, I realized I had never paused the clocks when Grandma Pat was within sight. No wonder she'd gotten so far on her own. Every time I'd tripped up Father Time that night, in hopes of stalling my grandmother's escape, Grandma had kept on skipping.

There had to be a reason Del and Grandma, and a smattering of other people, didn't freeze with the rest of the world. What charmed thing could the three of us share in common?

"How do I get out of this tin can?" Grandma crowed. Turning herself around, she found the door latch and yanked up on it. But stuck-time made the door stick.

"Frizzle . . . rackin' . . . fiddlesticks!" Grandma cursed as she pushed her frail weight harder against the door. She leveraged one boot against the back of Nola's seat and the other boot against the side of Del's face.

Del tried to grab Grandma's ankle. But before he could get a good grip on her, the door swung open, out, and down. My grandmother rolled out and down too.

"Grandma!" I shrieked as I watched her land with a soft *thwump* in the snow at the edge of the creek. Grandma Pat lay on her back. As still as death.

"No!" I cried, sure she was dead, or injured beyond repair, even though she'd only fallen a few feet. A second later Grandma Pat opened her eyes and coughed. I sighed in relief. My relief was short-lived.

Instead of getting up and brushing the snow from her clothes and hair, Grandma lay in the snow and began to act . . . weird.

Weirder than usual.

She moved her arms and legs through the snow, plowing arcs through the white drifts. For a moment, I wondered if Grandma couldn't control her limbs; she looked like Bambi on ice, an awkward, splay-legged deer, unable to get up.

In one of Momma's what-to-expect lectures during the drive to Colorado, she had told my brothers and me how Grandma's illness would eventually affect more than just her memory. She said other things would become difficult for her soon too. Simple things—sitting up on her own, buttoning her clothes, feeding herself— would someday be impossible.

Had that day come so soon?

"Ha! Would you look at that, Specs? Your gran is playing in the snow."

"What?"

I looked again and saw that Del was right. I laughed too. Grandma wasn't losing control of anything—she was making a snow angel.

Del and I kept on laughing as we followed Grandma, unbuckling our seat belts and sliding down the open door of the SUV. But our laughter didn't last long. The car still hung sideways, halfway over the frozen creek, like a three-ton Christmas ornament dangling from an invisible thread—a thread I knew I would eventually have to cut. As soon as I restarted time, Mrs. Kim's car would plummet the last few feet into the water, at the exact speed it was going before I said *stop*.

Somehow, Del and I had to get everyone out.

While Grandma lay on the ground, acting like it was the first—or maybe the last—snowfall of her life, Del and I went to work. It was a challenge to pull the others out of the car; we were soon sweating from the effort.

"It's like you're Thumbelina and I'm Tom Thumb, and we're trying to get Ken and Barbie out of Barbie's plastic Dream Car," Del said. He panted as we tugged on Samson's bent form, dragging him down to the ground and depositing him next to Nola, like a cast-off toy. Del stopped to wipe his coat sleeve across his brow, and to undo his bow tie.

"I s'pose that was kind of a babyish way to describe our crazy situation," he said, giving me a sheepish smile.

"Not at all," I said, grinning back at him. "That's *exactly* how this feels."

I glanced up at Tucker. My little brother had frozen mid-somersault in the airspace of the cargo area; I silently vowed to never let him ride in a car without a seat belt again. Captain Stormalong Fuzzypants looked like Superkitty flying next to Tucker's outstretched hand. Her soft paws and teeny-tiny claws were extended in every direction. Her tail was a fuzzy exclamation point.

Del put his hand on my shoulder as we craned our necks to look up inside the SUV. With the nose of the car pointing down, its rear hatch was high off the ground.

Del sighed. "So, got any idea how we're gonna get your brother down?"

I nodded. "I think we're going to have to do some climbing."

Somehow Del and I found a way to get every kid and cat out of the SUV. We even managed to retrieve the wheelchair and the blanket we'd taken with us from Mercy Medical Center. We were all going to have bumps and bruises in the morning, but we were safe. As safe as we could be, now that we were officially stranded.

Grandma Pat had picked herself up out of the snow. Now, having built two-thirds of a lopsided snowman, she shuffled away from her creation to stand at a distance. Her tiara was crooked again. Her glasses foggy.

Her thistledown curls sparkled with snowflakes.

Grandma stood with her eyes closed, knee-deep in white. I watched her wave her arms slowly up, then down, not moving her feet. She looked like a swan flapping its wings in slow motion beneath the dull spotlights of the shrouded streetlamps, clearing away the snowflakes that hung in the air around her. I gasped. Whether she knew she was doing it or not, Grandma Pat was making an upright snow angel in the air, just as I'd imagined doing when Del and I first left the bus station.

I took a step back, forgetting all about time, the car, the clock tower, and being stuck in Denver. As soon as these worries left my mind, the moment became magical. As Grandma continued to make her standing snow angel, I looked around—really looked.

Breathing in.

Breathing out.

The snowflakes hung like poetry over the city. Surrounded by their spacious hush, it was easy to pause. To listen. To bend my ear to try to hear what the heavens had to say, without the timey chatter of the whole wide world muddling the message.

Not wanting to blink and miss a single whispery stanza of the sky's cold verse, I drew in another long, deep breath, filling myself with the timeless *now* of the winter night. Above me, there was only snow. And, to my surprise, the moon. A crack had opened in the white vault of the sky, revealing a treasure of stars laid out on velvet strips of darkness.

Through the break in the clouds, the moon glowed as round and as bright as a giant clock face shining down from the heavens. The storm was moving on—or it would be, as soon as I was ready for the world to turn again.

But I wasn't ready. Not quite yet. Being able to linger inside this exquisite moment was so much better than looking into, and dwelling on, the past and future. Maybe the switch had been an okay thing after all.

Before I knew it, I was twirling. Twirling, twirling, twirling among the timeless snowflakes, with my arms spread wide and my mouth open to catch ice crystals on my tongue.

"Uh . . . Specs?" Del's voice broke into my reverie. "I know the snow is pretty and all, but it's still cold out here, and we just lost our ride. What do we do next?"

What *were* we going to do?

I stopped twirling and looked at Mrs. Kim's SUV, now burned and crumpled on the outside, and sticky, stained, and wet with snow on the inside. My magical moment subsided as storms returned to my heart and mind.

"Once I restart time, Del"—I slowly shook my head—"the whole thing will come crashing down. There's no way to stop it."

"Well, you can't keep things this way forever, Specs, just to stop bad things from happening."

I knew Del was right, but it didn't make moving forward any easier.

"You have to let it drop," Del said, looking at the car. "There's nothing else you can do. Gravity plus time equals falling."

The image of Grandma Pat plummeting from the clock tower swam before my eyes. What if there was nothing I could do for her in the end, either?

What if *gravity + time = Grandma falling*?

"Let's just take each moment as it comes," Del said, guessing my thoughts.

I took one last look at the SUV, at the moon, at the un-falling snow. Then I put an arm around Grandma and settled her into her wheelchair. I tucked her Mercy Medical Center blanket around her and kissed her cheek, not even minding when she pulled her face away, like a little kid; like our roles were reversed yet again. Then I turned back to face the grim fate of Mrs. Kim's SUV.

I knew how to do it now. How to restart time. I made myself ready. I quieted my hammering heart. I soothed the fear from my soul, and I kept my eyes open. I spread my arms wide to welcome the future.

"Come what may," I said, knowing that the magic wasn't in the letters and the syllables, but in trusting what they meant.

There was a pause. A pull. A whoosh. The SUV continued its rolling plummet for a split second. Then it crashed into the creek.

Chapter 24

EVERY ONE OF THE SUV's windows shattered as the car hit the water and rolled, spraying a thousand ice-like pieces of glass in every direction. Samson threw himself over Tucker to shield him from the flying shrapnel. I wrapped my grandmother in a protective hug, and Del added his arms to mine, sheltering the both of us. Nola sat dumbfounded in the snow, obviously surprised to find herself out of the car. It didn't take long for the others to put two and two together, to come to the solution that I'd once again stopped time.

When we borrowed her mother's car earlier that evening, Nola had warned us not to make a mess. I doubted we could've made a worse mess if we had tried. Upside down, with its nose in the creek, the SUV groaned and pinged. It's tires spun for a few seconds, then stopped. The engine gave one final, death-like rattle.

I had a cousin who could transform scrap metal into art simply by concentrating really hard. I wished Ledger was with us now; he could've used his metal-bending savvy to turn the crumpled car into a stretch limousine. Or a robotic fairy-tale carriage. At the very least, he could've fixed some of the dents.

"I killed Mom's car!" shrieked Nola.

Overhead, the clouds continued to part, revealing more and more of the night sky. The snowfall was lighter now, the storm in retreat.

Samson stood carefully, flinching as he adjusted his sling, then began to brush clumps of snow from his T-shirt and jeans. Now that my brother's internal furnace had been thoroughly dampened, he probably wished he'd brought his coat. Especially now that we were stranded.

With his good arm, Samson grabbed Tuck by the scruff of his coat and hauled him upright. Tucker's rainbow whiskers had smeared in the snow, but you could still tell he was supposed to be a cat. Samson looked

Tucker up and down, patting his arms and legs and head, making sure our little brother was in one piece. Then he tweaked Tucker's painted nose.

"You good, Tuck?"

Tucker began to nod but stopped short. His face contorted into a comical, colorful, quizzical expression. He wiggled. He jiggled. Then he reached into his pants and pulled out Cap'n Stormy. The ginger kitten chirruped in distress.

I turned to look accusingly at Del.

Del shrugged. "I had to put that cat someplace where it wouldn't get lost."

Finished inspecting Tucker, Samson awkwardly held his good hand out to Nola, hoping to help her up from her cold, wet seat in the snow. But Nola didn't take Samson's hand. She didn't even look at him. She couldn't turn her eyes away from her mother's ruined car.

"Three weeks!" she wailed. "I only had three weeks before I was going to get my driver's license!" Then she burst into tears. Samson shuffled his feet in the snow, like he didn't know what to do. There was nothing any of us could do, or say. Everyone was struck dumb over what we'd done to Mrs. Kim's car.

"Come on, Nola," Samson said softly. "We've got to get everyone out of the cold. There's got to be someplace we can go. I'm lost here, but you and Del know the city."

With a sniff, Nola let Samson help her to her feet. She swiped at her tears with the back of her wrist, smudging the makeup that was already running in streaks down her face. While Nola dragged her cosmetics case and shopping bags out of the upside-down SUV, I told Samson about Grandma.

"I don't know why, Samson, but Grandma Pat is immune to my time-stops too. Just like Del."

My brother looked from me to Del to Grandma, then shivered. "That's spooky. I wonder what connects the three of you."

It was far too cold to stand around, dwelling on savvy mysteries. Samson led the group up the sloping walkway that connected the creek path to the street. Too worn out to melt any of the snow, he enlisted Tucker to help him stomp two grooves for us to follow—two grooves just the right width apart to accommodate Grandma's wheelchair. Even so, it was a difficult, nearly impossible job to push Grandma forward. Del and I did it together, shoulder to shoulder and hip to hip, the same way we'd pushed the grocery cart earlier. Nola lagged behind, weighed down by her shopping bags, and by the guilt of having just destroyed her mother's car.

"I'm tired. Where're we going?" Tucker whined, after we'd traveled a mere three blocks.

"We're all tired, Tuck," Samson said. Without a coat or his savvy to warm him, Samson's lips were turning blue. "I'd give you a p-piggyback ride, T-T-Tucker," he said, his teeth chattering. "But with this b-bum shoulder of mine, I can't."

"We're looking for someplace warm, Tuck," I explained. "We need to find a hotel lobby or an all-night coffee shop—someplace that's open, where we'll be allowed to hang out. Then we'll try to call Momma again, or Del's uncle. But our first priority is to get Grandma out of the cold. You only need to walk a little farther, Tuck," I said. "You can do it. You're big now, remember?"

Tucker gave a full-body sigh. "Sometimes I miss being little."

I covered my mouth so that Tucker wouldn't see me smile. I knew something he didn't, a secret I'd vowed to keep for the next five years. Back in October, on the morning of my thirteenth birthday, my very first official savvy vision had shown me Tucker's future. One I'd nearly forgotten about after the switch gave my brother a talent early. I didn't know if the switch would permanently alter the things I'd seen in Tuck's future. But so far, like it or not, none of my savvy visions had been wrong.

That was good news for the fun visions. Bad news for the not-fun ones.

I looked at my watch. It was 9:40. Del had said that the old high school clock tower hadn't worked in years. That its hands were permanently fixed at two minutes to midnight. Nonetheless, the closer we got to the eleventh hour, the more nervous I became.

"Look, Nola!" Samson stopped short. "It's your dream come true."

Nola gasped. I followed her gaze up the street. Rubbing the fog from my glasses, I stared forward into the lights of a bright sign that buzzed and flashed a block ahead of us. The sign's fizzing orange glow stood out like lava against the white snow shrouding the city. Part of the sign appeared to be broken, but even from where I stood, I could clearly read four flashing letters. I saw an *N* and an *O* and an *L* and an *A*. The sign blinked over and over again:

NO LA

NO LA

NO LA

"What are you looking at?" Tucker demanded as the rest of us stared up the street with our mouths hanging open.

"It's Nola's name, Tuck," I told him. "It's Nola's name . . . in lights."

Chapter 25

NOLA'S EYES DIDN'T WAVER from the flashing letters of the sign up the block. She stood stock-still in the snow. Overcome by the sight of her name in lights, she looked like she'd forgotten all about her mother's ruined car, and about how much trouble she was going to be in when she told her parents what had happened. Gripping her cosmetics case and shopping bags in one hand, Nola reached up and removed her hat, like she was about to start singing the national anthem.

"It's got to be a sign," she whispered.

"It *is* a sign." Samson chuckled softly. His eyes reflected the glittering snowflakes gathering in Nola's hair.

"A restaurant sign," Del clarified, breaking the spell

the lights had cast over Nola. "That's the sign for Volcano Laverne's. But it's broken."

"Oh! I've heard of that place." Nola's voice rose with excitement. She wiped away the last of her tears, smearing her makeup even more. "Volcano Laverne's Hawaiian BBQ and Waffle House. They have round-the-clock karaoke."

"That's right," Del said. "My gran took me there once. The place is legendary. No one but Laverne LaFlamme serves waffles and short ribs all day, every day. You haven't lived until you've had a plate of Laverne's pine-apple waffles. Or her kalua pork. Mm-mm-mm." Del rubbed his tummy, like he could still taste every bite of the meal he'd shared with his gran.

"Waffles?" Tuck's tiredness vanished. Still holding Cap'n Stormy safely inside his coat, he ran in the direction of the restaurant, pushing through the snow like a pint-sized snowplow.

"Come on, Gypsy! Come on, Grandma! We didn't have any dinner, but I see a tower of waffles in our future."

✳ ✾ ✳ ✾

It wasn't long before we were all standing beneath the flashing lights of the broken sign, staring at the entrance to Volcano Laverne's Hawaiian BBQ and Waffle House. Located between two high-rises, the restaurant was a squat, two-story brick building, with a rusted fire escape running down one side. Now that we were directly under it, we could clearly see that the sign's lightbulbs did indeed spell out: *VOLCANO LAVERNE'S*. Only, most of the bulbs were burned out, making it look like *NOLA* from a distance.

I still wasn't happy to be stuck in Denver, so dangerously close to Larimer High. But now that we had no car, nor any other means of transportation, I was relieved to find a place that was open and warm and welcoming. A place where Grandma Pat could rest, Tucker could eat as many waffles as he wanted, and Nola could sing her heart out, karaoke-style.

"Why are we just standing here?" Del grabbed the door handle, rolling his eyes as the rest of us stood shivering in the cold, staring up at Nola's name in lights.

Riding on a wave of noise, the heavenly aroma of hot

food washed over us the moment Del opened the door. I smiled as the thrum of laughter and the mellow sounds of slide-guitar and ukulele warmed me, ears to toes.

The inside of the restaurant was long and narrow, with booths along the walls, and tables and chairs jamming the center of the room, right up to the small karaoke stage. There was green shag carpet on all the walls, and the floors were wide planks of waxed pine.

The only brightly lit spots in the restaurant were the karaoke stage and the all-you-can-eat waffle bar. Both were festooned with pink and yellow twinkle lights, tiki torches, and colorful paper lanterns. Fake palm leaves and raffia streamers hung from the ceiling. A plaster volcano towered next to the doors to the kitchen, fake flames dancing from its crater.

We'd stepped out of the snow, into a wacky tropical paradise.

A paradise packed with people.

There was no hostess in sight, and no one appeared to have noticed our arrival. Everyone was too busy whooping and hollering, cheering loudly for the tall woman on the stage.

The woman had to be Laverne LaFlamme. She looked like the queen of the place. Lit by a web of spotlights, she wore a bedazzled, double-ruffled muumuu. A towering orange-and-yellow wig tilted precariously atop her head. Around her neck, she wore a lei of rainbow-colored silk flowers. She also had the longest false eyelashes I'd ever seen.

While we waited for someone to seat us, I watched Ms. LaFlamme, spellbound by her flamboyant glam and sparkle. Standing center stage, strumming a rhinestone ukulele, the restaurant owner belted out a song with a decidedly downhome Hawaiian-country flair. It was everything I'd always loved, and more.

"It doesn't look like there's any place for us to sit," Samson said, his voice barely audible over the noise. I scanned the booths and tables. Samson was right; every seat in the restaurant was taken. There was a group of young soldiers dressed in tan-and-brown fatigues, with big duffel bags at their feet. They sat near a table of teenagers with crazy hair and piercings. Even at this late hour, families with young children, and men and women in business suits, crowded the restaurant. At the center of the room, a rowdy bunch of ladies were celebrating a bachelorette party. There was even a collection of old veterans in ball caps sporting military pins and patches with the names of ships and wars from days gone by.

The people inside the restaurant were from every walk of life imaginable, and they were all part of the party. Everyone was eating. Everyone was chatting. And everyone—everyone—wore the same rainbow-colored lei as Laverne LaFlamme, giving them all at least one thing they shared in common. Inside Volcano Laverne's Hawaiian BBQ and Waffle House, it was like the blizzard, and the differences between people did not exist. Here, no one had to be alone during the storm.

As I looked around at the packed restaurant, hoping there was a place for us too, Laverne launched into her chorus:

> *We all ate red-eye gravy and poi,*
> *Luau chicken and hominy grits—*

"Aloha, kiddos! Good evening, ma'am! No need to lurk in the doorway." Laverne paused her song, still strumming plink-plunkedy on her ukulele. With an encouraging wobble of her sky-high wig, the restaurant owner called out, "Be sure the door is closed behind you good and tight! We don't want to invite mean ol' Mr. Storm inside, do we? Come on in and sit a spell." Then she hollered to the crowd, "Make some room, people!"

Laverne beckoned us inside, pointing us toward a space the bachelorettes were opening for us by squishing together and sitting double on their chairs. Our hostess put her lips right up against the microphone, paused in a breathless way that made the entire audience go quiet, and said: "For those of you who may have just walked in, I'm your hostess with the mostest, Laverne LaFlamme, and this here's my place." The crowd inside the restaurant went wild—some of the soldiers even stood up to cheer.

It was as if the car crash hadn't even happened. Nola's eyes sparkled with every light and sequin and bedazzlement. I could see her thoughts as clearly as if they'd been written in Twisted Tangerine across her forehead. Nola Kim was imagining that very same crowd cheering the very same way for her. Just as she'd always dreamed.

As soon as she finished her song, Laverne LaFlamme

invited someone else into the spotlight. "Marine Corporal Vasquez. You're up, sugar!" The chords of an all-new tune rose from a karaoke machine at the foot of the stage, and from speakers in every corner. While the soldiers raised another cheer, television screens lit up around the room, ready to display the lyrics to the next song. Shaking her hair loose from a tight, regulation bun, Corporal Vasquez slapped a few hearty high fives and jogged to the platform.

Laverne placed her ukulele in a clear plastic tub full of other playful instruments: kazoos, slide whistles, Boomwhackers, and tambourines. When she reached the hostess station, she grabbed a stack of menus and an armful of flower leis, batting her long eyelashes.

Grandma pushed aside her blanket and got shakily to her feet.

"I-I think I took a wrong turn somewhere. This isn't the winter dance. Cleavon will never find me here." Grandma turned in the direction of the door. But before she could take two steps, she teetered and swayed. Then she spilled to the floor, like a Hawaiian puka shell necklace with a broken string.

Chapter 26

"*STOP YOUR FUSSING! THERE'S* nothing wrong with me." Grandma slapped feebly at Del and me as we lifted her gently back into her wheelchair. Samson shot me a worried look.

"Mrs. B. is probably dehydrated. How did I not think of that?" Nola berated herself as she picked up Grandma's blanket and tucked it around her. "Old people get dehydrated really quickly."

"Who are you calling old?" Grandma snapped, adjusting her tiara.

Laverne looked us all up and down. Her warm expression radiated amusement as she took in Tucker's face paints, Nola's smeared makeup, and Samson's leopard-print sling. "Woo-ee! It looks like you people have been chewed up, spit out, and stepped on."

It was exactly how we all felt.

"Come on!" Laverne motioned for us to follow her. "I'll put you kids and the Empress of Fierce"—she gave Grandma a long-lashed wink—"someplace quieter and more comfortable."

As Corporal Vasquez belted out a song about love being a battlefield, we trailed after Laverne LaFlamme, making our way across the large, tropical dining room. With a swish in her hips and one hand in the air, the restaurant owner led us down a short hallway, past the restrooms. Laverne unlocked a door at the end of the narrow corridor and let it swing wide, revealing a set of stairs, going up.

"There's nothing wrong with me! It's just a leg cramp." Grandma Pat continued to object, her hands flapping like the wings of startled mourning doves. "I don't need all this trouble. Take me home! I'm missing my shows."

"I'm sure these young folks would like to get you home as soon as possible, ma'am," said Laverne. "Unfortunately, there is a storm outside that's got everyone stuck. But you're at my place now, where everyone is welcome. You can watch your shows on the TV in my apartment, sugar. I'll work on getting you something to eat and drink so that you can get your strength back."

"Waffles!" Tucker leaned forward to shout-whisper into Grandma's ear. "Ask for waffles, Grammy." *Grammy*. It was a term of endearment I'd never heard Tuck use before, and even though Grandma didn't respond to it, Tucker smiled as if she had.

The steps leading up to Laverne's apartment were steep and narrow. I knew it would be a struggle to get Grandma Pat up them if she really did have a leg cramp. But Laverne fixed that problem in a snap. Startling everyone—my grandmother most of all—Laverne bent down and swept Grandma up out of her wheelchair. Then she carried Grandma up the stairs like she was nothing but a dress on a hanger.

"Okay." Grandma's voice floated down the stairs as the rest of us followed. "I'll stay. But only if you can make a decent tuna sandwich, missy."

"Waffles, Grammy!" Tucker reminded Grandma as

he stomped up the stairs behind her. "I told you to ask for waffles."

Laverne's apartment was small, but it was colorful and comfy and warm, just like her restaurant. We quickly shed our coats and hats, admiring Laverne's overstuffed chairs, the purple velvet sofa buried under a dozen throw pillows, and a musical-motion hula dancer lamp. One entire wall of the apartment appeared to be made of windows. But tonight the blinds were drawn, shutting out the storm that had its nose pressed to the other side of the glass.

Soon Grandma was settled deep into the sofa cushions. With her feet propped up on a satin hassock, and the television remote held high in her bony hand, Grandma really did look like an empress, reigning over Laverne's TV, in her dress and her tiara. Once she had something to eat and drink, and found a show to watch, I couldn't imagine anything in the world pulling her away from such comforts.

And yet, we were still in the city. Grandma was still in her party outfit. I couldn't let myself relax.

❄ ❄ ❄ ❄

When Laverne handed me her phone, I took a big breath and let Samson dial Momma's number. Samson stood beside me as I held the phone to my ear. This time, Momma answered on the first ring.

"Hello?"

"Hi, Momma. It's me."

"Gypsy! Thank goodness!" Momma exclaimed as soon as she heard my voice. "Where *are* you? Are your brothers all right? Your grandmother too? Samson left two messages, but—you know your brother—he said very little. I'm so sorry, Gypsy," Momma babbled on. "I didn't know my phone was off. I had a small problem with the car—heh." She gave a short, self-conscious laugh. A laugh that teetered on the edge of hysterics. "But I'm back at Grandma's house now. I should never have left you kids all alone and in charge of Grandma Pat. Tell me what's happened."

It didn't seem right that Momma was the one apologizing, like it was somehow her fault we'd all gone missing while she was out. I knew, once she heard our story, she'd be demanding our sorries instead.

"We're all safe," I assured her, even though two niggling words kept hounding me: *For now*. We were all safe for now.

I told Momma the barest skeleton of our story, leaving out the bits I knew would upset her most: Tucker accidentally taking ownership of a kitten; me stealing a homeless person's shopping cart; all of us removing Grandma from the safety of the medical center. And, of course, the total destruction of Mrs. Kim's new car. Samson and I could tell Momma and Poppa those things later, together, when we were all face-to-face. With Momma stuck in Evergreen, and the rest of us trapped in Denver, it wouldn't do any good to freak her out completely. Laverne spoke briefly to Momma too, offering her own grown-up assurances that we were safe. Then I ended the call with a cross-my-heart promise to stay in constant communication until we could find our way back to Evergreen.

When I hung up the phone, Nola said, "We don't *all* have to stay up here with Mrs. B., do we?" She gravitated toward the door, like the music downstairs was a magnet and she was made of iron filings. "I mean . . . I could just sing one song, then come back up—"

"You wanna sing, sugar?" Laverne beamed at Nola.

"More than anything! It might be the last chance I get before my parents ground me for life, or worse. With the skills they have, they might surgically remove my vocal cords."

"Singing is Nola's dream," Samson told Laverne.

Nola clasped her hands and grinned at Samson like he was the first person who had ever truly taken her dreams seriously. If she had been a cartoon character, a halo of red and pink hearts would have appeared above her head and started spinning.

Nola's reaction made Samson blush and look away. "Well . . . it's the truth, isn't it?"

"If that's the case," said Laverne, "let's get you up on that stage, hon!"

"Yes!" Nola punched the air, then reached for her cosmetics case. "Just let me touch up my makeup first."

"Stop, stop, stop!" Del shouted before Nola could unlatch the case. For a second, I thought Del was trying to stop time, even though he knew now that he couldn't. But Del was only trying to stop any further makeover catastrophes from happening.

"I can't stand by and watch this go down," he told Nola, shaking his head. "My gran would never forgive me. You need to holster your lip liner and take a seat before you make a bigger mess of your face than it already is."

Laverne chuckled, raising one finely drawn eyebrow of her own as she nodded her agreement. Putting one hand on Nola's shoulder, Laverne gently led her to a tall stool next to the island in the kitchenette across the room.

"Just come down whenever you're ready, sugar. We'll fire up your tune of choice." Before she left, Laverne disappeared into the bathroom and returned with a fresh package of makeup-removing wipes; she slapped them into Del's hand the way a trauma nurse might slap gauze into a doctor's palm on the front lines of a war zone.

"Tell me more of that tall tale, little big boy, while I search for my shows." Grandma's voice drew my attention as she and Tucker scrolled through the channels on Laverne's TV. "I want to hear more about that girl who fell into the river and climbed out all sparkly and golden." I was surprised Grandma wanted to hear more about our savvy ancestor, but Tucker happily began to tell the story for the second time that night.

"Okay, Grammy. Once upon a time . . ."

As Tucker and Cap'n Stormy nestled next to Grandma Pat on Laverne's velvet sofa, telling stories and watching TV channels flip by, Nola looked at me and Samson, pleading wordlessly for us to stop Del from giving her a makeover. Neither Samson nor I made any moves to intervene. Samson slumped into one of Laverne's overstuffed chairs and closed his eyes, still worn out from his fiery efforts to get Mr. and Mrs. Walker to the hospital.

"All right, I give in!" Nola said, shoving her cosmetics case toward Del. "But I'm trusting you. Promise you know what you're doing? As artistic as Tucker's face may be, I don't want go onstage looking like a kaleidoscopic kitty cat. Don't you dare give me whiskers!"

"Relax," said Del. "All I'm going to do is take off those heavy black garage doors that have melted down your face. Then everyone will see the flashy sports car you've been hiding this whole time."

Nola perked up at that.

As Del began to scrub the tear-smeared makeup

off Nola's cheeks and eyelids, I sat down on one of the stools next to them. I peered into the jumbled trove of Nola's cosmetics case, bewildered by her collection of shadows and polishes, brushes and lipsticks, liners and applicators.

"Ooh!" I thrust my hand into Nola's case and pulled out a small pump bottle of glow-in-the-dark glitter gel. The cloudy goo inside the bottle sparkled with specks of opal and silver and white, reminding me of the glimmer of moonlight on freshly fallen snow.

Without pausing to ask Nola's permission, I pumped a big glob of the shimmering stuff into my hand, ready to slather it on my arms, or through my hair. But as soon as I felt the cold gel hit my palm, I remembered the way Grandma Pat had pulled her hand out of mine back in Evergreen, the way she'd used a glop of clear hand sanitizer to wash away any trace of savvy cooties I might have given her.

When I turned and looked at Grandma now, taking in her tiara and her gown, a different, more recent memory filled my mind's eye. I couldn't *savvy*-see into the past, the way I could before the switch, but I knew I'd never forget the way Grandma had raised and lowered her arms under the moonlight, like an aged ballerina performing the last dance of the dying swan, while making upright snow angels in the storm. It might be one of the few magical memories I'd ever have of Patrice Beaumont. A memory as wonderful as any from the savvy side of my family.

Still holding the bottle of glitter gel, I got an idea that made me smile.

Chapter 27

". . . *AND WHEN SHE* got out of the water"—Tucker
leaned his head against Grandma Pat's arm as he continued the tale of our first savvy ancestor—"Eva Mae
was covered in gold dust. Ha! She must have looked
like a goldfish. Get it, Grammy? A *gold*fish?" As Tucker
erupted into giggles, I knelt on the floor at the hem of
Grandma Pat's silvery skirts, careful not to block her
view of the TV and make her cranky. I cradled a gooey
puddle of liquid moonbeams in my palm, trying not to
spill any of the glow-in-the-dark glitter gel I'd nicked
from Nola's cosmetics case. Using the tip of my finger, I
began to dapple Grandma's crinkly skin with the glittery
goop, making her hands, forearms, and cheeks shimmer.

"What are you doing, Nettie?" Grandma looked at

me as I reached up to add some sparkle to the wispy snow-white ringlets that framed her face.

"I'm just helping you get ready for the dance, Patrice," I answered, happy to let my grandmother believe I was Nettie for as long as it took to apply the rest of the glitter. "It's going to be sublime, remember? You want to look your best for your beau, Cleavon, don't you?" I don't know why I said it. The last thing I wanted to do was encourage Grandma to try to get to the imaginary dance. But I had my own motives for applying the glitter, and I wanted her to stay calm so I could finish.

When I ran out of glitter gel, I wiped my hands clean on my leggings, making them sparkle too. I carefully removed Grandma Pat's glasses and cleaned them for her, wondering what *she* saw when she looked into the blur.

Gently, I returned Grandma's glasses to her face. I stood up and stepped back to admire my work.

"Patrice Beaumont," I announced. "I now declare you an honorary ancestor of Eva Mae El Dorado Two-Birds Ransom. But instead of collecting the rock-solid sparkle of gold dust, you have a power that lets you gather the shimmer moonbeams and the glimmer of freshly fallen snow."

Grandma gave me a funny look, then stared down at the sparkle on her hands and arms. "Well," she said under her breath. "Would you look at that? I *am* glimmer-shimmering. That's different." After studying the glitter a moment longer, Grandma looked up at me and smiled.

Smiled!

"Why, that's just fine," she said. "I didn't even have to fall into a muddy river to get some magic." Grandma's smile grew even wider. She liked the sparkle!

"Grammy?" Tucker turned to look up at Grandma as the show on TV cut to a commercial. "Grammy?" he said again, yanking on her skirt.

Grandma's eyes took on a confused, faraway look, as though the word *grammy* was as meaningless to her as the words *bumfuzzle, mumpsimus,* or *ratoon.* But eventually she said, "Yes?"

"Is there something you've ever wanted more than anything else in the whole wide world?"

Grandma reached up and absentmindedly adjusted her tiara. She watched her hand move as she slowly rested it back on her lap, turning her wrist this way and that to make the glitter catch the light. Grandma's voice wobbled as she answered Tucker's question.

"I think there was something I wanted . . . once," she said. "Only, now I seem to have forgotten what it was."

Tucker nodded as though Grandma had confided something important. "For as long as I can remember," he said, "I've wanted to be big. And I've wanted a cat." Tucker gently stroked Cap'n Stormy, who was sleeping in his lap. "This week, I got both—*and* you didn't spank me again, the way I thought you would. So that was good too." Tuck sighed happily. "Do you like cats, Grandma?" He looked up hopefully, wiggling his pink, painted-on cat nose.

Grandma furrowed her brow as she stared down at Tuck and Cap'n Stormy. "I . . . I don't think I do."

Tuck's rainbow whiskers twitched as he contemplated her answer. He shrugged his shoulders. "That's okay," he said. "You might change your mind after you've spent more time with one. But if *you* ever want something—something important—let me know. Now that I can grow big, maybe I can help you get it."

"Nice job with the glitter, Specs," Del said, glancing over his shoulder and nodding his approval of Grandma's sparkly makeover. The sound of music pumped through the floorboards as he redid Nola's eye makeup. "Now you and your gran have even more in common. You sparkle on the inside, and she sparkles on the outside."

Double spoonful, I reminded myself, trying not to blush. Del was all sugar. Sugar and playful pranks.

I adjusted my glasses, pushing them higher on my nose. For once, I didn't prickle at the notion of sharing a likeness with my grandmother. It helped, I supposed, that I'd finally begun to see small traces of ordinary magic hidden deep inside her. I'd gotten a glimpse of the young woman she had been before she decided that growing up meant toughening up. Before she forgot that the world was full of sparkle.

I wanted to take Grandma's crooked hands in mine and tell her that everything was going to be okay. Tell her that, magic or no magic . . . savvy or no savvy . . . memory or no memory, we were family.

Maybe Del was right. Maybe I was lucky to still have my grandma. I tugged on one of my curls—maybe I was lucky to resemble Grandma too.

"Grandma Pat and I even have the same birthday," I told Del, feeling my life-long horror at sharing a birthday with her begin to melt away. "We were both born on October eleventh."

"Seriously? No way!" Del dropped the palette of eye shadow he was holding, and bent quickly to pick it up.

"It's true," I said. "Right, Grandma?"

Grandma dismissed my words with a wave, barely listening now that her attention had returned to the television.

Del faced me. "October *eleventh*," he echoed, his tone disbelieving.

"Yes . . . why?"

"I was born on October eleventh also! It looks like all three of us have something in common."

"That could explain a thing or two," grumbled Samson, still sitting with his eyes closed across from me, cradling his arm in its sling.

"What do you mean?" I demanded. Samson's eyes

popped open. He looked from me to Del to Grandma. Then he sat forward with a wince.

"You said neither Grandma nor Del freezes when you stop time. Right?"

"Right . . ." I answered slowly. "And there were those two girls," I added. "The ones Del and I saw waving at us through the window of the dance school, after we left the bus station. They looked like twins."

"Twins? That makes sense too." Samson nodded. "Remember Tuvalu?"

"Tuvalu?" I repeated uncertainly. Then I did remember. "Tuvalu!" I thought back to the day Samson had searched for facts about shared birthdays on the computer, trying to reassure me that Grandma and I weren't connected in any cosmic, unpredictable ways, just because we had the same birthday.

"That's right," I said. "Millions of people celebrate their birthday every day. Even twenty-seven people in Tuvalu."

"Where's Tuvalu?" Del and Nola both asked at the same time.

"It doesn't matter," I said, climbing to my feet.

"Don't you see, Del? Grandma and I *are* connected by our shared birthday. So are you! I'll bet you anything those girls we saw earlier were born on October eleventh too. Why, there must be thousands of people in the city who aren't affected by my savvy. But they're all spread out."

Del's eyebrows drew together. "So you're saying that you stop time for everyone *except* the people who share your birthday?"

"Nothing else explains it."

Samson's theory had to be right. Whatever magic or science lay at the heart of my family's powers, it did have a fondness for toying with people's birthdays. Generations of savvy-folk could attest to that. And even most regular people know that birthdays are special.

Five minutes later, Nola was transformed. Del had cleaned off all of her tear-streaked makeup. Then he'd lightened and reshaped what was left of her heavy eyeliner, adding subtle hints of color and even a bit of shimmer. He'd scrubbed off the remains of her dark, plum-colored lipstick, giving her lips and cheeks a soft glisten of pink instead. Del had worked his own kind of magic, a magic passed down to him from his grandmother, taking Nola from raccoon-rebel to fresh-faced glam in a way that showed off her natural beauty.

"*That's* what I'm talking about," Del said, smiling in satisfaction as he set down his brushes and applicators and backed away from her.

"Wow," Samson whispered as he took in Nola's new look. Then, as if he'd forgotten he'd said it once already, he said it again. "Wow."

Nola blushed. Then she snatched her cosmetics case back from Del and pulled out a hand mirror. "Let me see!" She studied herself for a moment before she too whispered an almost silent "*Wow*."

"It's good, right?" Del said.

"It's great," replied Nola. After admiring herself for another few seconds, she lowered the mirror and said: "Now make me look more like myself, and I'll be ready to rock and roll."

Del dropped his chin to his chest and sighed, but he took up Nola's challenge. He quickly added a bold contour of black liner around each of Nola's eyes, then he wiped away her pink lipstick and replaced it with two rowdy swipes of Twisted Tangerine. After a few more artful adjustments, Nola was satisfied.

Nola still looked so beautiful, and Del brimmed with such unconcealed pride, I clapped my hands together and bounced on my toes. "You *do* have a savvy, Del! Or a superpower, or whatever you want to call it." I looked from Tucker's artistic cat face back to Nola's glamorous, pop-star transformation. "You could be a makeup artist to the stars, making other people shine every day. If you're looking for a new superhero name, Del, I think it should be Mr. Makeover Man."

"Really?" Del cocked one eyebrow thoughtfully. "You don't think being good at makeup is an embarrassing talent for a guy?"

"Don't be dumb," Tucker said, looking up from the sofa and twitching his rainbow whiskers. "Boys can like face paints and makeup too. Right, Gypsy?"

"Right, Tuck," I agreed, beaming fondly at my little brother. Turning back to Del, I said, "You're good at this stuff, Del, and you like doing it. Why should anything else matter?" Samson and Nola nodded their agreement.

Bolstered by our enthusiasm, Del squared his shoulders, puffed out his chest, and held up his arms like he was flexing mighty muscles. "Aw, yeah—get ready, people of planet Earth, Mr. Makeover Man is here!"

"Can I be next?" I asked, wanting to look and feel just as pretty as Nola. Wanting Del to work his same transforming magic on me.

"*What*?" Del dropped his arms and looked at me like I was crazy. "Nah, no way. You're all that without a speck of makeup, Specs."

I stopped clapping and stood still. Not sure what he meant. "All *what*?"

"All *that*," Del said again, dipping his chin for emphasis. When I continued to blink blankly at him, he rolled his eyes. "Are you trying to be thick? I'm telling you that you're already razzle-dazzle super-*Specs*-tacular just the way you are. I wouldn't change a thing about you, Gypsy Beaumont!"

My mouth fell open. I was still trying to let Del's words sink in when Nola popped up from her stool and snatched a blush brush out of Del's hand. "Here, let me do it," she said.

I was about to object, sure Nola would make me look like a clown if she were the one applying the makeup. Del must have been thinking the same thing; he reached out to try to stop her. But all Nola did was bop the brush against the tip of my nose, once. Like she was putting the finishing touch on a painting.

"There. Perfect." She smiled. "That's all you needed. Now you're ready too!"

"Ready for what?"

"Ready to be my backup singer, of course! I'm guessing that you, Gypsy Beaumont, can bang a mean tambourine."

Chapter 28

EVEN THOUGH I'D ALWAYS loved tambourines, I'd never actually played one. When I'd pointed to a ribboned one in a store once, Poppa told me the house was already noisy enough, just with Tucker in it. My mouth went dry as Nola hooked her arm through mine. The thought of standing on a stage in front of a roomful of strangers made me want to send up an S.O.S.

What if there were a million more people like Shelby Foster in the world? What if half of them were crowded into the restaurant downstairs, ready to turn their backs on me at the first clink of my tambourine? Faced with the possibility of making a fool of myself in public yet again, I tried to convince Nola that she should perform alone.

"Are you kidding me?" she said. "You and I are going to throw the switch on this place, *Miss Specs*. Get ready to get your karaoke on!"

"What about Grandma and Tucker?" I asked as the others push-pulled me toward the stairs. "I vowed I'd never take my eyes off Grandma again."

"Me and Grammy are fine," Tuck called out. "We're watching our shows."

"I promise, it'll only take five minutes," said Nola. "Less than five minutes! Please come with me, Gypsy. The boys can stay up here and look after Mrs. B. I know exactly which song I want to sing. But I won't go onstage without you. I've never actually sung for anyone before. You're a teenager; you know what it feels like to have everyone staring at you. I really need a friend with me."

Teenager? Friend? Did Nola really see me as those things? Inside, I secretly began to twirl. Or maybe that was just the nervous twist of my intestines.

"You can do it, Specs," Del said. I looked to Samson for help, but all my big, dumb brother did was smile.

Two minutes later, I was standing on the karaoke stage. Holding a tambourine. Squinting into way too many lights and faces, and sweating in my pinching snow boots. How I wished my toes were free to wiggle!

If ever there was a time to *stop* time and run, it was now. But Nola looked so excited, I didn't want to be the dark cloud that dropped a foot of snow on her parade.

Tap-*clink*.

Still uncertain, I bumped the tambourine once against my hip. Heart thumping, I looked out into the crowd. Everyone was smiling.

The music started with an energetic piano slide. A ten-second countdown appeared on a screen at Nola's feet and on the monitors situated throughout the room.

3 . . . 2 . . . 1 . . . and Nola's first lyrics popped up on the display.

At first, I tapped my tambourine as softly as I could, trying to match the song's cheerful disco beat without looking too daffy.

Tap-*clink*.

Tap-*clink*.

Tap-*clink*.

Then Nola began to sing and I stopped tap-clinking altogether, forgetting my part in the production. Nola sang with the same zeal and gusto she'd shown when Samson and I had watched her through her bedroom window. It was an upbeat song. A song about a dancing queen who was seventeen. The only problem was . . .

Nola Kim couldn't sing.

At all.

Her voice plummeted down . . . wavered . . . squeaked . . . wobbled . . . and then lifted high into the key of *yikes* for the chorus, making me flinch involuntarily.

I looked quickly around the room, overcome with collywobbles. My stomach somersaulted and my cheeks burned with embarrassment for Nola. I wanted to save her. I wanted to shoo her from the stage before the bachelorette ladies began to boo. Before any babies in the crowd began to cry. Before the soldiers began to throw whipped-cream-covered waffles. It was Nola's moment in the limelight; I didn't want anyone to make her feel like she was less than she believed she was.

Should I stop time? I wondered. If I did, I could drag Nola's time-frozen body from the stage, rescuing her the same way Del and I had rescued everyone from the SUV before it crashed.

Feeling like a traitor, I inched backward into the shadows. But I soon saw that what Nola lacked in talent, she made up for in enthusiasm. And her enthusiasm appeared to be contagious.

As Nola kept singing, I realized that all my worry had been for nothing. There was no reason to stop time. There were plenty of reasons to savor the moment instead.

The bachelorettes weren't booing; they'd raised their glasses, looking like they were having the time of the lives. The soldiers weren't throwing things, but were clapping along. Even Laverne was dancing with a busboy half her size, executing two-handed loop-de-loops that made her towering wig jiggle.

I stepped out of the shadows, feeling terrible for having abandoned my duties as backup singer and tambourine player. Nola was counting on her friend. I refused to become another Shelby Foster. I wouldn't turn my back on Nola Kim, no matter what.

Gripping my tambourine with fresh determination, I began to tap-*clink* it against my hip again—this time, with the same enthusiasm that filled the rest of the room.

I was surprised to see Del and Samson standing in the entrance to the hallway, enjoying the show. They were supposed to be upstairs with Grandma and Tucker. Apparently they hadn't wanted to miss Nola's debut performance. Samson glanced repeatedly over his shoulder, keeping watch over the door to Laverne's apartment. He was staying vigilant—that was good.

My brother must have seen my concern; when I caught his eye and pointed upward, wordlessly indicating Grandma and Tuck, Samson gave me a reassuring thumbs-up, followed by an "everything's A-okay" hand signal. Then he fixed his attention back on Nola, like she was a nightingale from a fairy tale and he never wanted to stop listening to her sing.

Nola's dream was coming true right in front of us. It didn't matter that the real-life version wasn't precisely how she'd pictured it. Or precisely in tune. There was a triumphant spark in her eyes, and her face was luminous. It was clear that in those few precious moments onstage at Volcano Laverne's, with her name in lights outside, Nola wasn't embarrassed. Nola was a pop star.

Following Nola's lead, I began to tambourine my

heart out, not caring how I sounded. I became so absorbed in the tapping and the clinking, I was the last person in the room to notice the commotion, the last person to see the sweating, red-faced man who was clutching at his throat. It was the startling *thunk-clunk* of Nola's microphone hitting the floor, and the deafening, high-pitched *skreeeeee* that followed, that drew my attention at last.

"Someone call 911!" Nola pulled the plug on the karaoke machine and leaped from the stage in one fluid motion, headed straight for the choking man.

There was a moment of confusion, a murmured hullabaloo, and then the room fell silent. No one spoke. No one even whispered. We all held our breath as Nola set to work trying to clear the man's airway. First, she gave him five hard blows to the back where he sat; then, when that didn't work, she used the Heimlich maneuver to deliver five quick thrusts to his abdomen.

Once again, all eyes were on Nola. Only this time no one was dancing, singing, or tapping toes to a beat. The choking man's face went from red to purple. His eyes looked like they were about to pop out. Several of the soldiers moved forward to try to help. But Nola quickly warned them off.

"Everyone, stay back," she cried just before a short rib popped out of her patient's gullet and flew across the room.

The man sagged heavily in his chair, breathing in ragged gasps. His family flung grateful arms around Nola, thanking her. When Nola freed herself from them and turned around, the crowd exploded into deafening applause. Laverne leaped onto the stage and stood next to me, motioning the crowd to its feet.

Hopping up and down, I cheered too, hooting and hollering until my throat hurt.

Laverne waved Del and Samson into the dining room to join the party. Caught up in the excitement, they followed Nola as she waded through a sea of handshakes, fist bumps, and more group hugs from total strangers.

I stepped off the stage to follow too, but found my way blocked. Someone put a flower lei around my neck, making me a part of the Volcano Laverne's family. Everyone wanted to congratulate Nola and tell her what an amazing job she'd done. By the time she reached a table that had enough seats for all of us, she wore three color-ful leis around her neck and a plastic bachelorette-party cowboy hat with the words *Bride's Posse* written on the front.

Nola may have felt like a pop star while she was singing, but now she was an honest-to-goodness hero; judging by the way she glowed, that felt ten times bet-ter. She'd gotten her standing ovation, and she'd gotten it for something she was really good at.

I reached the table seconds after Nola and the boys did, just in time to see the four veterans who had pre-viously been seated there salute her. The vets moved to join another table, relinquishing command of their maple syrup and chili sauce.

Still shaking, Nola took a sip of someone else's hot chocolate, then said: "That was amazing! But did you hear my voice when I was onstage? Wowza! I sound *waaaay* better in my bedroom, with my music turned up loud. Maybe I should become a doctor after all. I didn't realize a bit of first aid could bring down the house."

"You should keep singing too," Samson said ear-nestly, nudging her awkwardly with his free elbow.

"Do you really think so?" Nola reached for Samson's hand and laced her fingers through his, her eyes shining extra-bright. Samson shifted nervously in his seat, but his hand tightened around Nola's fingers.

"Definitely," he replied, nodding a few too many times. "I mean . . . you know, because you love doing it so much."

Del raised a skeptical eyebrow and began to shake his head. He stopped when I kicked his leg under the table.

What would Nola become? I wondered. Would she be a doctor, a singer . . . a stunt car driver? I hoped she'd find a way to be everything she wanted to be. For the first time in months, I didn't think about lowering my glasses to try to look into the future. Maybe it was better to see how things turned out *as* they turned out. Or maybe I was just too occupied watching Samson lean closer to Nola, and Nola lean closer to Samson, waiting for them to—

The crowd in the restaurant erupted into a second round of applause as Nola and Samson kissed.

Why hadn't I seen *that* coming in any of my future visions?

Del grabbed a handful of paper napkins from the dispenser on the table and jokingly scrubbed his eyes. "Aw, man. I did *not* need to see that," he said, laughing. "Somebody, please just blind me now."

As if in response, the overhead lights flickered once . . . twice. A third flicker made the room fall silent. Then a collective cry went up as all of the lights went off. The evening's Big Bad Storm had made one final huff-and-puff, taking the power out. Leaving everyone inside the restaurant fumbling in the dark.

Chapter 29

MY ELDEST BROTHER, ROCKET, was fourteen years older than me. He had gotten his powerful electric savvy before I was even born. Power surges, smashed lightbulbs, and pitch-dark rooms had always been a part of my life. Blackouts didn't frighten me.

As soon as the lights went out inside Volcano Laverne's, everyone began to talk at once. Dim fluorescent emergency lights flashed on, casting eerie shadows across the carpeted walls. It wasn't long before the murky room was alight and sparkling with the firefly glow of phones and tablets as people began to use them as lanterns and flashlights.

"Grandma Pat!" I said, suddenly remembering that we'd left her upstairs, alone with Tucker.

"Tucker!" said Samson. "I'm sorry, Gypsy. I told you I'd look after them." I was sure Samson and I were picturing the same things: Tucker and Grandma upstairs without light or power; Tucker knocking over Laverne's hula dancer lamp; someone stepping on Cap'n Stormy's tail; Grandma Pat falling down Laverne's steep stairway in the dark; Tucker getting scared—then huge.

"Nobody panic!" Laverne's voice rang through the darkened restaurant, like she was talking directly to Samson and me. "Everybody, please. Just stay in your seats until we can get more light in here."

"Let's go," I said. The others were already on their feet.

"We'll follow you, Gypsy," said Samson. I wasn't sure why my brother put me in charge; maybe it was because I'd always seen things nobody else could see, and he thought I was the best person to find an invisible path in the dark. After all, I'd always been able to see *him* when he was invisible. Now I wondered if I'd merely been seeing where he was *about* to be, or where he'd just been. Showing signs of my savvy early, before I turned thirteen.

The four of us clasped hands to keep from getting separated, forming the links of a small human chain. I led the way around tables and chairs and people. But getting from one side of the restaurant to the other turned out to be more difficult than expected; despite Laverne's instructions, nobody stayed seated.

In the time it took us to get to the stairs to Laverne's apartment, Grandpa Bomba could've carved another president into the face of Mount Rushmore, using nothing but a toothpick, if he'd still been alive. With every winding step through the dark, I grew increasingly afraid that things upstairs were not as they should be. I was more certain than ever that I shouldn't have let Grandma and Tucker out of my sight—*again*.

I was right. By the time we reached the top of the stairs, Tucker and Grandma Pat were gone.

"No, no, no, no, no," I said, tearing off my rainbow-flower lei. Why did I keep letting Grandma get away from me?

"They have to be here somewhere," Del tried to reassure me. We searched Laverne's apartment quickly; it wasn't big. There were few places where Tucker and

Grandma could hide. We looked in the bathroom. The bedroom. Behind the sofa. Samson found a flashlight in a drawer in Laverne's kitchenette, but we didn't really need it. Grandma and Tucker had opened the blinds while we were downstairs. The apartment glowed bright with moonlight.

While Del and I continued the search upstairs, Samson and Nola ran back down to the restaurant with the flashlight, checking to see if Tucker and Grandma had rejoined the crowd when none of us were looking. They returned a few minutes later, panting from running up the stairs.

"We couldn't find Mrs. B. or Big Tuck," said Nola. "But it's such a scene down there, I'm not sure we'd see them if they were standing right in front of us. We told Laverne they're missing. She's spreading the word. That squad of marines is getting people organized. They're forming a search party as we speak. Are you guys having any luck, up—?"

Nola abruptly stopped speaking. I followed her gaze to see why.

Both she and Samson were staring out the windows

like they'd been struck dumb by the beauty of the moon and the sight of the snow clouds blowing away to the east, revealing a sky full of stars. The lights of Denver had gone out. But it wasn't the moon or the stars or the shadowy city that made Nola and Samson pause.

I stared out the windows. Not blinking. Not even breathing.

"Is that—?" Samson began. He trailed off, already knowing the answer to his unspoken question.

I nodded miserably. "It *is*. Grandma and Tucker must have pulled the blinds when the lights went out," I said. "Grandma must have seen—"

I found my coat where I'd left it before going downstairs to play the tambourine. I fumbled through the contents of its pockets, pulling out empty candy wrappers and the invitation to Grandma's high school dance.

With shaking fingers, I held the invitation out in front of me, comparing the architecture of the building engraved upon its face to the shape of the building I could see clearly in the distance.

I tried to swallow but couldn't. I felt like I was choking on one of Laverne's short ribs.

I looked again at the image of the Larimer High School clock tower at the top of the invitation. Moving my eyes three inches to the right, I looked out the windows, seeing the ramshackle face of the actual, real-life clock tower. Its broken hands pointed just shy of midnight. The hands on my watch read 10:45. But the time no longer mattered.

What had I done? All I'd wanted was to keep Grandma safe. But everything I'd done that night had been for nothing. In the end, I'd delivered Grandma Pat straight to the front door of her doom. What good were visions of the future if I couldn't change bad things before they happened? What good was stopping time, if I couldn't stop Grandma from moving closer and closer to her fall?

"You don't think—?" said Nola.

Next to me, Del nodded, still staring out the window. "We're all thinking it."

"Grandma Pat and Tucker are headed *there*," I said, pointing to the clock tower. "They've gone to the high school. But how did they get out of the restaurant without us seeing them?"

"Here's how," said Samson. He pulled aside a wicker screen in the corner near the kitchenette, revealing a door. The door led to the fire escape we'd seen outside. Tucker and Grandma hadn't closed the door all the way behind them. The crick of cold air that crept through it made my teeth chatter.

I was jamming my arms into the sleeves of my red coat, ready to plunge through the door and down the fire escape after Grandma and Tucker, when the apartment filled with people. A hardy quartet of youthful marines and a rusty trio of old veterans stormed into the room.

Whether we needed them or wanted them, reinforcements had arrived.

"OORAH!"

I wasn't entirely sure I wanted an entourage of strangers joining our chase. On the one hand, our small, four-kid brigade was now a part of something bigger, a makeshift army of people bound together with one sole purpose: To find Grandma Pat and little Tuck, before anything bad could happen to them.

On the other hand, it was problematic—maybe even

dangerous—to be surrounded by so many people. So many soldiers. The company that joined us now knew nothing about savvies, visions of the future, or little boys who could grow to colossal proportions.

I needed to keep it that way.

Earlier, I'd imagined working for the government as a way to help pay for the damage to Mrs. Kim's car. I'd pictured myself using my savvy skills as a spy, or to stop bombs from exploding. But what would really happen if the military found out about my family and our unexpected talents? Would they try to turn my brothers into weapons? Would they control Tucker with rations of gummy bears, kittens, and face paints? Or would they lock us all up in Area 51 with the aliens, ready to study or dissect us?

Before we set off on our mission, Corporal Vasquez questioned me.

"It appears we've got a real soup sandwich on our hands, kid. Why do you think your brother and your grandmother are headed for the old high school? That building is dangerous. It should be demolished."

I showed Vasquez the winter formal invitation.

"Grandma Pat is sick. She thinks she's still a teenager. She thinks she's going to this dance."

"How can you be sure? If she's that ill, she could've wandered off in any direction. She could be walking around in circles!"

"You need to listen to my sister. She . . . er, knows things," Samson answered carefully. He pulled me closer to him, ready to guard my six. Then he said, "When Gypsy is sure about something, she's sure." Samson shivered in the cold draft still slithering through the apartment. One of the veterans, a man too old and bent to join the rescue party, saw my brother preparing to brave the cold wearing nothing from the waist up but a T-shirt and gauzy leopard-print sling. He took off his army coat and handed it to Samson.

"Thank you, sir," Samson accepted the coat with gratitude, pulling it around himself as best he could.

"Come on, people," Del spoke up, trying to herd the rest of us out the door. "We need to go."

"Yeah, we're wasting time," Nola added.

Time.

What was I going to do about time?

If I halted the ticking seconds now, Del and I could set off on our own. We could leave the soldiers and everyone else behind. But it wouldn't help. My time-stops had no effect on Grandma Pat. She'd keep moving, all the way to the clock tower. She might even leave Tucker behind, wherever he happened to freeze. Then we'd all be scattered again.

Now it was my turn to shiver. Would this be Patrice Beaumont's last night on Earth? Or would she and I get to share more birthdays?

Stopping Tucker and Grandma Pat from reaching Larimer High School was my number one priority. If the squad of soldiers wanted to help, I wasn't going to stop them. Maybe I wouldn't be alone in the end after all.

Chapter 30

DOWN ON THE STREET, surrounded by tall buildings, I immediately lost sight of the high school. It didn't matter; I knew where it was now. The marines appeared to know too. Grandma and Tucker had a head start, and even though they wouldn't be moving fast, I knew from my vision that Grandma could and would get to the top of the clock tower. I knew Grandma Pat was going to fall, and that I had to be there to try to catch her when she did.

How could I explain *that* to Corporal Vasquez and the other marines and veterans who had come along?

A soldier who'd set off at a run in order to scout ahead soon called back over his shoulder. "I've got their tracks, Corporal."

"Show me, Private Anderson!" Corporal Vasquez lifted her camouflaged knees high as she jogged through the snow. The rest of us ran behind her, trying our best to keep up.

Two sets of tracks lay ahead of us: Grandma's shuffling Sorrell treads, and little Tuck's tiny, hopping boot prints.

"We don't need to follow their tracks," I whispered to Samson. "We already know where Grandma and Tucker are going."

"They don't know about your savvy, Gypsy. They don't share the faith I have in you and your visions." After we'd hustled a few more yards, Samson surprised me by asking, "Do you miss them? Your old visions? Or do you like stopping time better?"

I didn't answer right away. As we hurried after the soldiers, I took my glasses off to wipe away the fog from my labored breathing. I paused before returning them to my face—thinking maybe, if I tried hard enough, if I wished powerfully enough, I could get my savvy to switch back. I could find a way to look forward in time, just once more. To see what was going to happen next.

But I already knew, and that's what frightened me.

"I'm not completely sure yet," I told Samson as we made our way closer and closer to the high school. "I think I might like my new one better. What about you?"

Samson also hesitated before answering. Then, sounding almost embarrassed, he said, "I prefer my new one too. I never thought I could ever like being so . . . so bright. So *seen*. So—"

"So hot?" Nola teased. My brother's face turned fire-engine red.

"You guys are nuts," said Del. "If I had the chance to have amazing powers, I wouldn't quibble over which one I liked best. I'd take anything."

"What the—?" Ahead of us, Private Anderson stopped short, pointing at the two sets of footprints he'd been following. "If I didn't know better, I'd say these smaller tracks are getting *bigger*."

It was true. With each step forward, Tucker's footprints grew larger and larger, and farther and farther apart. Three blocks south of Volcano Laverne's, in the middle of the empty, snow-bound street, Grandma Pat's prints disappeared altogether, baffling the band of military trackers. It wasn't long before just one of Tucker's boot prints was big enough for six soldiers to stand in, all of them shaking their heads in disbelief.

"Who are we following?" asked one of the old men. "Paul Bunyan?"

Unlike the soldiers, I could easily guess what had happened. Somehow, for some reason, Tucker had gotten big, Big, BIG. Bigger than he'd ever grown before. Then he'd picked up Grandma Pat to carry her over the snow. It was the only thing that could explain the tracks.

I pictured Grandma Pat sitting criss-cross-applesauce on Tucker's giant palm, like he was King Kong and she was his damsel in distress. I hoped Grandma Pat was holding Cap'n Stormy, and that the kitten wasn't clinging by her teeny-tiny claws to Tucker, a burr stuck inside the lining of his winter coat.

"I-I think we must have lost them somehow, Corporal," Private Anderson said. Looking around, he took off his cap and scratched his head. "Maybe this is where the kid turned into Bigfoot. Ha-ha!" Nobody laughed at Private Anderson's joke.

Samson shot me a worried look. But I knew we

couldn't fret about savvy secrets now, or stand around while the soldiers scratched their bums and britches. The clock hands high up on the high school may have been permanently stuck at eleven fifty-eight, but that didn't mean we needn't hurry.

Pushing through the snow, I crossed the street, jogged on, then crossed another, leaving the others to follow me. With the rest of the search party on my six, I rounded a corner, waiting for my hulking little brother to appear before me at any moment.

"There it is," Del said, reaching my side just as I looked up and saw the high school.

Surrounded by a bent and drooping fence of chain link and barbed wire, the decrepit building stood four stories tall beneath the clock tower. The tower itself added another twenty feet. The doors and first-floor windows were boarded over with graffiti-covered plywood, and plastered with orange signs that read DANGER: NO TRESPASSING. Burdened with heavy swags of snow, veiny tendrils of winter ivy twisted and twined over the bricks of the upper stories. All of the upper-story windows were smashed and broken, leaving dark spaces and eerie, gaping holes.

The lofty architecture of the high school pictured on the winter formal invitation had long since fallen into disrepair and ruin. But it was easy to let my imagination drift back into the past, to a time when the school had been a prominent feature of the city. A proud and noble building.

"Gypseeeeee! S-S-Samsonnnn!" Little Tuck's cries made me forget about buildings and bricks and barbed wire. His voice sounded small and far away. Was he still a giant? Or had he already shrunk back down?

"There!" one of the veterans shouted. "The boy is over there." We all turned to see where he was pointing. Tucker was a tiny ball at the base of the high school. His painted-on cat face had lost all nine of its lives, leaving his cheeks a tear-stained mishmash of rainbow colors. One by one, we slipped through a jaggedy hole in the fence.

"Tucker!" Samson cried as he rushed toward our brother. "Are you hurt?"

"What happened?" I said, when I reached him a second later. "Where's Grandma?"

Tucker looked up at Samson and me as we bent down beside him. He was so upset, at first he didn't even notice the small army we'd brought with us. He sobbed and hiccupped, hardly able to catch his breath. Then, with a tremendous howl, he cried:

"I lost Cap'n Stormy!"

It took nearly two full minutes—two precious, frightening, tock-ticking minutes—before Tucker calmed down enough to be able to tell us what had happened.

"The lights went out in the apartment, Gypsy." Tucker snuffled, wiping his nose on my sleeve.

"There was a blackout, Tuck," I explained, trying to keep my voice calm. "The snow must have knocked out the power." I gestured toward the darkened city. The electricity was out for miles.

"I-I was okay, Gypsy. Rocket makes the power go out all the time when he comes home to visit." Tuck sniffled. "I wasn't scared of the dark. But Grandma was. I opened all the blinds, so she could see better. Then

Grandma saw this building out the window, and she said she wanted to come here—"

"So you told her you'd bring her," I finished for him.

Tucker nodded. He'd made himself big for Grandma. Not because he was upset or angry—but because he loved her and wanted to fix her fears and help her get the thing she wanted most. He'd wanted to make her happy the only way he knew how.

"Grandma had trouble in the snow, Gypsy. So I concentrated really, really hard and got big. Bigger than I've ever been before! Big enough to carry Grandma."

"That's great, Tuck." Samson nodded, making his voice as reassuring as possible to keep Tuck talking. "When Momma and Poppa find out," Samson went on, "I bet they're going to be super-proud."

"Really?" Tucker looked up at us with tear-filled eyes.

Samson glanced at me and shrugged. He and I both knew that Momma and Poppa were probably going to be hopping mad at all of us. But we needed little Tuck to be okay, so that he could tell us exactly where Grandma was—and so that he would stay little in front of all the soldiers.

"I got so big," Tucker went on, "I forgot about Cap'n Stormy. She was in my coat. But she fell out somewhere along the way." Tucker wailed again, sobbing huge sobs between each word as he said, "I . . . set . . . Grandma . . . down so I could look for my kitten. Then I got scared and small again, and I couldn't—"

"You set Grandma down?" I interrupted him. "Where, Tuck? *Where* did you put Grandma?" I had a terrible feeling that I already knew the answer.

Tucker shook his head, like he didn't want to say. Like he was too afraid to tell us.

"You're not in trouble, Tuck. We're not going to get mad."

Tucker sniffed again. Then, slowly, he pointed up. Straight up, in the direction of the clock tower. I craned my neck, but as hard as I tried, I couldn't see Grandma Pat.

"Do it again, Tuck," I said. "Get big. Get Grandma back down now!"

"I caaaan't," Tucker howled. "I tried, Gypsy. But I just stay small and fart, fart, fart. Grandma will be safe up there, won't she? There was a really big ledge for her to stand on."

"Tucker!"

"I have to find Cap'n Stormy!" Tucker disintegrated into a flood of waterworks. Nola took Tucker's hand, nodding to me and Samson.

"You guys go." Nola jerked her chin toward the clock tower. "You already knew Mrs. B. would be up there, Gypsy. I'll help Tucker look for his kitten. He won't be any help to anyone until he finds his fuzzy friend, and someone needs to look after him. Go! You're running out of time."

Time again.

Time, time, time, time, *time.*

I stood up and turned to face the others. Del's fists were clenched; he looked ready for action. The four marines and the two veterans looked befuddled.

"Here's what's happening—" I said. Talking as fast as I could, I briefed the soldiers. "Tucker's kitten is missing and our grandmother is stuck up above us on a ledge on the *outside* of the clock tower. She could fall any minute. I don't have time to explain how any of this is possible. We have to get up *there*." I pointed straight up at the clock tower. "ASAP!"

"Roger that." Corporal Vasquez nodded, understanding the need to follow orders and act without question. Without another word, Vasquez, Anderson, and their fellow marines went to work on the thick wooden boards that covered the nearest window, prying them loose. Giving us a way into the school.

Nola rousted Tucker from his tears and they began to scan the snow, walking away from the rest of us in ever widening circles, searching for the tiny orange kitten. The two old veterans, worn out from their first heart-pumping adventure in decades, quickly fell in step beside Nola and Tucker. Lending their experienced eyes to the search for Captain Stormalong Fuzzypants.

Corporal Vasquez threw her jacket over the fangs of glass that rimmed the broken window. She sent Private Anderson into the building first. Then Vasquez and the other two marines—Private Casey and Lance Corporal Parker—helped boost the rest of us inside.

"Maybe I should have gone kitten hunting instead," Samson grumbled, after he'd been unceremoniously dumped inside the building.

It was dark inside the old high school, and creepy.

Samson held the flashlight he'd taken from Laverne's apartment out in front of him, shining it around the dusty old classroom in which we found ourselves. I glimpsed a chalkboard covered with graffiti, piles of trash and dried-up leaves, drooping cobwebs, and a single broken chair turned on its side.

Following the beam of Samson's flashlight, we moved out of the classroom and down the empty hallway. Our wet boots squeaked against the cracked and dirty floor tiles.

"We have to find the main staircase, then look for access to the tower," barked Corporal Vasquez. As we neared the school's lobby, Vasquez stopped short. She raised a tight fist, barely visible in the dark. A signal for the rest of us to halt.

A loud groan, and the sound of a metal bar scraping across the floor, made the hairs on the back of my neck stand up. My first thought was: *Ghosts!* My second, more rational—more hopeful—thought was: *Grandma Pat!*

I was wrong on both counts.

Chapter 31

IT WASN'T A GHOST or Grandma Pat who haunted the front lobby. It was B-Bug. The soft-spoken bully with fists the size of bricks. The same boy Grandma Pat had mistaken for her beau, Cleavon Dorsey.

"Byron!" Del shouted, pushing his way to the front of the group. B-Bug turned toward us in the dark, gripping a long metal pipe and looking as scary as all get-out. I moved to stand next to Del, ready to stop time if the huge bully lifted the metal pipe and charged.

"Del?" B-Bug raised his hand, shielding his eyes from the flashlight beam Samson leveled in his direction. Byron Berger was covered in dust. His coat was torn.

"Is that you, Del?" B-Bug's breath puffed out in a cloud in front of him, yet even in the dull light of the electric torch I could see he was sweating. "I know you probably hate me, Del—hate Tripp and me both—but will you help? Part of the ceiling caved in right after we got here. Now Tripp's legs are stuck. He's not hurt . . . I don't think. But I can't get him out."

Corporal Vasquez grabbed the flashlight from Samson. She lowered the beam, scanning the rubble and debris strewn across the lobby, stopping when the light fell across Travis Kaminski the Third's pale, spotted face.

Pinned to the floor, Tripp looked up at us from beneath a mound of masonry that buried him from the waist down.

"Help me, Del," cried Tripp. His eyes rolled wildly in the flashlight's yellow beam. "Help me, and I'll forget everything. I'll delete the picture. I'll leave you alone. I'll never step foot inside your uncle's store, or steal anything again, I promise. I'll even let you give me a makeover every day for a week when we get back to school—in the middle of the cafeteria, during lunchtime—just to make it up to you."

"Huh! My gran would have considered that a waste of good makeup," Del muttered at my side.

"I've been trying to free Tripp for hours, Del." B-Bug shook his head. "But I haven't been able to. Not by myself. I'm strong. But not strong enough. Maybe you and your friends could help?" B-Bug squinted into the light again. I wondered if he could see exactly what kind of friends Del had brought with him. I doubted Tripp or B-Bug had expected Del to appear flanked by a platoon of United States Marines.

Why were Tripp and B-Bug here? How had they known Del was going to be at the high school? Not even Del had known he'd be coming here when he left the bus station with me. He thought he was taking me as far as Aardman's Flowers. Tripp had sent that text, telling Del they were coming for him. But Del thought the message was only meant to scare him.

Next to me, Del said nothing. I could tell he was just as baffled as I was by the appearance of the bullies at the high school. Vasquez moved closer to Tripp and B-Bug. The other soldiers followed, stepping out of the shadows.

"Who . . . who are you?" B-Bug demanded, his eyes widening in surprise. He raised his metal pipe defensively, looking like a baseball player coming up to bat, ready to swing at the strangers in front of him. But as Vasquez drew closer, B-Bug dropped the pipe and said, "Have you guys come to help?" As soon as he said it, I remembered why I was there.

Drat and dragonflies! I was wasting time. I had to get to the clock tower. I had to reach Grandma Pat.

Chuffing out my breath, I pushed past the others, heading in the direction of a wide concrete staircase I'd seen when Samson's flashlight beam passed over it. I adjusted my glasses. Already, my eyes were growing accustomed to the darkness. It wasn't completely pitch-black on the stairway; moonlight peeked in through the dozens of broken windows above, dappling the steps with jagged shards of dim light. Samson and Del were right behind me.

"Hey, wait! I don't want you kids going up there on your own," Vasquez called after us. I ignored her. There was no way I was going to risk my grandmother's life to help rescue a thieving bully like Tripp. There were four strapping marines who could do that without me.

"Anderson, Parker, Casey!" The echo of Corporal

Vasquez's voice followed Samson, Del, and me up the stairs. "You three stay down here and get this kid out of the rubble. I'll go up to the tower to help look for the old lady." The corporal's boots were on the steps behind us a second later.

Vasquez left the flashlight in the lobby with the other three soldiers, giving them a light to see by while they worked to free Tripp. I didn't have any more time to waste wondering how Tripp and B-Bug had come to be here. My only thoughts were for Grandma Pat. My vision was coming to pass, but I still didn't know how it would end.

I glanced down at my red coat sleeves. Would I have the strength to catch Grandma and hold on to her? Only time would tell.

I took the stairs two at a time for the first three flights. When I stumbled at the top of the fourth flight, breathing hard, Del caught my arm, keeping me from falling.

"You good, Specs?"

"I'm good," I said, relieved to see a crooked spiral

staircase right in front of us—a listing, twisting iron ladder that led straight into the heart of the clock tower.

Corporal Vasquez may have been a United States Marine, but I was still the first one on the stairs. My boots clang-clang-clanged up the rusted metal steps as fast as my feet could go. I was heedless to the way the staircase swayed. I was deaf to the way the rickety metal fittings creaked and groaned. The others couldn't match my speed.

I counted the steps the same way I counted heartbeats whenever I stopped time: Ten . . . twenty . . . thirty-three . . . forty-seven . . . fifty.

Fifty steps up, I found myself standing in the small square room that housed the clock machinery. Rods and beams jutted here and there, leading from a large wooden gear box in the center of the room to the four separate faces of the clock. One face for each direction. North, south, east, and west.

The room glowed, drenched in filtered moonlight. Cobwebs hung like party streamers. Powdery gray grime was thick upon the floor, like forgotten stores of fairy dust. Grandma Pat was outside, hugging the V shape of the Roman numeral five, balancing precariously on the ledge that ringed the tower. All I could see of her was her silhouette, a shadow puppet of a time-forgotten Cinderella swaying against the glass of the southern clock face. The clock's giant hands both pointed heavenward above her, forever stuck at 11:58 as if it were always just a hairsbreadth away from pumpkin hour. The hour when magic failed.

Without pausing another moment to think—or to wait for Del, then Samson, then Corporal Vasquez to reach the top of the spiral staircase, one after the next—I raced across the small room at the top of the tower, tripping over a riffraff of fallen clockwork parts. I pressed my hands against the inside of the clock face. I could see no trapdoors or any other openings in the glass in front of me. No way to pull Grandma Pat safely inside.

A metal rod rolled away from me as I kicked it, making a ringing, clanging sound. I hunted at my feet, searching for something I could use to break the glass. Finding just the right piece of metal—a solid tube of steel short enough for me to wield, yet heavy enough to do some damage—I called out to my grandmother. I spoke softly at first, not wanting to startle her and be the one to make her fall.

"Grandma! It's me, Gypsy. Or . . . or Nettie Arbuckle. Or whoever you need me to be. Just hold on tight and don't be scared. Stay right where you are. I'm going to break the glass so you can come in from the cold. Try to hang on!"

I braced myself and pulled back my arm. Then, with every bit of strength I had, I struck the thick glass with the metal rod. My first blow only cracked it. A fine line ran across the entire pie-shaped wedge between the six and the nine. I kicked as hard as I could at the glass below the Roman numeral seven, then I struck again with the pipe . . . once . . . twice . . . three times, until the entire wedge-shaped pane shattered outward, raining down into the deep drifts of snow, six stories below.

"I think I'd like to go home now," I heard Grandma say in a shaking voice.

As the others raced toward me, I peeked out of the hole I'd made in the clock face. I watched Grandma turn to look at me, the glitter gel making her own face sparkle and glow in the moonlight. I saw her boot slip and her shimmering hands reach out to grab . . . nothing.

Nothing but air.

It happened exactly like my vision. Grandma's mouth opened in a surprised O. Her tiara flew off as her milkweed curls floated up around her face. Her skirts flew up too, exposing her skinny legs.

When I'd had my premonition, staring into the mirror in the church bathroom, *this* was the moment I'd closed my eyes. From this split second onward, Grandma Pat's fate was a mystery to me.

I reached, reached, reached for Grandma. And in the best and bravest moment of my life, without a thought for the sixty-foot drop below me, I made a leap of faith.

Or a leap of sheer stupidity.

Throwing myself out of the hole in the clock face, I scrabbled to catch hold of Grandma. My fingers found her wrists and held on tight. Only then did I realize that I was now falling too.

If only my switched-up savvy had given me the wings I'd longed for, or the power to levitate. Those abilities would have been much more useful.

Then I felt hands wrap around the ankle of my right boot. Breaking my fall. Jerking my body to a painful stop and making me feel as though I was being ripped in two. Even as thin and frail as she was, Grandma Pat's weight threatened to pull my arms out of their sockets as she and I dangled below the clock.

"Uff!" The wordless sound puffed from my lungs as I hung on to Grandma with all my might. I refused to look down. I didn't want to see how far away the ground was.

"I've got you, Specs." Del's voice sounded strained. For the first time that night, I was thankful my snow boots were so snug. If my right boot had been any looser, Grandma and I would've already fallen.

"If you've got me, who's got you?" I called up to Del.

"Me—I do!" Samson's voice came from somewhere above Del. "I can't hang on much longer, though, my shoulder's killing me. Corporal Vasquez!" Samson cried. "I need your help."

Turned out, Samson was holding on to the back of Del's belt with his one good hand, leaning backward with his feet braced against the clockworks. Del was halfway out of the clock himself, having thrown himself against the ledge to grab my ankle.

"I've got you covered, kid," came a woman's voice. Then I felt myself being slowly lifted up. I gripped Grandma Pat's wrists with renewed resolve, knowing that Corporal Vasquez was helping now. Grandma made a whimpering noise that nearly broke my heart.

"It's going to be okay, Grandma," I told her. "We're not alone. You'll never be alone again, I promise." But as my palms began to sweat, and my fingers began to slip, I knew the others were going to be too late. They might be able to rescue me, but I couldn't hold on to Grandma by myself much longer. After everything we'd been through, in the end, Grandma Pat was still going to fall.

That's when I hollered for the one person who still had a savvy that could help. The one person who, against all odds, had gotten a switched-up savvy five years early.

"TUCKER! I need you! I need you *right now*!"

I screamed for little Tuck, and capital B-I-G *BIG* Tuck came.

Chapter 32

SOMETIMES WE SURVIVE OUR falls. We catch ourselves, or someone else catches us. Or we go down, scraping our knees, our chin, our elbows, or our pride. We might cry a little, then get up and find some rainbow-colored Band-Aids. If we're lucky, life goes back to normal.

Anderson, Casey, and Parker were still inside the school, helping B-Bug free Tripp from the rubble. Nola and the two old veterans were racing around the corner of the building, moving toward us. I was relieved to see one of the vets cradling a ball of orange-striped fur in his arms. As far as I could tell, Corporal Vasquez was the only member of the expanded rescue party who'd seen Tucker grow . . . Grow . . . GROW. Vasquez was the only one from her platoon who'd watched Tucker catch Grandma the moment she slipped from my grasp. And she was the only one to hitch a ride back down to the ground with us on Tucker's open palm.

Visibly shaken, Vasquez had watched Tucker shrink back down to his normal small size. Even I had been stunned by Tucker's goliath feat. I'd had no idea he could get so very, *very* large.

The corporal recovered surprisingly fast, all things considered. I supposed that Vasquez, in her time as a soldier, had probably seen plenty of things that I'd never seen before. Things that might be equally unbelievable, in their own way. Perhaps watching a little boy turn into a giant—becoming as big and as brave as he knew how be, in order to save someone else—well, maybe that was something Corporal Vasquez could understand completely.

Still, the experience left the corporal stammering and off-balance. She kept looking around, like she'd just been monumentally pranked by her buddies and was now waiting for someone to jump out with a camera, and yell: "Gotcha!"

"Is . . . is someone going to explain to me what just happened here?"

Little again, Tucker cupped both hands around his mouth and shout-whispered to Vasquez: "I got really big and saved everyone."

"Yeah . . . I got that. Outstanding. But—but . . . *how*?"

"Could you maybe forget what you just saw, Corporal?" I asked, hoping she wouldn't pull a satellite phone out of her jacket and call for a team of helicopters, a supply of elephant tranquilizers, and a giant net with which to capture my youngest brother.

Vasquez gave me a long, stony stare. Then she swore under her breath and shrugged. "Forget what? I didn't see anything, kid."

When we all looked at her in surprise, Vasquez held up her hands and said, "If I start talking about the jolly young giant here, I'll get kicked out of the Corps on a psych discharge, quicker than a boot-camp haircut. *Improvise, adapt, overcome.* That's what we marines are trained to do. Right now, kid, I'm adapting."

I felt as though I'd been doing the same thing all night: Adapting to my switched-up savvy; improvising the rescue of my grandmother; trying to overcome every new fear and obstacle in my path.

"I think your grandma needs some rack time," said Vasquez. She continued to shake her head, like something inside it had rattled loose and she was trying to knock everything back in place. "Let's get the old lady inside, out of the weather, and see if the others need help freeing that other boy from the rubble. Anderson was going to call for help—a rescue team should be on its way here shortly. They'll have blankets and water for everyone. Your grandmother will be taken care of. She should be out of danger now."

Relief washed over me. My final savvy vision had come to pass and Grandma and I had both survived the fall.

This time, we entered the abandoned high school from the back, finding a gap in the plywood sheeting that led us into an old gym at the rear of the building. It was a quicker and easier way inside than the one we'd first taken. I wondered if Tripp and B-Bug had gotten into the school the same way, looking for Del.

Vasquez wanted to carry Grandma Pat inside. But Samson and Tucker insisted that they be the ones to support our grandmother as she shuff-shuffled back into the building. Grandma Pat shook and shivered, mumbling about TV shows, tuna sandwiches, and loud boys with enormous hands. Her eyes were unfocused behind her glasses. Her tiara was gone for good. I hoped her Old-timer's would make her forget the trauma atop the clock tower, quickly.

My arms ached and my spine felt like it had been stretched three inches longer. I didn't think I'd ever forget the sensation of Grandma Pat slipping from my grip, six stories up. Or the relief I'd felt at not having to be alone at the end of my adventure. My brothers, my friends—even the United States Marine Corps—had been there to help. Someone had been looking out for me after all.

Our footfalls echoed as we entered the cavernous gymnasium at the back of the building. The gym's wooden floorboards had been torn out long ago, leaving a rough surface of hard-packed dirt and cracked concrete. We kicked through the dry leaves, aluminum cans, and shredded plastic shopping bags that had blown inside over the years. Here and there, snow lay in strangely patterned drifts across the floor, where it had gusted through the broken skylights in the roof.

It was shadowy inside the gym, but not completely dark. With the skylights smashed out, and most of the windows gone, the moonlight held free rein; it speckled the gymnasium floor and lit the backboards of the rusted basketball hoops. Moonbeams illuminated dusty rafters and rotting bleachers. Powerless electrical cables hung down from the ceiling like dead vines.

I didn't know when Del had linked his fingers through mine again, but I was happy that he had. We'd done it! We'd gotten through the scariest vision of the future my savvy had ever shown me. After jumping from the clock tower, taking a leap of faith that somehow everything would be all right, I knew I had the strength to face whatever time brought next. I'd just take life moment by moment, trying my best to keep my eyes open as I moved forward.

Samson and Tucker deposited Grandma Pat on the nearest, most solid-looking bleacher. Then, as Nola and the two vets fumbled their way into the gym, Tucker rushed to the man who held his kitten.

"You found her! You found Cap'n Stormy."

We didn't have to see if B-Bug and the marines needed our help digging Tripp out of the rubble. They found us a moment later.

"Oorah!" barked Private Casey, marching into the gym.

"We got him out," said Lance Corporal Parker, right behind him.

Anderson and B-Bug carried Tripp into the gymnasium between them. Using a two-person hold, they clasped each other's arms to make a seat for the skinny boy.

"What the heck, Del?" Tripp snarled when he saw us. "I thought your girlfriend said there was going to be a party here tonight! Were you two plotting the whole time, trying to lead me and B-Bug into this death trap? Is that why you left that stupid, bloody note? You're going to regret messing with Travis Kaminski the Third. Give me back my phone! I'm gonna ruin you."

A party? Had I told Tripp there was going to be a party? I supposed that, in a way, I had. When I first met Del at his uncle's store, I had asked him if he'd seen my grandma, explaining that she thought she was going to a dance at Larimer High. Tripp had overheard only a part of our conversation. He'd jumped to the wrong conclusion.

"I said, give me my phone, Del," Tripp snarled again.

I looked at Del, wondering what he'd do next. I couldn't see into his future. Would he run away? Would he stand his ground, cuss Tripp out, or smash Tripp's phone into a million tiny pieces?

I closed my eyes and stopped time without a whisper of a word. Then I crossed my arms and turned on Del. With the others frozen, and Grandma Pat still resting on the bleachers, Del and I may as well have been alone inside the gym.

"Exactly what's so bad about the picture on Tripp's phone, Del?"

"You stopped the clocks just to ask me that?"

"Yes!"

Del laughed. But he also looked pleased, like it made him happy that I'd stopped time for him.

"Why does that horrid boy think you wouldn't want anyone to see your sister?"

"Um, Specs?" Del laughed again, a bit nervously this time. "I told you back at the bus station—I'm an only child."

That's right, I thought. He did tell me that. I knew something had felt wrong earlier, when Samson asked Del about the photo.

"So, explain," I said. "There may be two thousand people in this city, and twenty-seven in Tuvalu, who are wandering around right now with us, but I'm certain not one of them cares about some silly picture on a bully's phone. Show it to me?"

Del hesitated, then he fished the phone out of his pocket and displayed the photo Tripp considered so embarrassing.

I understood what I was looking at immediately. It was a picture of Del. Wearing makeup.

"It was the first day you stopped time, Gypsy—" Del began to explain, rolling his eyes and then looking down at his feet. "Last Sunday. Remember? That was the first time you killed the clocks, right? Man, that day went on forever!"

How could I forget the day everything switched? It

was the day Poppa told us Grandma Pat was sick and she needed to come live with us; the day Samson caught fire and Tucker grew big for the first time; the day I'd spent feeling endlessly alone, cleaning the house and eating cereal straight from the box, doing everything I could to keep bad things from happening. I had walked to the highway and back. I had tried on all of Momma's jewelry, and her makeup. I'd played with makeup that day! I smiled. Apparently, I hadn't been the only one.

"I was working in Uncle Ray's shop when you made the world stop turning," Del continued to explain. "For a while, I kept stocking the shelves, not sure what was happening. But soon I ran out of stuff to do. I ate potato chips. I played tic-tac-toe by myself. I wandered around the bus station, switching everybody's hats around. Tripp and B-Bug were there, frozen halfway down the escalators. If I could've seen into the future the way you used to be able to do, I might've turned Tripp and B-Bug around, or tied bells to their shoes or something. If I'd known Tripp was on his way to Ray's store to steal stuff and threaten me, I would never have started messing around with all of the makeup behind Gran's old cosmetics counter."

I listened to Del tell his story, feeling sorry that my time-stop had caused him trouble.

"I wish you'd figured out how to restart time sooner, Specs. I was bored out of my mind! So bored, I decided to give *myself* a makeover. I should've noticed that something had changed the minute people in the bus station started moving again. But I didn't. I was too busy trying to put on a pair of fake eyelashes—those suckers are tricky! I looked up from the mirror and Tripp and B-Bug were standing right in front of me. Tripp already had his phone up in my face."

Del frowned. "For the last week, Tripp's been trying to take something my gran taught me to love, the one thing I'm actually good at, and use it to make me feel bad about myself."

I knew how Del felt. Shelby had made me feel bad about myself too, when I was in Flint's Market.

Del stared long and hard at Tripp, then said, "I'm going to let him do it, Specs. Go ahead and restart time. I'm ready to face this guy."

"Are you sure?"

"I'm positive."

As soon as I set the world into motion again, Tripp cackled: "Maybe we should start calling him *Delphine* now instead of Del. Right, B-Bug?"

"Really, Tripp? *Really?*" Del shook his head. "I'm pretty sure I remember you begging for my help a few minutes ago. I didn't think you'd go back to being a horse's backside quite so fast. I don't even *care* about your stupid picture. Here, you can have your phone back." Del tossed the phone in Tripp's direction, letting it clatter to the floor. "Go ahead, Travis. Send my picture to anyone you want. I look *smokin'* in that snap. My gran would've been proud."

Private Anderson, who was still helping B-Bug hold Tripp aloft, looked from Del to the slippery salamander boy in his arms. Anderson scowled at Travis Kaminski the Third, and dropped him like a hot potato. "Kid, I get the feeling you can walk alone."

Tripp landed squarely on the floor. B-Bug had dropped him too.

Chapter 33

AS TRIPP GROANED ON the floor, B-Bug drew a crumpled and blood-stained paper napkin from his pocket. He held it up with an apologetic half smile. "Next time you run away from someone who's about to clock you, Del, you might not want to leave a note saying where you're going." Tripp and B-Bug had found Grandma's note after Del discarded it. The note that read:

I don't care what you think.
I'm going to the dance at Larimer High tonight.
Don't come after me!

"So, where's the dance?" asked B-Bug. "Wasn't there supposed to be a rave here tonight or something?"

"Cleavon!" When Grandma saw B-Bug across the shadowy gymnasium, she leaped to her feet with the energy of someone closer to sixteen than seventy-six. "Cleavon Dorsey! I've been waiting for you for ages." Grandma's eyes shone brightly, as though she saw a thousand twinkle lights and silver streamers no one else could see, decorations for the winter formal going on inside her mixed-up mind.

When B-Bug saw Grandma coming, he dropped the napkin. Grandma's note floated away from him, riding on an invisible current of air and joining the rest of the debris time had littered in the shadows.

Samson moved to block Grandma's way as she shuffled toward B-Bug. "That's not Cleavon, Grandma," he said softly. "That's—"

"Don't, Samson," I said, stopping my brother from interfering. "Let her go. It'll be okay. Trust me." I crossed my fingers, hoping I was right to place so much hope in Byron Berger. It was a smaller leap of faith this time, not nearly as big or scary as the one I'd made up on the tower. But Grandma needed this. She'd never gotten to go to her winter dance. It was time she did.

I watched Grandma shuffle-twirl across the room toward her mirage of Cleavon Dorsey. I knew there would be many un-magical moments in Grandma Pat's future. Her illness—her *Old-timer's disease*—guaranteed it. But for one shiny, happy moment, Patrice Beaumont's inner world was as full of enchantment as a thrice-charmed fairy tale.

"Oh, Cleavon," Grandma sighed when she stood in front of B-Bug at last, reaching up to lock her fingers behind the boy's thick neck.

B-Bug went rigid, and his eyes darted wildly between Grandma and Del. But he didn't step away. He didn't push my grandmother to the side or tell her to back off—not even when she leaned one cheek against his wide chest and said, "I never thought this night would come, Cleavon. You don't know what I've been through to get here. Daddy told me I had to toughen up, and I did, for a while. But it wasn't any fun. It feels like I've been dreaming of slow dancing with you for sixty years."

B-Bug, to his credit, patted Grandma gently, if awkwardly, on the back and said:

"Er . . . me too?"

Then, as if he knew that he alone had the power to be Patrice Beaumont's prince for a brief turn, Byron put his hands around her waist and slowly, carefully, began to waltz her around the gym.

Sometimes it just takes one person to change everything.

Next to me, tough-as-nails Corporal Vasquez sniffed sentimentally. Maybe love wasn't such a battlefield after all.

"That's just beautiful." Vasquez sniffed again. But her expression turned Marine Corps–tough when Lance Corporal Parker glanced her way, looking poised and ready to ask her to dance. It didn't matter. Soon everyone was dancing. Everyone but Tripp, the two old veterans . . . and me.

There wasn't any music, but no one seemed to care. Samson held a single pinkie finger out to Nola. Nola hooked her own pinkie around his and dipped a playful curtsy. Vasquez bent low to link her arm through Tucker's, before Lance Corporal Parker could take another shot at asking her to dance. The rest of the group cut loose on their own, to whatever music they hummed, or heard inside their heads.

I hung back. I wanted to dance—I did. But it had

only been a week since I'd danced through the aisles of Flint's Market, leaping about to the tune from *The Nutcracker,* with my arms filled with boxes of soap. A lot had happened in a week, but a few of Shelby's barbs were still stuck under my skin.

Before I could linger too long over painful scenes from my past, Grandma Pat broke away from B-Bug and grabbed my hand.

"Dance with me, Nettie!" she crowed. "Don't be such a wallflower." Grandma wrapped one arm around me, then let me go again, sending me spinning. I couldn't believe it. Grandma Pat had hugged me! She'd danced with me! I didn't even care that she'd called me Nettie.

Sirens sounded in the distance, growing louder, reminding me that Private Anderson had called emergency crews to our location. Our magical winter formal would soon be over. The pumpkin hour was drawing near. But now I knew that, even after the most frightening falls, we can pick ourselves up and dance.

"Come on, Gypsy," said Del, catching me by the hand as soon as I stopped spinning. "I'll teach you how to moonwalk."

I took off my glasses, wiping away tears of happiness. I was about to return my sparkly purple spectacles to my nose when I stopped.

Staring into the blur around me, I imagined that I still had a savvy that let me see into the past. I pictured the old high school building as a living, breathing character, allowing me to peek into its dusty history—letting me watch every prom, homecoming dance, and winter formal that had ever taken place inside its rubble-strewn gymnasium. In my mind, I saw a hundred different parties. A thousand transparent dancers overlapping. And among these ghostly figures, a small group of solid, living, breathing ones: Grandma Pat waltz-shuffling slowly, back in B-Bug's gentle arms; Corporal Vasquez bending down to swing-dance wildly with little Tuck; Del moonwalking next to me, waiting for me to mirror his smooth steps; and Samson and Nola, slow dancing to whatever love song Nola might be softly singing.

While Tripp and the old veterans rested on the wooden bleachers, and Privates Casey and Anderson, and Lance Corporal Parker, all boogied on their own, I let myself take it all in. Until—*Mew! Mew!*—Captain

Stormalong Fuzzypants rubbed up against my leg, trilling and mewling and being button-cute.

I put my glasses back on and picked up the tiny kitten. I had no doubt that Cap'n Stormy was now a permanent part of the family. In fact, I suspected we might return home to Kansaska-Nebransas with not just one cat, but two. If Tucker had any say in the matter, the growly old cat that sunned itself on Grandma's stoop would probably be coming with us as well.

I wished we could take Del and Nola home with us instead. After everything we'd been through together that night, I'd miss my new friends when we left Colorado.

"Hey, Gypsy!" Tucker hollered, snapping my attention back to the present in time to watch Vasquez spin him around in a swing-dance pretzel. "Aren't you going to keep dancing with the rest of us?"

I laughed, knowing that I would keep twirling, now and forever. Nothing would ever switch that up again.

Chapter 34

IT TAKES TIME TO recover from a storm. Days, even weeks, may pass before the sun comes back, warm and bright, melting the ice and snow of an unexpected blizzard. Sometimes the fingers, toes, and hearts of the storm-struck stay cold and numb forever. Other times, clear blue skies return faster than expected, leaving everything glistening and serene. Leaving us standing stronger for having made it through rough weather.

Poppa got to Evergreen a day later than expected. But he got there. Once he heard about Grandma Pat's great escape, and the madcap adventure my brothers and I went on to rescue her, the world would've had to break in two to keep him away.

"What were you kids thinking?" Poppa asked, after

giving each of us a big, long hug as soon as he arrived. But after Samson and Tucker and I took turns telling him our tale, after we explained every crazy choice we'd made, and exactly why we'd made it, Poppa rubbed his knuckles against the scar on his bald head, and said:

"I'm very proud of you all."

When Tucker and I grinned, and Samson's eyes glowed crimson with pride, Poppa's face grew stern again. He quickly added, "Let's just hope none of you have to do anything like that again." Then he hugged us all a second time, and a third. He hugged Captain Stormalong Fuzzypants, and when Grandma woke from her nap, Poppa hugged her too. To my surprise, she let him.

"My baby boy has come home," Grandma Pat cried, pinching my father's cheeks.

"I've come to *bring* you home, Mother," said Poppa. "You're going to live with us now."

Grandma wrinkled her nose in distaste. "With you and that so-called *perfect* woman you married?"

I glanced at Momma, waiting for her to trip, poke herself in the eye, or fall face-first into a piece of cake. But Momma didn't do any of those things. She simply laughed, and her laugh was like church bells ring-a-ding-dinging on a daffodil-spring morning.

She said, "I don't think you need to worry about that 'so-called perfect' woman anymore, Patrice. I'm not sure *that* woman will ever be returning."

As far as any of us could tell, the switch was a permanent phenomenon. "Do you think Grandma Pat has a savvy after all?" I asked Momma quietly as Poppa settled Grandma back in her recliner. "Do you think Grandma has the power to change people? Could that be why our savvies got switched up?"

Momma wrapped one arm around my shoulders as she thought about my questions. "Maybe, sweetheart, when faced with a situation we can't change, we find extraordinary ways to change ourselves instead."

I squinted at her, unsure how being less-than-perfect could ever be extraordinary.

Momma chuckled when she saw my doubtful expression. "If I can learn to laugh at my mistakes, Gypsy, my new talent for blunders guarantees I will never, *ever* stop laughing. A sense of humor can work wonders when it comes to softening the harder parts of life."

Unfortunately, a sense of humor alone wasn't wondrous enough to fix Mrs. Kim's annihilated SUV. Momma and Poppa were a thousand times more understanding about our misadventure in the city than Nola's parents were. But just because we Beaumonts had been dealing with savvy marvels and mishaps for years and years, that didn't mean my brothers and I were off the hook. Like Nola, we had to face the consequences of our actions. Even though the Kims' insurance helped cover the cost of replacing the SUV, we had to make amends for destroying it.

Before leaving Colorado, Nola, Samson, Tucker, and I faced a tribunal of parents. The four of us sat across from the four of them and pled our case:

"We were trying to save Mrs. B.!" said Nola.

"We didn't mean to cause so much damage," Samson mumbled, working hard to keep his cool in front of Nola's parents, now that his fiery savvy had begun to rekindle.

"We aren't a fiendish horde of rabble-rousers," I said. "We're—"

"We're heroes!" Tucker crowed, interrupting me. "Really *big* heroes. Wanna see how big?"

"No, Tucker, they don't!" everyone shouted at once, startling poor Mr. and Mrs. Kim, who were already looking at my family like we were a herd of neon-green elephants.

Samson had asked Nola to keep our secret from her parents; then he blew our cover himself by standing in Nola's front yard and drawing blazing hearts in the air, in the middle of the night, not realizing that Mr. and Mrs. Kim were both home and watching him through the window.

After squirming in our seats for an uncomfortable length of time, we were told that each of us would have to choose our own penance. Each of us would have to pick a way to show how remorseful we were about the past, and how responsible we could be in the future.

Nola immediately offered to do volunteer work at the local hospital. "I'll also wait until I'm seventeen to get my driver's license," she added quickly, beefing up her punishment without even being asked. After steering her mom's SUV over an embankment and into an icy creek, Nola was in no hurry to get behind the wheel of a car again anytime soon.

I expected Samson to choose a quiet and solitary task for his act of atonement, like shelving books in the shadowy stacks of the public library. He surprised me when he said, "I'll contact the explorer program at the fire station when we get home and see if they'll take me on as a junior firefighter."

"Yeah, and I promise to send Mr. and Mrs. Kim every piece of candy I get the next time it's Halloween," Tucker said, nodding solemnly as if he was making the biggest sacrifice of all.

Remembering all of the old photos and mementos I'd sorted and packed at Grandma's house, I knew right away what I wanted to do.

"I'd like to help Grandma decorate her bedroom in Kansaska-Nebransas—to make the future she has left as nice as it can be. I want to create a memory album for her too, so she can look at the scenes and the people from her past that she can't remember anymore."

No one objected to any of our plans.

My wild ride through the stormy streets of Denver had taught me a lot about scumbling my new abilities. I looked forward to stopping the clocks when we got home again. I'd be able to pet newborn fawns in spring-time without frightening the does. I'd be able to freeze the firework finale on the Fourth of July, so that I could enjoy it longer. I'd even be able to stop time just to dance a hundred merry, barefoot circles around Shelby Foster and her new friends if I wanted to.

And yet, there were nineteen million people I couldn't forget about. Nineteen million people who shared my birthday. A Dutch boy in Holland, a tour guide on the Great Wall of China, twin girls who took dance lessons in Denver . . .

None of those people knew about twirly-whirly Gypsy Beaumont from Kansaska-Nebransas, and her time-stopping savvy.

But one boy did.

One sweet and funny boy, who had a remarkable talent for transforming other people and helping them see the best in themselves. Just like he'd done for me. Antwon Delacroix had told me I was razzle-dazzle super-*Specs*-tacular just the way I was. And I believed him.

Before saying our good-byes in Denver, Del and I

had made a solemn vow to remain friends—and Time-less Crusaders—for as long as there were clocks on walls, and people who needed rescuing. I told him to call on me whenever he needed time to stop for a little while, and he promised he would.

Occasionally, I thought back to the first, swirling-whirling savvy premonition I'd had on the morning of my thirteenth birthday. I had seen . . .

Tucker.

Older.

Blowing out thirteen candles on a cake, and then—*Gadzooks!*

If my vision of Tucker's thirteenth birthday came to pass, the way the rest of my savvy visions had, Tucker's savvy was destined to switch again. Maybe Tucker would still be able to grow big-Big-BIG in the future. But the moment he blew out his candles, he would also be able to become SMALL-Small-small.

In just over five years, Tucker was going to shrink down to the size of one of his plastic army men and ride off on his own adventures astride Cap'n Stormy, chasing mice and squirrels and bullies and bad guys. Both imaginary and real. Proving once again that time brings unexpected and extraordinary changes for everyone.

A week after we moved Grandma Pat to Kansaska-Nebransas and got her settled into Grandpa Bomba's old room, Momma and I took her with us to Flint's Market. We needed to restock the pantry. We also needed to get Grandma away from the clamor of drills and hammers. Carpenters and electricians were still working to repair the giant Tucker-shaped hole in the front of the house, and the racket was too much for Grandma to bear. Momma hoped the familiar aisles of a grocery store might put her at ease.

Mr. Flint's eyes nearly popped out of his head when he spotted us. But he softened when he saw me holding the arm of a frail old woman wearing a flannel nightgown under her winter coat, and he didn't bar us from the store. Mr. Flint didn't even kick us out when Momma tripped and fell, knocking over a towering display of tissues.

After helping Momma pick up all the tissue boxes, I led Grandma to the floral department, where bright clusters of balloons floated above the flowers and the potted plants. Mr. Flint had taken down the winter holiday decorations, at last. "The Little Drummer Boy" no longer *rum-pa-pumm*ed over the loudspeakers. Now love songs filled the air, and everything was decorated in Valentine's Day pinks and reds, reminding me of the way Samson and Nola had secretly kiss-kiss-kissed behind Grandma's house, right before we left Evergreen. Since we'd gotten home, every day had become a lovey-dovey, broody-moody sweetheart's day for my older brother. He'd even started writing poetry.

Buoyed by the sights and scents around me, I sighed happily. I almost wished I'd run into Shelby Foster again inside Mr. Flint's store, just so I could tell her that I didn't give a flying fig about what she thought of me or my silly, dancing, flower-picking ways. I didn't care what she'd think about me having a grandmother who wandered through the grocery store in a nightgown, either.

"What are we doing here?" Grandma asked as I held up different blooms for her to smell and touch and see—a rose, a lily, a carnation. Even a bird of paradise.

"You never got to buy a boutonniere for Cleavon," I

told Grandma. "You wanted to get him a flower for his lapel, remember? I thought you might want to pick out a special posy now—something to remember him by, even though the dance has come and gone."

"Dance? What dance?" Grandma scowled and waved one hand dismissively. "I don't know what you're nattering on about, girly. What . . . what are we doing here?"

"We're here to buy tuna, Grandma," I told her simply, thinking tuna fish was something she might remember and understand. But Grandma's eyes grew cloudy and confused.

"Tuna? Do I like tuna?"

Instead of answering, I reached up and stuck a spray of baby's breath into her white curls. Then I plucked the biggest, brightest yellow daisy I could find, and tucked it into my own ringlets. One blossom quickly led to dozens more, until Grandma and I looked like we'd had our hair done by a fanatical frenzy of flower fairies.

Gently, I took Grandma Pat's hand and raised it high, hoping she would twirl beneath my arm. She planted her feet instead—stubborn to the end. Life with Grandma Pat was going to be hot and cold, and as blustery and changeable as the wind, for as long as she was with us.

"Take it moment by moment, Gypsy," I reminded myself.

When Mr. Flint suddenly loomed large before me—scowling at the ten acres of garden in my hair—I closed my eyes and whispered, "Stop, stop, *stop*." Stubborn or not, this moment with Grandma was one I intended to enjoy a little longer.

Nowadays, my thoughts turned immediately to Del whenever I stopped time. If Del had been with me in the grocery store, he might've made a mad dash for the toilet paper aisle, then the cosmetics aisle, bent on giving Mr. Flint a masterful mummy makeover. I considered doing the same thing myself, just so I could laugh with Del about it later. But mummies and makeovers were Del's style, not mine. Instead, I removed a red rose from behind my ear and stuck its stem between Mr. Flint's front teeth.

"Humph." Grandma peered at the store owner and huffed in disapproval. "This sour-looking man could use a bit of sparkle, don't you think?"

I beamed at her, and said: "Yes, Grandma. I do indeed."

A thousand heartbeats and two bottles of glitter gel later, I stood tall and strong, ready to let time loose again. Ready to let time dance and spin along its natural course . . .

Come what may.

ACKNOWLEDGMENTS

I'd like to thank my editor, Kate Harrison; my publisher, Lauri Hornik; and my agent, Daniel Lazar, for their invaluable insights and their patience. Time is precious. Thank you all for understanding that, and for giving me such unceasing and boundless support. Kate, this book wouldn't be what it is without you. In fact, if it weren't for you, I'd probably still be lost somewhere in Georgia, and the freezer aisle in Flint's Market might still be filled with gnomes.

Many thanks to Regina Castillo, Jasmin Rubero, and Kristin Smith, who contributed their talents to the design and edits of this book, as well as to everyone at Dial Books for Young Readers, Puffin, and the entire team at Penguin Young Readers Group. Brandon Dorman, thank you for another stellar cover.

For giving me valuable advice, feedback, support, or information, I extend my gratitude to the following people: Sean and Matt Morris, Fio, Christine Ambrose, Derek Ward, and Kappie & Randi at HearthFire Books in Evergreen, Colorado. Also to G.K.S. and D.E.M.—and anyone else whose names or initials I've forgotten to mention here.

For always being at the other end of an email or Skype chat, for reading early drafts, and for never failing to cheer me on, I send only the most magical acorns and the deepest red Twizzlers to Deborah Kovacs and Linda Urban (my very own Myra).

Thank you Ellen Oh, for being willing to read my manuscript at the drop of a hat, and for sharing your thoughts. And thank you to the community of kid-lit writers in Colorado and places more distant, for giving me such a lovely and talented group of friends.

There are people in this world who make you more courageous just by knowing them . . . my sprog, you've made me braver. Never forget how loved you are.

Final notes: I would love to take credit for having thought up the song "Red Eye Gravy & Poi," but I did not. It is a real and utterly delightful song sung by Melveen Leed. Inspiration for this book came to me from many places; the late Barbara Park will never know the importance of the role she played in its creation. Nor will the countless other people who wrote books, filmed documentaries, and created websites about children and teens dealing with grandparents suffering from dementia or Alzheimer's. Mine is a fantasy story—a work of sheer fiction—but there are many young people who have their own stories to tell, stories they *need* to tell. Let's not forget to listen.

About the Author

INGRID LAW (www.ingridlaw.com) is the *New York Times* bestselling author of two other books for young readers, *Savvy* and *Scumble*. Her books have been placed on more than thirty state reading lists, and have earned accolades from *Publishers Weekly*, Oprah's reading list, the *Today Show*'s Al's Book Club for Kids, and the Smithsonian. *Savvy* was named a Newbery Honor book in 2009. When she's not reading, writing, or creating new stories, she can usually be found in a movie theater, listening to music or audiobooks, or walking around her favorite lakes and ponds. Ingrid lives in Lafayette, Colorado.